NICK SNAPE

# The Scorching: Just Press Play

Book design by GetCovers.com

www.nicksnape.com



First edition

ISBN: 978-1-0686411-2-1

This book was professionally typeset on Reedsy.
Find out more at reedsy.com

# Prologue

A red haze lit the ocean. A stunning radiance that desperately tried to raise the beauty of the brown scum that rode the water's surface – a display of nature's wonder as the sunlight broke into shards above the horizon.

"Fuck me, here it comes." The wave of heat rolled in, touching my bare feet with the first breath of thermal wind sliding under the concrete balcony. I pulled them in closer to my chair and glanced at the thermometer on my tablet. It rose another couple of degrees as the dawn heralded yet another day in fucking hell.

Can you tell I'm in a good mood?

My tablet flashed, a tiny icon appearing in the top corner letting me know I had mail. Mail. Shit.

I was about to lose the last bearable time of the day, and someone decided I needed to read their drivel right now? Can't even enjoy the final few minutes before I have to retreat to my room.

But it might be a recall. A chance to get out of hell and back to where the water is cool, and the food doesn't taste of dust.

I shifted my rebreather, dropping the mask down a little so the tube didn't cover the screen. Clicking the icon, I watched the data stream – pictures, words. My life on display. Everything about me and my family. Bastards.

I lost a good friend last week. My only friend. All I wanted was some peace. Time to grieve. And now this.

At the bottom of the message was a voice note.
I pushed my mask back on and listened.

# Joshua Nkosi's Vlog Channel

Replay – The Life of an Underwater Ranger Force Sea-Cop
Narrator/'Tuber: Joshua Nkosi.
Likes: 0
Subscribers: 0
Theme: Humour, mainly.

***Is The World Sitting Comfortably?***
***Then Press Play***

# Chapter 1

"Welcome," I said. "This is Josh Nkosi, speaking from the corridors of the Mining Platform *Socorro*. When I say platform, that's a throwback to the days of old, as we're around two thousand metres under the ocean." I dropped the camera into my URF shirt pocket, its gimbal ensuring the technological marvel maintained a steady view of the metal corridor I strode along. The ring of boots echoed off the grey walls as the entire four-hundred odd population of the *Socorro* seemed to be out for a morning stroll. I nodded to the few I recognised and smiled my way past the rest. Hey, when you're a cop, you've got to keep in with the locals. Besides, it isn't the generously paid workers of the platform that I police. Well, not yet. And the responding smiles are worth the effort. It's great to see people's lips and teeth in the ocean depths, rather than rebreathers and breathing masks up top.

I adjusted the camera. The feed into my eye-mod showing I was mainly pointing at the crew's asses as they busied themselves on the way to work. "Well, that isn't what you tuned in to see, is it now? I didn't spend a month's wages on this set up just so you can watch their feet slide by. Hey Nakina, want to say hello?" I slid my arm into the crook of Nakina's, the submarine tech giving me the side-eyed response that I think meant WTF.

"WTF?"

See, I was right. Part of a URF cop's job is to know your people, read their signals and explain yourself before the punches land.

"Just, erm, recording a little vid. For my fans."

"Record? Fans? You been at the potato juice again?" Nakina twisted her lips into something akin to a smile, but I wasn't convinced it was fully meant. Up top, body language had become a struggle to understand. The demands of interpreting vocal tones distorted by radio and frustrated hand signals, adding more to the complex mix of languages. The majority of people rarely spent time without a breathing aide. I'd seen an old vid, can't remember which, where the entire planet had masked because of the 'rona, some bug or other. Same thing, children lost most of their language skills with their development set back years. Just makes you think what might be happening right now in the slums of Johannesburg or Rome.

"Old style. Pre the Scorching. The whole world was doing it, recording their lives for others to watch. Some, and I'm not even razzing you, had millions of followers. It didn't matter if you were powerful, or rich, you could be another's equal on camera." I gave her my best smile, full pearly white teeth and a little twitch of my nose that I'm convinced is a winner with whatever woman takes my eye. Except Nakina, and Jezze, oh and Margarite, and ... never mind. Some day, that twitch will snag me a woman of substance.

Nakina smiled back. I'm sure there was pity in there – emotion is good, it's a start.

"Followers, huh? And who is going to watch this film of yours? How many of these followers have you got?"

"Well, none. Yet," I replied, remembering to keep my head up instead of letting her downer force my eyes to the floor. Some people don't respect talent. "But you never know. All those 'tubers had to start at zero, so why can't I?"

Nakina slipped her arm out, squeezing my forearm. Pity, definitely pity. The magic of the nose twitch lost upon her indifferent brown eyes. Maybe she missed it?

"This is me. I got reassigned to Captain Hinch's dredger. Going down in the world, if you know what I mean."

"Wow, that's amazing. That in dry dock, or...?"

"I'll be hitting the 4-5k, I reckon. She's been targeting the polymetallics approaching the Mathematician Ridge, so it's going to be some trip." Nakina turned to the pressurised door, swiping her hand over the glowpad that registered her chipped code. Stepping in, she dropped her kitbag to the lift floor and looked back, a wink accompanying the smirk. "And no filming anything I wouldn't while I'm gone. You'll get a reputation."

"Chance would be a fine thing," I said, the low whisper unheard over the swish of the door closing. Nakina is a good friend, probably my best, other than Marc. Maybe I should save that nose twitch for someone else.

"Well … where was I? Ah yes. The corridors of the *Socorro* teem with human life, but the oceans …"

* * *

Stepping out of the lift, the dock pulsed with humans going about URF business. Techs and mechanics roamed the bay, many trailing magno-lifts behind them as they streamed from section to section. Three subs waited for their service, the biweekly swap of submarine and personnel. One fault, and an expensive piece of equipment comes to a watery end, either crushed or lost to the ocean floor. Of course, the operator goes with it, but hey, you can train another cop desperate for clean air in their lungs and real food in their belly.

Like me.

And knowing that, it's time to keep shtum and stop filming with the pocketcam. I can always add a little something later, you know, a voice over with something ominous, like *I am unable to film my super secret role in the Underwater Ranger Force.* I've always found the name funny – reminds me of those cartoons you can find on the viewscreen databases, with their nefarious villains who never seem to stay in jail. Or dead, for that matter. Unlike the real world, both out in the black and above.

Death. Yeah. Not so funny.

I hustled over to my sub, its gleaming metallic surface a welcome sight after a week's downtime. Post-service and shined to perfection, its bulbous centre boasting room enough to stand and move about, cook and … *ahem*

... you know, defecate, for a week. Low down at the front lay the twin robotic arms, flexible yet powerful – the long arm of the law! See what I did there?

Anyway. The stern is in fact a second super-sub, tight and wrapped around the operator (me – I guess you worked that out, but just in case you forgot, I'm the hero) that cuts through the water at a much greater speed and level of agility. Short on range, and short on pressurisation, they have two uses. One to chase down those nefarious villains with a burst of speed, especially if they enter somewhere a little tight. The other to rag the shit out of the ocean like a mean, lean swimming machine. Now that I *got* to film.

I climbed the ladder, running my fingers over the sheer beauty of the URF pursuit sub, my smile wide. On reaching the hatch, I let my hand slide over the internal glowpad, following up with a right-eye retina scan. Can't be too careful with *tech* this good. I slid on in, donning the waiting integration suit that would be my home for the next week. Unless, of course, there was a big bad out there and I saw some action. Then we'd be *hightailing* it back to base. I think that's the right word.

It's at this point the sub fully wakes up. The internal systems recognising the interconnected suit and activating the emergency life support backups attuned to my last medical check. That, of course, was two days ago. After all, if you lose the operator, you might lose the submarine if it fails to make its own way back, or the dumb human breaks something while they die. With the internals all in the green, I fiddled with the camera, musing over the best time to switch it back on, and waiting for the MARC unit's usual grumpy meet and greet. She hated being left in the sub and usually gave me both barrels on my return. Her wit was nearly as sharp as her tentacles – but don't tell her I said that.

"Hi Marc."

*"Is that it? No 'did you miss me, Marc?' How are you doing? What have you been doing Marc while I've been chilling with my friends, watching vids and playing basketball?"*

"You got that new sarcasm chip sorted? Sounds to me like it's tuned a bit high," I replied. My apologies. Can't resist feeding the troll. Never quite sure where that childhood saying comes from, or what a troll is for that matter, but hey, old stuff's all good by me.

*"I think the medtech has it just right. You, however, need an empathy check. Need to scrub up your 'small talk and genuine interest and concern for your partner' algorithm."*

"Wow, *partner*? That's an upgrade. Let's compare pay cheques, shall we?" I gave up on the camera, a creeping sense of the inevitable warning screams from the WPF surveillance system playing on my mind. The sub techs never spoke about them, but I'm convinced the black box (yeah – its bright green and with a far better buoyancy aide than those reserved for mere humans) runs a constant security scan. This sub tech is badass and not something to share. The lingering suspicion it may also have a self-destruct has never left me, either.

*"You'd lose, especially spending it on junk like you're carrying. That an eye-mod? How'd you get that past security? Oh wait, you are security."*

"Hey, out of my brain, Marc. None of your business, and it's between you and me, yeah? No need to spread it about. I'm – you know – going to record myself. My life. Not the cop stuff, but the—"

*"—boring stuff. Who's gonna watch? Apart from the URF when they lock your ass in the brig. You could film that last glimpse of light as the door closes."*

"You definitely need that chip testing. Running system procedural checks." Okay, so I cut her dead. Sometimes you get outclassed, and you have to circle the horses (or something like that). "How are we doing, *partner*? The sub's systems all in the green?"

*"Looking good, Josh. All systems connected. Oh wait, there's an organic glitch. Damn, someone let a human drive."*

# Chapter 2

Now you might think that being a URF cop, with your own sub – and dare I say it – hot super-sub ride, would be all glamour and glitz. The action hero flexing his muscles, ready for the enemy squad to swoop in and take you down, responding in a blaze of bullets and chases. Well, for 99.99% of the time, that's completely wrong. Okay, maybe I'm exaggerating a little. Sometimes a bit of seaweed floats by while you're on guard, or the odd carcass from above drifts down to the seabed, ready to be consumed by the waiting horde of crabs and bottom-feeders. You see, in the old days, before the Scorching, the seas teamed with life. I know that may come as a surprise to my 'up top' fans. But yeah, from what I heard, out in the blue and away from any shallow continental shelf or ridge, it could be sparse, yet there. One of my favourite vids shows humans using diving bells, pre-Drathken tech, dropping into the ocean's rifts and finding abundant life. And yeah, it's still around, but only a fraction of what I saw on film. And the variety, well, we don't have much now. When the world heated up, the seas suffered the most. You'd have thought that people would have noticed. It's not as if it wasn't right in front of their eyes, or their stomachs, for that matter. Some of the documentaries ... ah, another time, perhaps. We work, that's what we do. Work to survive, to provide for ourselves and the Drathken. What's the alternative?

The Deep Ocean Harvester lay about forty metres below us. A hundred metres long, with its front end nearly thirty wide, the toothed scoop scraped the ocean floor clean. Everything, and I mean everything, enters its maw to be sifted, compiled and compressed into neat bundles of precious metal or useful minerals out of the arse end. As it makes its slow, laborious way across the ocean's abyssal plain, the section of the seabed between the continental shelves and ridges or trenches, nothing remains unscathed. Many believe it leaves a trail of debris behind with the sea full of silt. But no. You see, that would be inefficient. The rear of the mighty machine smooths, compacts and calms the waters. For if the waste silt rises, it would make the operation much harder, filling the already oxygen-poor water with more debris. When you're this far down, where else do you get your water and oxygen from? If you could see, remembering that 2000 metres down darkness reigns, to look back across its movements, then the abyssal plain would appear like the manicured lawn I'd seen in a picture. All lines and systematic rows, until the currents have their sway.

Of course, the Harvester also picks up the real survivors of the Scorching – the shellfish and crabs that feed upon the dead and dying. Food for the workers, once it's been purged, obviously. A no-lose process, so they say.

Did I mention the boredom? Then why, you might ask (go on, I know you want to) do you need a guard? Or three?

"*Is that a blip?*"

Well, today's your lucky day.

"Naah, it's just a shadow. Likely Bennita's sub, she's ... oh shit."

See, told you.

"*Shit – roughly translated: not at that speed and direction.*"

"We are moving in. Full lights activated." Now you might have expected my *partner*, Marc, would be in control. But no. Don't get me wrong, she does have an amazing brain. No, hang on, brains – I always forget that. But she doesn't think in the same dimensions as a person. And the sub is designed for human use. If I let her have control, we'd be scraping ocean and cave rock, and before you know it, my lungs would be the size of an orange, or a pea. Not really sure I want to find out which. I swept the submarine downwards, powering up the main engine to drive the propellors towards maximum. Now I know what you're after – it *must* be time for a high-speed chase. We can reach 50 knots, but it takes time to get there. Unlike the dolphins and whales of times past, ocean-going life able to reach that speed with far higher rates of acceleration. Probably why the modded Cuvier whale was sweeping downwards into the wake of the Harvester right now.

"Ah crap, we're on, Marc." I swung the submersible round, timing my intercept speed against the radar and computer calculations. What they couldn't do, however, is predict with any certainty. You see, the whale was human controlled. Nothing more unpredictable than an ocean-going animal following a human's directives. I should know. The Cuvier swooped down, driving for the rear of the massive Harvester. More blips glowed back at me from my radar, but those were for the others to monitor. I had my target. URF cop and cetacean wrangler. Great combo.

The lights finally picked the beaked whale out. Its bulk sheathed in a gleaming metal harness, the bottom of which latched onto a bundle of polymetallic nodules excreted from the vast machine. The admin team on the *Socorro* would know its exact value to the Drathken. Personally, I just saw fresh air and good food wrapped in its metallic claws. With a drive of its tail, the Cuvier rushed onwards, this human adjusting the sub's trajectory to the new direction. I dropped just in front of the whale, ready to hit the stunner when it powered on past, leaving eddies rippling in its wake and disrupting my acceleration.

*"You sure you took the refresher training?"*

"You're not helping." I looked over at the super-sub button, dreaming of cutting through the water and lassoing the mighty whale on my way past. Yeah, right. Not that a beaked whale's agile or anything. Sighing, I upped the power to the last notch on the engines, hoping the modded creature's stamina would fail before we did. The chase lasted another five minutes before I felt the first complaint from the engine and, easing back, found we were losing ground.

"They're driving it too hard. Its body will give out."

*"They don't care, Josh."*

True. You can grow an animal from its cell structure *en masse* if you have the tech. More difficult to mod it to live long enough to be useful, but that would come. The radar blips sped up, the pings letting me know we were closing in. Our lights caught the failing creature, its tail and fins only managing tired movements, barely cutting through the water. We picked up pained clicks emanating from inside it – a creature grown, exploited and then used up. Nothing changes. An explosion tore it apart, the body mere meat in a moment of horror. The flash was accompanied by a second echo, a bag expanding, lifting the creature's harness and its cargo away from the ruptured torso. The speed it rose was beyond the sub's capabilities and its safety parameters (as well as mine).

"Ah, crap." Having already passed the surging balloon, I swept around, taking aim and releasing one of the robo-arms at the front of the submarine. Now I know what you're thinking. Thousands of metres below the surface of the ocean, in the dark, with currents surging, there's absolutely no chance for me to hit. Except, of course, you forget the 99.99% boredom factor. When you spend most of your time doing nothing, you search for anything to fill your breaks. In downtime, the URF cops get ever so slightly competitive. And yes, you guessed it, you're looking at the cop who came second at least five times out of a hundred. Still, a bit of luck helps.

The arm snagged the rising balloon, ripping across its surface. It blew instantly, the deep pressure forcing the gas out, and the bundle of polymetallic nodules dropped. My luck didn't hold out, the other arm missing its mark, the precious metal spiralling its way into the black.

"Shit." I nudged the nose down, running through the positioning software as the propellers drove us on. If it made the seabed as predicted, we'd be approaching the limit of the sub. I cut through the murk, chasing the nodules downwards, the light catching the harness straps as it hit the ocean floor. Then the current swept it into a crack between two bulges of volcanic rock. Bloody typical.

Checking the depth limits, I dropped just above the floor, keeping the propellers angled up and away from the sediment. Adapting the speed and engaging the computer to adjust for any changes, we sat stationary above the crack.

A metallic, multi-jointed tentacle tapped me on the shoulder.

*"Only if you ask me nicely."*

"Please will you collect the stolen goods, oh wondrous Marc?"

*"Now that sounds good. Keep that up, and I might even refrain from mentioning how far you missed the cargo by."*

The weight dropped from my shoulders, the tapping tentacle now pulling along with seven others, slipping down into the membraned hatch. Yes, Marc. Multi-purpose, All-terrain, Recovery Cephalopod. As insane as it might seem, inside that tin can had been a real, live common octopus. Yeah, modded and all. Why an octopus would need an exoskeleton shell should be plainly obvious – the pressure is as bad for some cephalopods at this depth as us. But they can go just about anywhere, with their ability to squeeze into tight spaces, and morph with their surroundings. Useful when in need of a handy recovery tool outside the ship. And chipped too. You see, cephalopods use light and colour to communicate, and we don't. But the suit translates back and forth straight to a chip in my brain. When we talk, it's all in our heads (hence the cheesy voiceover). Yep, I'm modded too. A guy's got to eat. And breathe.

I watched Marc as her tentacle tips wafted in the current. Her body pulled in tight as she drifted down to the floor. Suddenly caught in a stronger eddy, she spun, head down and the tentacles expanding before rushing forward. I love to watch her swim. She uses jet propulsion, sucking water into a cavity before her suit muscles contract, forcing it back out a siphon. Did you know they steer by adjusting the direction of the jetting water? Of course, the exo-suit mimics all this, adjusting to her brains' impulses. There's more tech in her suit than in my life support systems – just saying.

She reached the gap, and those tentacles slipped in, stretching out until the suckers took hold and dragged her inside. I watched the last of her limbs disappear before bringing up her tracking icon. The chip gives me a sense of direction, but no more, and the forty-metre range lets me judge things just fine if we're free swimming somewhere shallow. We trained ... I say we ... she trained me how the link worked snorkelling near the surface before Marc had grown enough to wear the original exo-suit. The sub's viewscreen threw up the beacon, mapping behind my cephalopod pal as her suit sent back data about the tunnels. Not being an expert on geology, I'm guessing they went deeper, but Marc soon had hold of our stolen goods, pulling herself back with her other four limbs. Three jet bursts later and the same silvered tentacles slid through the membrane, grasping the hand (tentacle) grips placed for just that purpose. Behind her bulbous body, the package followed, a wonderful sight that sent the radiation metre into overdrive. The nodules lit up my domain in glorious red. I slammed the containment box down on it, thanking the Drathken for the suit I was wearing, adapted from the original deep-sea miners' kit. The alarms cut off, bringing peace to my world and Marc's, who had auto-shut down her light sensors.

"Way to go, *partner*." I held my hand up, palm out, ready for my high tentacle. Marc never said a word. If a metal suit can show indignance, that's what I got as she left me hanging.

*"I despair. Can't you act a little more professionally?"*

Now I would like to mention here that the chip may be sending its interpretation of the colour changes, but where, in the scorching hell of this planet, does an octopus learn the word 'professional' or 'despair'? The longer I spent with Marc, the more convinced I became they'd messed about with octopi intelligence a bit too much. It isn't right that a cephalopod should have a better vocabulary than the human operator. Sorry – human *partner*.

I took the controls again, setting the radar to provide alerts as we headed back to the platform. Yeah, we had the stolen goods, but whoever grew, controlled and sacrificed modded whales had serious intentions on the nodules back in that containment box. I doubt they would have any qualms about doing the same with the sub and me. With the Harvester in the direct path, I checked in on the way past, finding Bennita and Jeremiah were back on station.

"Hey, Benni," I added a smile. The radio is non-visual, but it's a habit, okay? Besides, Benni has a tendency to make everyone a little happier. There was that time after the potato juice ... and that table collapsing while she danced ... yeah. Not important now. Let's just say everyone winced when she landed and leave it at that. Except the bar manager. He just passed out after her boot caught him under the chin.

"Yes, my little video star. How can I help?" See, I bet you even used a smiley voice in your head.

"Hey, how'd...?"

"We live in a tin can two clicks under the ocean. What else is there to do but talk? And drink?"

"Nakina? I thought she'd be halfway to the ridge by now."

"They waited until the excitement was over. They're not risking the dredger while we have terrorists around."

"Terrorists? Is that what they're saying? The polymetallics and minerals are worth a fortune in air, food and tech. I was thinking more deep-sea piracy." I stopped smiling at this point. You know that feeling you get when everything is going right? I wasn't having that feeling.

"Just reporting the news, not making it. Yours was the only modded Cuvier to get through the net, so you'll be up for debrief ASAP. I'd get that not so cute ass back to the bay, mister star-in-the-making."

The radio cut off, but not without a couple of clicks on my receiver. To the lay person it was just static, to a URF cop on security detail, it was a friend telling you to watch your back.

# Chapter 3

I sat in the metal chair, the most uncomfortable piece of furniture known to humankind. My ass was cold, my heart colder. Next to me was my metallic cephalopod partner, her tentacles tucked tight around her. A protective gesture. All we needed now was the man in the dark suit opposite to shine a light on her – then the ink really would start flying.

I'd been sat there an hour, going over the same story again and again. The Underwater Ranger Force HQ was not exactly salubrious (hey, I've an octopus's vocabulary to compete with here). The metal table scratched and worn, the window at the side of the room as clichéd as they come. Did I mention the walls were grey metal? See, I used the right word.

The dark suited Drathken WPF officer (that's World Pissant Force in my view, but supposedly it's Police) sat opposite. Not that he was an alien or anything. No, you won't find anything that wide down here in our tiny corridors. As human as his mods allowed, and right now I'm betting he's had surgery, or even gene modding, if he was high ranking. Able to breathe unaided in most places above. Mind you, can't say that the *Socorro* was the most likely place to find a high up.

"So, Josh, tell me about the explosion again. You say the bag erupted at the same time?" He smiled like I always imagined a tiger would just before ripping the squirrel apart, or an antelope, whatever it was they used to eat. You know the ones, all teeth and menace.

"It was a second explosion. I think the whale blew first, to release the harness. The remains of the straps were still attached to the cargo. You have the evidence there."

"I'm aware of that, Josh. But you're filling in the gaps, here. The sub's recording systems can only film so much with the lighting, and everything happened so fast. Humour me." Not a chance of that. This man had less funny bone than a half-eaten sandwich. Probably my sandwich.

"The Cuvier blew first. If you want my guess, it was in a preordained spot so they could collect the pressure bag. The whale was tiring fast. Whoever was operating pushed it near to death, knowing they were going to kill it anyway. Sick bastards." And I meant it.

*"Tell him I concur."*

"The MARC concurs with me."

The officer nodded in response. "Agreed. I'll send my report in. You're stood down until Drathken Command respond, understood?"

"But ..." There goes the rest of my sandwich. I could also see my three meals a day disappearing before my eyes.

"On pay. You're not under direct suspicion, but Command is wary. There are too many terrorist groups up top who'd want that cargo, so they need to be seen taking action."

"By standing the recovering URF cop down?"

*"And his partner."*

"And his recovery cephalopod? What's that going to achieve?" You know that time when you shouldn't push your luck, but you still do? "You're making me appear guilty here. Everyone on the platform will be looking my way. This isn't on."

It was at this point he reached inside his pocket, removing a stunning piece of tech that cost a month's salary. I bet that gimbal was working beautifully, keeping the picture steady as it dropped onto the table. I swear he raised an eyebrow at me.

"Hard to argue when you have contraband on board. This tech is forbidden within all Drathken facilities, and you are a cop, so don't tell me you had no idea. Luckily, we were able to download the ridiculous stuff you were recording, or you'd be fertiliser for the plantations."

On some of the vids I watch, there's usually ominous music at this point. Me, I get an octopus with *'I told you so'* on repeat. Inside that suit, I imagined her flashing like an old-fashioned Christmas tree.

For a change, there was not much I could say in return.

"Does that mean I'm not getting it back?"

* * *

I wandered along the corridor, Marc attached to my back. Two tentacles hooked either side of my neck, two around the waist, and the others slid into the environment power unit for a recharge. They'd rushed us in for the debrief, and she had been in overdrive with the stress she'd been exhibiting. Marc's internal systems usually self-charged off her movements, but she had remained still for too long.

Right now, my paranoia had kicked in, convinced that every glance my way was to pronounce my guilt. Remember how Benni knew about my vids? Tin cans are nowhere to be when the rumours fly. I may as well have had a neon sign flashing my suspension for everyone to see. I'd sat in the canteen alone, with none of the usual crew coming over to say hi or chew the cud. It could have been the dark cloud above my head, not that I've seen many lonely clouds being from Brazil. It was either fucking hot or fucking wet.

*"Where are we heading? This looks suspiciously like the way to the URF docking bay."* See, intelligent.

"Maybe it is. Wanted to check on your power pack. You were sitting still for a long time." Now you would have thought that an octopus would not be socially adept. At least with humans. But lying was a trait Marc understood. I put this down to her use of camouflage to 'lie' about what and where she was. Yet one was physical, the other conceptual. And, as you perhaps noticed, she'd mastered sarcasm, or her chip had. Go figure. We humans perhaps underestimated cephalopods in the past. The Drathken certainly hadn't.

*"But I'm trickle charging now. Everything will be fine. Except you're not, you seem on edge. And your colours are pulsing, like waves."*

"I can't think why I'd be on edge, can you? I've just been stood down, suspended. I am in deep shit, Marc, even though we did our duty. It doesn't feel right, and I'm one step away from losing my commission. If they take exception to the camera, they could choose to send me up top, even to the Drathken factories."

*"Or the slums."*

"Not helping. Think about it, Marc. If they decide I am guilty of something, or even need a scapedog—"

*"—goat. Scapegoat."*

"A scapegoat. Then what about you?"

*"Me?"* Now we get to what cephalopods can't do. Predict the future. That ability to look beyond the immediate consequences of actions. For instance, eating that shellfish will lead to nutrition and all is well. Eat all the egg-laying shellfish in an area, and I'm left with nothing to eat, so I move on. Keep repeating that and you have no food at all. Oh, hang on. No. That's humans who do that. Never mind, you know what I mean.

"Yes," I said, standing a few metres away from the docking bay's entrance. "We are interconnected, chipped. The software is keyed to us, and experimental. There are only eight other operators who have MARCs, the rest are using awkward recovery drones. If they send me up top, you won't have an operator and it'll be too expensive to match, train and chip another one." I didn't add 'due to your lifespan'. I'm not heartless. Yes, Marc's lifetime should have been longer than those in the lab, as they are able to mate. When octopi breed, they are affected by a process called senescence, a breakdown of cellular function without repair or replacement. Marc could have mated, but the plan had been to wait until she was much older. A last act of motherhood.

*"You mean I'll be discarded?"*

Now I know I can't translate emotions that are spoken into my mind by a chip. But you had to be there to get the full impact of that statement. It was like someone held my heart with one hand, while stabbing it with a knife in the other. It's just an octopus, isn't it? Of no consequence, with human and Drathken of far more importance in this world.

I held back.

"Yes. You will." Okay, I lied. She has a right to know. At that moment,

Benni opened the docking bay door, and I strode forward, arm out, ready to use my ID. She threw me a smile that lit up my day, blue eyes shining as she finished laughing at something Jeremiah said from behind. I grabbed the bulkhead, letting her pass.

"Hey Jeremiah." Cool as you like. "Hold the door, man. Coming through." Now protocol says this is not the done thing, and as you can guess, URF cops are sticklers for procedure. Jeremiah moved aside, a twist of his neck and a wink under his tight dreadlocks.

"Yes sir, anything for the vidscreen star." His English drawl did not match his looks, but we don't get to choose where we're born.

"Not you as well. Giving that up. Can't handle the attention." See, I didn't lie. I slapped him on the arm, slid past and headed for the sub. If I timed it right, the hatch would be up for the standard system check. If not, I'd be standing suspiciously at the exit door, waiting for someone to leave. I had no idea if my ID would work, but this way, no one would know I had been here. Sneaky, huh? Watching all those old shows sure gives you some ideas.

I tried not to move too quickly, but the tension strumming through my chest wasn't helping. Anyone observing would have laughed at my stiff-necked stare straight ahead and the awkward, stiff-armed walk. Did I say I was stiff? Luckily, a URF cop in the URF docking bay, heading for a URF sub, was the last thing to draw any attention. Even if he did walk like a robot on a suicide run.

It was about now I remembered I was wearing the integration suit. Yeah, the one designed so you could spend a week independent of the platform if needed. The one I didn't have time to take off before the bloody debrief. The one I'd be expected to return to the techs for cleaning and a reset. Can you hear the face slap from there?

My usual smooth walk returned as I calmed down and approached the sub a little more relaxed. My tech, Martin, was nowhere in sight but the hatch was wide open. Peering over, it was empty, the dials and screens all aglow. I promise I didn't look around suspiciously before dropping in. Okay, maybe once.

Marc detached, ambling over to the recharge unit, carrying out what she thought we were here to do. I sat in the pilot's chair, flicking through switches, looking busy.

*"That's the ship's internal recording system, Josh. What are you doing?"*

"Just checking something while I'm here." I ran the internal camera view; one the WPF officer hadn't bothered with. And there it was, something my partner and I had both missed. Maybe enough to deflect attention from us, if I played it right.

* * *

"I shouldn't be doing this," Benni keyed in the autopilot on her sub, eyes constantly flicking back to me as I ran through Marc's data stream on my tablet. Behind us, *Socorro*'s last vestige of light was absorbed by the black.

"It's not as if you're breaking the rules. More, bending them. I was the one stood down, but on full pay. You're piloting. Me and Marc are just here for the ride. I checked through the deposition on my work log, and nowhere does it state that Benni McAndrew shouldn't provide said suspended cop a ride into the black. Your sub is due a maintenance shakedown, so it all fits."

"I meant more, you know, Jeremiah. He might get a bit jealous if he knew…" she let her eyes fall on me as I twitched, eyes wide, pretending to be shocked.

"You and him? My, the whole station would never have guessed. Bloody hell, Benni. This place is rumour central. Don't need a vid channel to get any news out." I rummaged in my suit pocket, withdrawing the chit I'd been saving. "Shit. I lost," I said, waving it at her before tearing it up, "I had four weeks and three days after you were assigned the same shift. I lost a week's wages on that bet."

Now the problem with URF subs is that, though capable of supporting a crew of two, they were a little tight. Benni's swift jab smacked into my upper arm. That was going to bruise, but the half-amused grin and scowl combo she also threw me was worth it.

"Bastard."

"I have another piece of paper that proves I'm not."

We headed directly to the lava field and, after thirty minutes, with the current favourable, passed the Deep Ocean Mining vehicle. In operation twenty-four hours a day, seven days a week, Benni called in to the security detail running shotgun today. Once they knew what she was doing, she manoeuvred on past, soon out of radio contact range. Another fifteen minutes and we were at the site. Marc did her thing, which totally impressed Benni, it has to be said. Her underwater drone far too big to have made it into the crack, never mind manoeuvre around. However, the other half of the buried treasure was nowhere to be found. Ah, damn. I do get ahead of myself. The nodules *we* already recovered were only half of those stolen. That was why the WPF officer from hell was so awkward and evasive. He could have just told me some were missing.

It was at this point Marc revealed her party trick. Apparently, cephalopods are quite sensitive to radiation. Modded octopi even more so, and particularly in the saliva glands. Who knew! I have a suspicion that the Drathken were thinking of other uses for my octopus partner when they added that upgrade to her suit.

*"There are traces of the uranium in the rock, but this is stronger, definitely from the nodule."*

My tablet blipped, and Marc's beacon faded in and out, along with ear-piercing static.

"Losing you, Marc. Go in further, but carefully. You get trapped, and there's no way to get you out down here."

*"I'm an octopus."* Was the only answer I got to that, though the accompanying image in my mind was of her escaping from under the lid of her tank. She'd shared it so many times, it now popped in unasked when I queried her abilities. Apparently, the scientist had forgotten to feed her, so she went and collected her own. *"There's a taste of oil in the water, a bit like your sub. Engines? Yuk. And there're scrapes on the inner rock. Going through."*

I showed Benni the data feed coming in, and she nodded impatiently, finger tapping on her control panel.

"Can you take the sub over the other side, looks like Marc's exiting somewhere else."

"Sure thing, not that it's a complete waste of time."

She added a deep-throated cough to continue her unsubtle hint that she wanted to be gone. But hey, we were here now. Might as well do it right. Benni is a fine pilot, not the best even if I do so say so myself, though her close quarter manoeuvring outmatches the URF's basic AI systems. It's almost like Benni feels the submarine's movements, how I imagine the larger sea animals would have done it – micro adjusting naturally. She glided us around the lava bulge, reaching the crack on the far side where two flows merged, metallic tentacles wrapping around the hole before Marc pulled herself out. The beacon's static dropped, but there remained a background hum, and she sent me the images gathered on the inside.

"There's been something here," said Benni, bringing up her viewscreen, filling it with a 3D model of the sea floor around the lava bulge. "Look." She pointed out several smaller rocks, the surrounding sediment disturbed in circular patterns, though the current was slowly shifting again. Benni recorded a few, saving the 3D model as she peered my way. "Some type of submersible. Can you throw up Marc's photos? Here, that scrape, and again here. Propellors. I reckon ... yes." A drone appeared on the screen, a model I didn't know but Benni appeared to. Not modern by any standards, but flexible and more importantly small, and able to reverse. She looked at me with that smile, lighting the sub.

You see, I'm slow on the uptake sometimes. Yes, I'm a cop. But I'd put Benni's nervous ticks down to being impatient, not the worry that I might have actually done something against the law.

# Chapter 4

"Me and my big mouth."

*"I never said a word."*

"You don't. You just flash that bloody skin of yours, and then I get in deep shit."

*"They were impressed. I am not sure you can blame me for any of it."*

"Yeah, yeah, yeah. I had a cushy thing going on down there. Then you have to come across all professional."

*"Someone has to."*

Now I need to digress a bit. We've missed out how we ended up in the decompression lift in the first place. Oh, I didn't tell you about that either? Right. We live and work two clicks under the ocean. For most of that time, we operate in a heavily shielded space where the pressure is maintained by the Drathken's technical wizardry and knowledge of physics. All beyond me. However, spending so much time down there leads to a few issues when rising from depth. Like death. Oh, and extremely painful death. And then there's dying in screaming agony. Something to do with the body's adjustments, etc. So, after a few failed attempts, they built staging posts used by us humans to wait for the appropriate bodily changes. Now the Drathken are known for their patience, but we humans are not, and that impatience led to problems around claustrophobia and going stir crazy. Hence, using Drathken tech, we devised the sea lift. It allows a steady rise to the surface, while being fed a cocktail of drugs via the atmosphere in there. Healthy, huh?

Where was I? Oh yes.  Why we're *in* the decompression lift.  Bloody cephalopods.  You see, as explained, the internal vid showed the retrieved polymetallic nodes were only half of those taken. When Benni and I took a looksee and found that the rest had been removed, I, as an upstanding cop in the URF, reported this to try and get my ass out of the sling I found myself in. Now, I think my friendly neighbourhood WPF Officer has trust issues, as he sent all the evidence up the wire to the surface. And here we are, on our own way up. Did I mention where Marc insisted I tell them about her radiation tasting abilities? And that she could probably match the residue from the thief's submersible if given the chance?

And that was the rub. She told me, I told him, etc, etc.

Now here we are, aboard the ascending ocean bloody ladder to meet with WPF Command. Apparently, we've been temporarily reassigned. Could life get any better?

Don't answer that.

Right now, I am beginning to wish I had used the human ability to predict the consequences of my actions, and my words, and stayed quiet.

I sighed heavily, and just to make sure my cephalopod pal got the hint, I did it again. Getting up from the deeply cushioned chair, I pressed both hands into the small of my back before approaching the portal. The designers had seen fit to add a viewing area on the outer rim of the elevator and I walked around the central cylinder that housed the thick wire we rode to the surface, taking in the beauty of the ocean. We were at the point where the darkness fades, with light encroaching into the deep.  Its starkness is breathtaking, and for some the cause of the claustrophobia that the engineers were trying to mitigate. Maybe they should have checked with a psych first. The ones the *Socorro* admin team use to evaluate whether we would crack up at two clicks down. You see, as I sat in my second uncomfortable chair of the day, with three other surface seekers beside me, all you take in is a vast shade of blue. Your mind stretches outwards, attempting to fill the void, searching for life to populate it. If you do this too much, you get one of two responses. A complete sense of wonder at the vastness of the sea, or an understanding of how small and insignificant you are and the meagre box you're travelling oh so slowly in. Imagine that. And you're sucked back in, all that water, that emptiness, pressing down. No wonder some people end up in a psych ward, or worse. Of course, I bring my own kind of shallow to the party – able to shrug anything off, no deep well of thought here.

* * *

*"Josh."*

The metal tentacle tickled under my nose. Some girl out there would see that twitch and fall at my feet – I can dream. Well, I was anyway. In a rather good one I'll have you know, involving an action-packed sub chase through the streets of Madrid. Don't ask.

*"Josh, five-minute warning. We're at thirty metres."*

My eyes shot open. Clearing the sleep-filled blurred vision, I held out a hand, tentacles wrapping around the forearm and up over my back. With a metal octopus on my shoulder, I pressed my nose against the thick poly-glass to stare out into the almost blue – and not so empty. Life finds a way.

There were fish, ugly, often with blisters and perturbances, that swam in and out of the elevator's floating platform. Growing outwards, corals formed. Not the bleached and broken pieces you find littered on beaches or smashed against ledges beneath the waves. These were alive, and if the light caught them right, vibrant. Their twists and curved branches shot off tangentially. Some forming upwardly curved tables, others intertwined, snaking through the struts of the platform. Darting among all this stunning chaos were the nursery fish, the tiny offspring desperately clinging on to life while being hunted.

Life.

The elevator system brought up cooler currents from beneath, these plumes enabling the old life of Earth's coral reefs to cling on. Beautiful.

*"I don't have the colours for this,"* the tentacles squeezed a little tighter. *"Do you have a word for me, Josh?"*

"I think you would call it longing, or yearning. A pain that sits in you, stirs every time a memory of this moment creeps in."

*"I like both. And the way you describe it. I will train the chip."*

"Yeah, you do that."

Out in the blue, a shadow hung heavy over the water. I'd heard a few things about what it might be, but I'll save that for later. Much later.

The elevator whined, the noise reverberating through the shell and on into my feet. Then a moment of darkness as it was swallowed by the platform, before emerging onto the brilliance of the dust-ridden receiving deck. I reached down, lifting the backpack containing my worldly goods. I travel light. Not much choice. Marc wrapped herself around, the usual position, though I'd be giving up the internal connection suit soon enough. Otherwise, you would find me broiled on the outer deck and about twenty kilos lighter. In a rare moment, I squeezed her tentacles before carrying the bag out into the furore. Opening the door was like transcending from a serene symphony of quiet contemplation, into the cacophonous reality of a new Earth. First the heat, at least 43°C at my first guess, then the dust you taste on the wind. Finally, the noise crashes in. Machines, people, stress. All in a maelstrom of bustle. See, spend time with a learned octopus and you become almost poetic.

"Nkosi," said the sweat-ridden platform administrator who wore a *very* expensive rebreather. You work for the Drathken Deep-Sea Mines, you get some perks. Food and decent air. She handed over my version, wrapped in plastic, stamped with the sterilisation and production date. I was being treated like a king! Tearing it open, I wrapped the coil around my neck, resting the filter and mech-lung on Marc who huffed in return. The DDSM administrator tapped at her tab, the viewscreen flashing up my details. She turned it to face me, expectant. The look wasn't bored, more 'is he about to make the same comment as everyone else?'

"Really? You want my ID? Who the hell is going to impersonate me two clicks down in a pressurised tin can?" I hate to disappoint. After a wrist swipe and thumb scan, she pointed towards a waiting doorway, ignoring me from the moment she looked back to the tab. Not even time for a nose twitch.

*"I don't like it here."*

Marc shifted on my back; I could almost feel the thrumming of her three hearts. The memories of our last visit here still on the chip. The beautiful and the bad, when the MARC 1 internal life support had kept her moist with oxygen recycled through a film of water. It had met her physical needs, but psych wise? Not so much. I pushed those memories away, far too raw.

"You're with me. If it had gone to shit on the *Socorro* that might not have been the case." I squeezed one tentacle, receiving the same back. Partners. I may only have the one heart, but sometimes that's all you need. I peered through the door, rubbing the dust out of my eyes and wishing for some decent eye-cover. "Looks like the WPF have a welcoming party. We need to play this cool, Marc. Don't go slipping any of those comments into my brain that somehow end up in my mouth, okay?"

*"Cool? That a joke? I'm cooking in here."*

"Like that. See, 'cooking' is in my head now." I pushed the door open, to be met by another. Atmosphere locks, an upgrade on the last time I was here. When the entrance sealed behind me, a fan and suction system whirred, the green-lit timer above the inner door probably counting down towards the end of my cushy life.

When it hit zero the seal released and I pressed against the metal door, smiling at the WPF Officer waiting in the corridor beyond. Same suit and tie, with a haircut to match. I wondered if the differing eye colour was deliberate, so it didn't confuse the Drathken. That, and this was clearly a woman.

"Welcome, Nkosi," her voice was rich, smooth, and didn't match the exterior. I need to stop jumping to conclusions. The hand she proffered made me start, but I responded in kind, allowing the pearly whites to show. But not the nose twitch. Nope. The shake was firm, but warm, and it hit her eyes too. The cynical version of Josh Nkosi would assume this was all a ruse to put me at ease. It was working, and a weight lifted off my shoulders. Oh, hang on. Not Marc – I mean the stress lifted. "I'm WPF Officer Dulik."

I slid the rebreather off. "Thank you. This is all a bit – I dunno – rushed? One minute I'm under suspicion and the next I get a first-class ticket up top." She turned, her hand out, directing me to walk with her. The corridor smelt of chlorine and polish. Strange, welcoming smells amid the hum of the air conditioning. Like a home away from home. Or platform away from platform, at least.

"That's because we are in a hurry. You intercepted a terrorist raid, and your MARC has the radiation signature and the capability of tracing the raw nodule. Lead Officer Rainsford will tell you more." We walked side by side, stopping at a door and window combination. Glancing in, I picked out a man in his fifties, distant grey eyes covered with black-rimmed glasses. He wore a different suit, same cut, and the tie was at a more relaxed angle. A tab lay on his desk, a second, larger screen on the wall with a rather handsome looking URF cop smiling back. My details scrolled by, followed by Marc's specs. She huffed, my chip feeding her the visual via my chip.

*"Short of my shoe-size, they know everything about me."*

"You don't wear shoes."

*"Exactly."*

Dulik knocked and opened the door, and to my surprise the Lead Officer smiled and pushed his chair back, rising with hand out. "Mr Nkosi, welcome." I shook it, a little shocked. Where were the bright lights and handcuffs? *Cooking* under interview lights. Damn it – I knew I'd use it. Cephalopods. It took me a second to remember I was reassigned, but authority always gives me the shivers. I never know which face to show, the mask to wear. I put away the Nkosi grin and settled on attitude. "Take a seat. We are time poor right now, so forgive me if I jump in with the nitty-gritty."

I love that word. Or is it words?

"Go ahead, please." I sat, with Dulik waiting by the door, leaning against the wall and her arms crossed. The smile had faded, shit was about to go down. I'm a cop, I know these things.

"Good." He turned to the big screen, tablet in hand and tapping away. "You signed the Silent Accords when you joined the URF. You understand? Yes? Anything we say here, or you engage with in your new role, comes under that jurisdiction. Am I clear?" The jovial version of Rainsford appeared to have taken a holiday. I nodded, and when clearly this wasn't enough, verbally agreed. "And in accordance with the Accord—"

"My brain gets fried if I talk. Yeah, I get it. Signed, sealed, delivered."

*"Cooked."*

Cephalopod humour can be so ill-timed.

"How long have you been under, Josh?"

"A few months since my ... my enforced break, give or take. My third stint." And I was hoping for more. Yeah, the air might be tinged with a little chlorine, but it was my kind of air. You know the type, the one full of *oxygen*.

"When you went under, the Jo'berg faction of the HLA," (That's the Human Liberation Army between you and me), "had just taken out the Liaison Parliament building, yes?" I nodded. It had been all over the vid news, we even had the Drathken delegate on screen for weeks afterwards, espousing the virtues of their new experimental programmes to gene-alter algae and re-oxygenate the atmosphere. I told you the Drathken were patient, right? Not so sure the word 'decades' was particularly calming. But they were trying, more than humanity ever had pre the Scorching.

He continued, "That was just the start. Stockholm, Vancouver, even what's left of Rome have had systematic incidents. Then it stopped." The pause was either for dramatic effect, or the contemplation over how much I could be told. A nervous tick started behind my right ear, where the chip had been implanted. His face contorted a little, decision made. "We think we uncovered a lot of the terrorist cells, took out a few leaders. But all the info we have points to them seeking resources for an advanced dirty bomb."

And there we have it. Now you might have expected there to be loads of already enriched uranium and plutonium around in those nuclear weapons humans loved so much. And in the nuclear plants. Well yes, and no. There's nothing like the end of the world to get everyone all pacifistic. That, and the need to piss off as fast as possible and leave the rest of the planet in the fuck up you made of it. The rich and the powerful suddenly became best mates, whether Ruskies, Yanks, Europhiles or Eurasian. No one gives a shit about religion or political affiliation when your ass is on the line. The Drathken, bless them, turned up in their spaceships and shared their tech with humanity to save the great and the not-so-good – the brightest of our people, who just so happened to be the richest too. Go figure. Somewhere out in the other *black*, there's ten massive spaceships careering towards whatever their chosen destination was. Some set of numbers associated with a solar system or other. Not my bag. It may surprise you to know, I wasn't even a twinkle in my poor-as-hell parents' eye when they left. Nor were they the right type to be considered. According to my *pai*, my father, they needed a pair of *creatives* like them far more than the nuclear engineers, and every scrap of radioactive material they could lay their grubby hands on.

Anyway. Nuclear stuff. The Drathken stayed, their intention to save the Earth. Recalibrate our atmosphere if they could or adapt the remaining biosphere to cope with it if they couldn't. Any useful mineral or metal goes their way, hence the deep-sea mining, to help with that cause. And what remains of humanity – at some point I'll mention that – works to that altruistic aim. But remember what I said, Drathken are patient. Humans? Fill in your own gaps.

"Okay, I get it. The raid was aimed at getting the raw material. We intercepted, and the MARC has the ability to detect the exact radiation markers. But surely you have specialists for this? And the unit's data can be downloaded, shared. I'm just a sea-cop."

"All true. And we'll be doing that, but we're stretched to hell and back, and the Drathken are fretting. They're talking of pulling contact with the Liaison Parliaments until we cut off the heads of the HLA cells. We need a symbol of intent, and quick results. Your MARC is special—"

*"Someone appreciates me."*

"—ly adapted, the exo-suit can operate on land with a few tweaks."

*"I'm a 'she', not an 'it'."*

"DDSM hold your contract, and now reassigned to us. This isn't a choice." That was Dulik, smooth voice, bitter words.

"Afterwards? What then?" I fished for a bribe, I'm only human.

"You go back down. A little richer and with a warm heart knowing you've done humanity a favour." Now that sounded better. A hero, and with creds to spend on real food. Win-win. Except this was the last thing I wanted to do. Too many opportunities for things to go wrong, too many people I didn't want to meet. Informed people.

"Not that I have a choice but call me a willing partner. I'm in."

*"Harrumph."*

"We're in, the MARC and me."

*"Better."*

"Good. Dulik will get the download and software upgrade sorted. And we'll need to get you up to speed."

# Chapter 5

The helicopter was internally air-cooled, the reconfigured systems running a stream through the hold to ensure all those suited and booted inside could cope in such a small, enclosed space. The noise was awful, but with the helmet replaced by a set of air defenders and a rebreather in place, you traded one discomfort for another. Dulik sat opposite, eyes scanning over a tablet as information poured through the comms headset she wore. Interspersed amid the grimaces were the odd moments when she'd glance my way. I decided it was less a reassurance, than an assessment of how I was taking the ride, and the prospect of engaging with potential terrorists.

Personally, the helicopter ahead of us filled with WPF Marines, and the pair of high-speed intercept frigates now steaming their way towards a third suspect ship, allayed any fears I might have. I'd been twiddling my thumbs back on the platform for three days before the call had come in, only for us to get halfway out over the Pacific Ocean and then be recalled. This was the fifth day, and the third ride, and we were past the halfway mark. I looked up from my personal tablet, pausing the vid I'd acquired with a few creds from the platform's security team. To them, it was just empty ocean scanned routinely by the elevator's AI for any danger. To me, it was beautiful and calming, living and swimming free amid the coral coils and branches. Got to have a few pleasures in life.

*"Play that bit again, where the nudibranch is lit up."*

"Aye, aye, partner." I rewound, the stunning sea slug emerging, its multicoloured tentacles across its back and around its mouth caught in a shaft of light from the surface. My heart ached.

"Nkosi," I glanced up, automatically pausing and then switching off my tablet. Dulik motioned me over, handing me a pair of cans to replace my air defenders. I dropped in beside her as she focused the tab screen on something less than beautiful. The ship's image was surrounded by known data – registration, home port, name, etc. Each had been crossed out by Dulik, a second note written by their side. To my eyes, it looked like one of the old whaling ships, with an added water tank and crane at the rear.

"Look," she enhanced the image of the external storage tank. It'll come as no surprise that two whales swam slowly in there. An orca and a Cuvier's beaked whale, same species as the one we had chased. Both were modded, head surgery complemented by an additional metal collar wrapping behind and underneath the dorsal fin. There was no way they were sharing a tank otherwise or could survive in the food depleted ocean for very long. The crane added to the burden of guilt, the dull-grey, bulbous submersible at its base explaining its purpose.

"How long until intercept?" I asked.

"They're playing fast and loose with the weather, plotting a course towards a storm, but the Frigate *WNF Carson* will cut them off. Then it's boarding. Dangerous if they resist, especially as we need to safely recover whatever evidence they have on where the nodules have gone."

"Gone? I thought ..."

"If we hadn't been on a wild goose chase with the others, then yeah. We might have got here in time, but not now." I didn't ask what a goose was, she was in a moment.

"So why am I here?"

"The modded whales, Nkosi, are not illegal nor proof of involvement. All the evidence blew up two clicks down. I need to know if there's any trace of the same radiation signature, and if your MARC unit is right, the same oil residue. They match, the WPF can tear up the place legally. It makes things easier. Keeps the higher-ups happy."

"And what if they don't?" I knew the answer, but felt she needed to affirm how important this all was for the newbie. I can be obliging.

"Then we rip it up, and the Liaison Parliament will be receiving depositions left, right and centre. But, for once, the Drathken are in a rush. They say, we do. It's the way the world works."

"Fine by me. I'm in."

*"Me too. Those whales …"*

* * *

The frigate had it harder than Dulik painted it, the ex-whaling ship more adept in the deep swells than I thought possible. The weaving dance came to an end when the second WNF vessel caught up, cutting off any chance to escape attention. Two shots from each frigate's main guns over the bow went unheeded, and unable to risk damaging potential evidence, the WPF Marines hit the water in fast intercept boats. Under the cover of the ships' helicopters, both managed to reach the sides before responding small arms fire tore into the *Carson's*. It blew, half the boarding squad engulfed in the explosion, the other half hauling themselves up the hull as the helicopter raked the deck clear with 20mm cannon fire. The second frigate's Marines were halfway up the starboard side when the ex-whaler's crew pulled sheets back to expose twin barrelled heavy machine guns swinging on 360° pivots. They had a huge circular sight at the end and looked as ancient as the boat itself. Two bursts sped across the heaving water towards WNF *Carson's* helicopter, catching the side doors and peppering the cockpit. Paired missiles responded, the impacts' glow lighting the dull-grey sky as the storm moved in.

"Take us in!" shouted Dulik, my stomach jumping into my throat as the 'copter dropped, hitting an air pocket. The pilot wrestled on through it, carrying us towards the errant ship.

"It's not clear yet!" I responded, now convinced we were boarding a terrorist ship, or worse, one crewed by pirates and sea scavengers.

All I got was a look of disdain. Where had that warmth gone? Oh yeah, I said *yes.*

I buckled up, pulling the restraints tight as the helicopter pitched and yawed.

A crewmember started adjusting a pulley system, its cradle whipping about as wind and rain lashed the chopper. I squeezed my eyelids shut, wondering which God I'd recently forsaken might help first. Then it hit me, the cradle was for me, us. I'd seen no landing pad on the ship below.

"Fuck," I said aloud.

*"Yeah, procreate."*

A clatter of the door pulling back cut through the self-pity, and I opened my eyes to see Dulik cinching her helmet strap. She prodded me with her toe, and I nodded, tightening mine as Dulik attached herself to the pulley. She then removed her rebreather before being winched down. I watched as the rope swung beneath the fuselage, and back, trying not to think about my turn.

Now, suffice to say, that my lovely breakfast didn't stay down. I am proud, however, that no other bodily fluids were forthcoming, just a few external bruises when the 'copter yawed right as I swung left. Dulik gathered me in at the bottom, a pair of Marines covering while she unclipped the shaking sea-cop. Me that is.

Once on deck, my lungs decided it was safe to come out of hiding, and I sucked in a breath.  It was hot, sticky, wet and salty all at once.  Foul. Remembering the rebreather, I slotted it back in, Dulik shoving me towards a door guarded by another Marine. Once inside, the noise abating, only the ship's movements gave any hint we were in a storm. Those I could cope with. Home territory.

"This way, ma'am," shouted a voice along the rusty white corridor. Dulik pressed ahead, stepping over the bloodied bodies left by the Marines' advance inside. She bolted up the internal steps, and I followed close behind, pleased to see I was the steadier this time. Another Marine waited at the bulkhead, spinning the door lock to let us both through into the most modern part of the vessel – the bridge – its captain dead upon the floor, another man sat in the navigator's chair. Asian, balding and probably in his fifties, with a scar across the top of his nose. He looked ruffled, eyes darting from Dulik and back to me – trying to decide who was in charge. He chose wrongly, making eye contact with me, and went to speak. Dulik whacked him on the jaw. Apparently, I was 'good cop', and not in charge.  She hit him again as a WNF operative appeared, one in a standard navy uniform and soaking wet. She didn't give any of us a second glance, immediately approaching the ship's wheel and navcom systems.

A third *umph* returned my attention to Dulik, who stepped away from the bloodied prisoner, glancing back at the Marine on guard. "Take Nkosi to the sub. I need the info on the radioactive material and the engine in the next five minutes, so I know whether I'm in my rights to kick the rest of the shit out of this asshole."

"On it," I said, feeling Marc adjust herself against my back. I nodded towards the soldier, and we headed off. I sensed the ship begin to turn, the subtle shift of the waves' impact thrumming through my boots. The soldier seemed confident, so I let her lead, assuming she'd studied the expected layout before the assault. A few level drops, bypassing the odd dead body, we came to an external bulkhead. Lifting the bar, we were hit by a combination of wind and sea water, though relief from the stifling internal heat was welcome. We were one level from the crane system, so we grabbed the rails, noting the entire ship was wired with safety cabling to clip onto – not that we were prepped for that. We staggered the last ten metres and descended the steps to arrive near the strapped down sub. It was old, I'd say pre-Scorching, but robust, with minimal portals to reduce any risk. Visuals were dependent on camera systems, and the external limbs in great condition. I made a guess that whoever maintained it, piloted it, knowing the machine like the back of their hand because their life depended on it. Marc wriggled, and I felt her slip off my waist and shoulders. I knew the Marine was gawping. I sent her a wink and added a nose twitch in case I got out of practice. My tentacled partner slithered across the wet deck, metal tips wrapping around the rear propellers and settling in.

"*Analysing,*" she said. After a minute, data streamed into the chip. "*It's the same taste, and taking into consideration engine particulates, and lubricating oil, it's a yes from me.*"

I relayed that to the Marine, who immediately accessed her radio. The thought of the man in the navigator's chair flickered through my mind. Ah well.

Marc let go of the propellors, using her tentacles to range out and grasp the gentle curves of the submersible. She dragged herself along the hull until she reached the first of the metal limbs protruding beneath the bow and entangled herself amid the grapple arm. After another minute, she dropped, heading for something I'd missed. Underneath the main body, there was add-on housing bolted on with a box secured to it. Curious, strong tentacles soon had this apart, exposing a UV drone similar to that Benni had shown me two clicks under the ocean.

*"It's singing,"* said Marc. *"Definitely. This vehicle has been in contact with the cargo. Bang to rights."*

I let the Marine know, Marc dropping to the deck before hitching her way up my spine and settling into position.

"You're to go back to the bridge. Be okay to find your own way?" Gunfire cut through the wind's howl, and I ducked down, only for the soldier to look over to her left, clearly unfazed. "Getting rid of stuff we don't need," she spouted, glancing my way. "The whales."

The words took a while to sink in. Marc's grip on my waist tightening as once again I found myself standing outside of the info loop, looking despairingly in. I headed towards the source of the sound, the Marine's protests swept away by the wind, or ignored, I don't know which. Climbing the steps up the tank side, I peered down into the now dark red water. Two heads bobbed sideways in the too small tank, one glassy eye from each staring back, accusations of being late as usual slung my way. My mind refused to accept their deaths, and I found my hands reaching out, touching the orca's skin. The connection was absent, as if the soul had already left, and the light from within that mournful eye faded while I watched. The three intertwined aerials protruding from its skull, surrounded by poorly healed scar tissue, sunk beneath the blackening surface. Acid rose from my empty stomach, burning the base of my throat. The Cuvier flopped, rolling. A clicking emanating from deep inside the body, before it too weakened and eventually slipped away. Its antenna adorned corpse joined the other beneath the bloodied water, with an accusing black eye the last to slide beneath the surface.

*"Why?"*

I had no answer. I still don't. Not only to maim a creature by hacking it open, but to then end its life as if it were inconsequential. Discarded.

"Hey, man," said a WPF Marine to my left, climbing the ladder she had clearly just descended. "I've done that job. You're wanted. If you ain't there in five, Dulik will blow a gasket, or three." She winked at me, attempting to pull me into her world. At first, my heart hammered, and I could sense Marc tensing up. But then the tentacles shifted, one either side pressing into the base of my neck, easing my tension. I put back on the face I show the world, a mask to hide my thoughts behind. I nodded to the Marine, looking back to the tank. "Yeah, you did your thing. My bad." I moved past the soldier, clapping her on the arm on the way, giving her the pearly whites. As I took in her green/grey eyes I swore I'd remember her face. She sent a grin back, one I let sink in before descending the ladders and heading towards the bridge.

I fully expected the bald sailor-cum-navigator to be black and blue by the time I arrived, but no. The spark had left his eyes, however, with investigator extraordinaire Dulik working out he was far more than just the navigator when she spotted how big his clothes were, and the supposed ship's captain's far too small. A few minutes of discussing field surgery techniques and he was singing like one of those goose we had been chasing.

My thoughts back on the helicopter were half-right. Pirates they had been until the ship was bought out from under them and retrofitted with the crane and tank. The captain and half the crew had just stayed on, preferring the money and the reduced danger. Until the WPF came knocking.

"He says he knows nothing about the cargo, that he was just following orders," said Dulik. "I can get enough drugs in him to get the bastard to turn canary."

(Ah, see, I knew it was a bird that sang)

"But that'll have to be back at base, under Rainsford's supervision," she continued. "I was thinking your recovery unit could have a little taste, see if he has any traces of the cargo on him?"

I nodded, still mentally sore but being useful would help. Marc's four tentacles detached from my shoulders, and she slid down, landing on the steel floor with a slight clang. My eyes never left the old pirate, my tight smile turning into a full beam as he watched Marc pull herself along the floor towards him.

*"Stop enjoying this."*

"No." I said, mind on the modded whales' last pleading looks. This man had accepted them on board, and the people who'd either dissected and modified intelligent animals for their own gain or paid for it. Same thing. "The whales."

Marc wrapped a tentacle around his ankle, then the knee of the other leg, pulling herself upwards. The captain's eyes widened with each tentacle movement, fear of the unknown and the sheer strangeness drying his throat. Only a hoarse 'no' escaped as she reached his shoulders. The two Marines on the bridge were halfway between shit-eating grins and primal revulsion. I enjoyed that too.

*"There's traces. He's been around the cargo. Can you get him to put his hands out?"*

I'm more than positive Marc was playing with the man at my behest. The data running into my chip was enough to incriminate the old bastard without prolonging it. Ah, but you have to humour your cephalopod, and she'd picked up my mood.

"Put your hands out." I said the words slow, letting my smile tighten and pull wide. A little maniacal glint in my eye. Okay, maybe I imagined the last bit. Shaking, he extended his hands, still mouthing 'no' as Marc crept down his shoulder and along his arms. On reaching the wrists, she let her metal body glow a shade of red.

"Something new?"

*"If I showed you everything at once you might get bored of me."*

Dulik had already taken the hint, and by the look of the old pirate's reddening face, she'd be losing a source of information pretty soon if I let Marc loose any longer. "Yeah, he's handled the cargo." Marc unwrapped her tentacles, dropping to the floor in one smooth motion and headed my way.

I can't remember much of the conversation after that, only the waves smoothing out and the dropping of the wind as the ship's new WNF navigator turned us away from the passing storm. Amid the walk back to the stern to prep for the returning helicopter, the only word that sunk in was Tijuana.

# Chapter 6

During the debrief back on the WNF *Carson*, things got interesting. Apparently, my reassignment was going to last a little longer. Having ascertained that the cargo had been off-loaded onto a seaplane along with two well-dressed women whose names were clearly false, and four others of a far different ilk, the seventh member of their little terrorist cell lay with a bullet to the brain wearing the captain's attire. He'd been the sub operator and mechanic, Marc ascertaining the man had received an unhealthy dose of a familiar nodule sourced radiation markers. According to our goose-cum-canary, the pilot was a loose cannon after a bottle or two of cactus juice, and one of the women decided his fate after combining a sedative with his favoured tipple. Nice to know they were as callous with human life as they were with cetacean.

"We need to get you equipped," said Rainsford, somehow making his office on the fast frigate as bland as the one back on the platform. Maybe that's how they all were? So that in the fast-moving world of the WPF Lead Officer, he could orientate himself swiftly, be ready at every turn. Or maybe it was cheaper.

"Equipped?"

"Yes. Tijuana is a burning, fiery shithole. Not a place to go unprepared." Yeah, save that snippet of information for last. My geography isn't great. I know I mention places, stuff I've seen on vids, but this was one subject I showed little interest in. Did I tell you I was home educated? No? As the sea level rose, and Rio flooded, the powerful and the monied left. The best places to survive and rebuild were already taken by the favelas, and no one fancied clearing those out. And with them, went the teachers, with only a few saintly ones staying to set up basic education in those favelas where the local gangs offered protection. Now my parents had been educated—rare you say in Rio's slums—but that wasn't their home turf. No. I mentioned they were 'creatives', right? The type unwanted on board those starships sailing towards whatever system the Drathken had pointed them at. Well, they were creative with *data*. The kind that wings its way between info systems, data centres – oh, and banks. Not that they ever got to see much of it. They were the monkey, not the piano grinder. So, for their 'protection', they ended up as the gang's 'live-in' hackers. And that included me. Yeah, I could roam the streets, and with more freedom than most as I enjoyed an equal amount of protection. Made me an asshole at times, did some mean things. But my *mae* and *pai* would always find out, and that meant extra lessons. Usually geography. What was the point with the world drowning, burning or both?

Where was I? Oh yeah.

Tijuana. Rainsford brought up a map, highlighting the delightfully named city. I researched it later, the name supposedly means 'by the sea'. You can find it next to 'irony' in the dictionary. Most of the river valley it was built on was now under five metres of seawater. Not near enough the equator to be uninhabitable, just, but in spitting distance. Of course, it would dry up the second it left your lips, while the air sucked the remaining moisture from your mouth and came back for more. Fiery shithole was an understatement. I've seen the vids – those of Darwin, Sri Lanka, and on a dark day, Nairobi. Hell on Earth. A good place to hide then.

"That MARC upgrade had better be top-notch."

*"Something I should know?"*

* * *

Now there are fiction books out there that depict a full-body suit worn on a distant planet, one where you consume your own bodily fluids in a continuous cycle. That's how the original MARC exo-suits operated, and though resources get depleted, they can keep the cephalopod alive for an extended period. Longer if it drew seawater from around it.

*"Welcome to my world, partner."*

What I didn't expect, was for me to need the human version. Mine, however, was rubbery, the inner lining strange against the skin. Come to think of it, I felt more like an octopus than Marc. There were breathing and water tubes pinned either side of my neck, and a full mask with eye-cover due to the irritants prevalent on the hot winds. Near my left hand was the additional reservoir, and to the right a holster for the standard issue Glock I was registered to wear. Dulik had ditched the sharp suit, and let's say her collection of weaponry dwarfed mine. It made me feel so much safer that we were going into a place where she needed the pump-action shotgun and flash grenades. None of the ultra cool weapons here. In this heat, reliability was king (or queen or whatever monarch you want). Behind her in the cacophony of the helicopter, a team of four WPF Marines prepped. Let's just say I was imagining Tijuana as a fiery shithole, with its own personal war zone.

"You stay with us," bellowed Dulik in the radio. "You do not, and I repeat, do not get distracted and leave your team. Understand? I've seen your file, Nkosi. You've watched enough of the old films to know how many pieces you can end up in if you leave the fuckin' path."

Now, I'm not sure which bit worried me the most, the fact she'd reviewed my records, or that they contained what I actually watched. A moment of horror washed over me. Did you know it's possible to blush under a rubber exo-suit? I can confirm it's possible. I mean, it's embarrassing. Those cartoons were for kids (cough).

"Yes, ma'am. Stay with my squad, stick to the path, don't wander the fuck off. If I see a pair of creepy twins beckoning me down a corridor – *I tell you* – not run after them." I'm not sure my tone came across right over the crackle of the radio and the thrum of the copter blades, but her look seemed to suggest it did.

"This is Alpha Squad. You only need to know them as Alpha One through Four. No names. One and two will stick with you, three and four will be on my ass. They are here to protect us, and they are valuable assets." I didn't baulk at that word, but Alpha 1 gave me a side-eye like you wouldn't believe. "And WPF want them back in one piece. They have permission, if you lose it, to make you more *compliant.*" The squad leader followed the side-eye with a smile I'd last seen on the WPF Officer back on the *Socorro*. Alpha 3, however, I'd already met.

The helicopter swung south, skimming the sea edge. The coastline here was hilly, the valleys filled with an angry ocean slapping against dust and rock. As you follow those ridge lines inland there are a few of the older buildings remaining, those not taken out by the rise in the sea level. Most, however, fell during the earthquakes – the population so battered by everything else they finally upped and left, taking whatever they had with them. It was a poisonous cocktail of fucked up mother nature and mirrored what happened all around the world. Those regions already suffering with high temperatures, and weather extremes, just couldn't take any more. It isn't as if no one lives here, just that those with money or connections left Dodge City, and those that didn't we were about to meet.

I unholstered my Glock, checked it over, and made sure my newly acquired WPF belt had the clips to hand. Over my exo-suit, I cinched in the combat armour, heavier than anyone would want in the heat, but I like my innards just where they are. Looking out the window, the sprawl of New Tijuana brought back a lot of distant memories. More of those later.

"We're coming in," bellowed Alpha 1.

"Ocean View Hills," Dulik sniggered. Yeah, I used that word. The battered and half-collapsed houses certainly had a close in look at the sea now. The helicopter dropped, throwing us all against the restraints, before being slammed back.

"Thermals," crackled the radio. "Like a fucking rodeo."

We got hit again, this time from the side, and then a drop that jarred my back before the wheels hit dirt. Alpha 3 dragged the door open, and the heat rammed in, sucked every bit of moisture it could, and deposited a shitload of sand. It didn't leave either. Alpha 4 went through, rifle high, with Dulik close behind. A tap on my shoulder and it was my turn, so the newly professional sea-cop jumped to the ground, rising with Glock in hand and scanning the wreck of a building in front. With a swirl of dust, my bodyguards were next to me, and the chopper was lifting off. And with that we were alone – dramatic, huh?

Alphas 1 and 2 did their thing, double teaming the building and giving the all-clear. With no concerns at our rear, a little tension eased off, and my body realised we were on the periphery of a bloody furnace. My face stung with the heat. The neck of the suit chafing where it ended, and the dust rubbed. Trickles of sweat ran everywhere. Somewhere inside my exo-suit some gizmo or other was collecting it for reuse. Lovely.

*"Humans live here?"*

"Only desperate ones. Or those that prey on them."

*"Why?"*

"Good question. I have no answer for you."

"Put your visor down, Nkosi," Dulik motioned with her finger, and I duly obliged. My world turned a little bluer, the Heads-Up Display blipping with welcome signs of Alphas 1 through 4, and Dulik her own special yellow. "Intel says we have two gang hotspots where the HLA have been cultivating support. Both Cartels run the drugs and water runs, tapping off the US reservoirs and hate each other's fuckin' guts. No change there." A satellite image dropped, one devoid of a 'you are here' red arrow – but I'm not picky. A series of dotted lines appeared, snaking through shanty-sided streets. "Stick to the path. We're heading for the T-Cartel first, the most tech minded."

I dropped in behind Dulik, her team running point. Two choices – you enter at speed and try to outrun rumour. Or you go in at night, quiet, and try not to make any. My visor's night vision kicked in, and we moved swiftly across scrub and shifting dunes, until we reached the town's edge. I was expecting wide streets and spaces between each slum to let the air circulate. But they were packed in tight.

"Your system's up?"

*"Yes sir. The only thing I'm getting is the occasional increase in background radiation from the dust. There's a lot of radon in the mix."*

"And?"

*"The system says it causes severe health problems in high concentrations, and it releases radioactive 'daughters' as it decays. If people are living inside to be out of the heat, and doing so without radon scrubbers, it'll exacerbate poor health. Their life expectancy's going to drop."*

I know – how does an octopus form a light pattern for exacerbate?

As for radon, well these guys have it easy. Russia, Norway, Canada? Screwed. Oh, and Alaska. You see, it might be hot as hell down here, but it only took a few degrees change in the cold north and south to cause a stack of problems. Permafrost – sounds cool right? Until it releases methane and radon by the bucketload. The latter kills you slowly, the other perpetuates (beat that cephalopod) the cycle of global warming – accelerating it. I saw this vid where some Innuit in a t-shirt set fire to the air by lighting a match. Sheesh. I digress – I know this crap because Rainsford had taken me through the satellite scans. The entire area glowed like a nuclear bomb had gone off when they used the electromagnetic spectrometer.

We were through the initial three streets, ankle deep in stuff I don't want to think about, when the first, distant shot rang out. I hit a crouch, weapon up, scanning the road with one eye on the HUD visor. Yeah, professional. The Alphas were tense, Dulik letting them work without a word. I glanced back, my Marines eying the eaves and roofs. A few kids appeared behind us, silent, just cloth masks and wide-eyed behind plastic goggles. After peeking out from the tight alleyway, one threw a ball into the street, another collecting it before running over to the other side while the rest chased. At night.

"Dulik. We've been made," I radioed. "They'll know we're coming."

"Just kids, Nkosi."

Yeah, right.

Alphas 3 and 4 signalled us on, and we rose to follow. Likely, some poor sap out there wouldn't be seeing the sunrise after the gunshot, not even if dust had dropped long enough. Two more streets and we would be in Dulik's red zone and on the hunt. Or hunted.

The lead Alphas reached the next crossroads, eyeing the alleyway, one swinging a rifle around with a corner sight, the image feeding into his HUD. Satisfied, Alpha 4 passed her, only for a shot to ring out, catching him low on the thigh. The bullet hit an armoured plate, pinging off into the murk. He spun, trigger already pressed, and the burst caught the kid holding the ancient pistol slap bang in the stomach. A second burst scattered the others, a blood splattered ball and child the only sign they'd been there as they melted into the alleyways.

*"Did she? Was that a…?"*

I didn't answer. She was disappointed enough in humanity. Another round clattered into Alpha 1 behind me, his grunt an affirmation it had hurt but that was all. The Marine spun, rifle up and picked his target. The single shot cracked into the forehead of a real gang member; the cloth mask a symbol of his allegiance. The blood flower a signal of its end.

From the opposite alleyway, the barrel of a shotgun emerged. Assuming it was a pump action similar to Dulik's still holstered on her back, I calculated my chances of survival would increase by joining the fray. My first shot slammed into the building corner, piercing the plastic sheeting. I let a prayer slip with the second, hoping whoever was inside remained unhurt. It struck the barrel as it turned my way. The weapon went off, the muzzle splitting wide as it failed. Dulik fired, the resultant crash of the weapon to the floor and the twitching hand a demonstration of her prowess.

"Move," Alpha 1 shouted, and we did. Upping the pace, now a race to clear the area before we were up to our neck in gang members, or wannabes looking to make a name. Moving at speed in formation is tricky, but I kept my end up, keeping cover on my fellow squad members as we crossed alleyways, helped greatly by the lack of doors and windows facing directly onto the street. Got to keep that heat out.

"Nkosi, we need your MARC unit up and running."

"She's purring away." I replied. "Nothing yet."

*"With the interference, the new system gives me fifty metres range if the cargo is still together, and not shielded."*

I relayed that, a sudden dread gripping my stomach. If it was shielded, then we were looking for a radiation needle in a shanty town full of hate. Shit. But that's why we had the big guns.

The next street really did feel like Dodge City. I counted at least ten gang members behind a couple of old jalopies they'd strung across the dirt. The first shot rang out, striking Alpha 1 on the helmet as he dodged into a side street. In a long list of mistakes a goon makes in life, that one was a doozy. The rocket-propelled grenade rammed into the gangbanger's vehicle, rusted metal tearing him and five others new holes. Alpha 2 opened up, his tight bursts cutting through the ancient cars. The sporadic return fire soon died off, cries for help muffled by cloth masks. Dulik and her Marines ran for what was left of the vehicles, Alphas 3 and 4 picking off those rising from rooftops when the temptation became too much.

We joined them, a brief stir of conversation agreeing we should stick together. Alpha 2 swung up her little tube of death and made an entrance into Dulik's target building before temporarily casting it aside.

Knock, knock.

And in we went.

# Chapter 7

"Sen-sors up!" I said, stifling a smile.

*"Eh?"*

Some cephalopods don't watch enough classic sci-fi vids.

"Never mind. You got anything?" I tapped impatiently on the dirty table in what I took to be a makeshift kitchen. The room now had a new door, not quite as nicely made as those on the *Socorro* – you couldn't even shut it to keep the heat and dust out.

*"It's difficult. This place is full of interference, not a healthy place at all. There may be a hint of something three metres up and ten metres back."*

Guessing my dimensionally astute cephalopod meant the second floor, I told Dulik, the sounds of assault rifles and flash grenades punctuating my radioed words. We met Alpha 3 and 4 at the rickety stairs, and with 1 and 2 sweeping the rest of the ground floor, they led us up. I kept my body on a half-turn, watching behind and casting only the occasional glance upwards for reassurance. The dust still flew below, but the dull thud of weapons' fire was lessening, so I felt reassured everything was going to plan until the bloodied gang member ran for the first step. She wasn't looking our way, the makeshift breathing apparatus probably masking me from view. I fired, the bullet searing into her neck. Blood spurted, and she died, her eyes catching mine as the momentum whipped her around. Now you might think I would find this difficult, being a sea-cop and all. Not many gunfights at two clicks down. But there are a few caveats you need to know. Firstly, I want to live. Secondly, I have a keen sense of responsibility to Marc who gripped my shoulders and waist. Thirdly, well, I'm far more used to violent death than most. I mentioned I'm from Brazil, right? To be more accurate, Rocinha's favela. From the tales my parents told, it was bad enough before the Scorching took hold and the seas rose. Afterwards? I'll let you use your imagination. And what was that you asked me? How did a kid from the favelas, with a name like Nkosi, which isn't even Brazilian, end up as an underwater cop? I'll get there – we're in the middle of a firefight here. Patience.

Gunfire rang out from above.

"Grenade," said Alpha 3, and the flash and roar pierced the dark. Heavy boots hit the steps and bursts of assault rifles followed. By the time I reached the summit, Dulik had swapped out to her shotgun, the rounds peppering splintered doorways and an intricate pipe system that ran across the ceiling.

*"Radon fan,"* said Marc. *"I think if I tune the levels out from that. Yes."*

A blue, flashing light appeared in my HUD. Left-hand doorway, the one Dulik decorated with her buckshot. "This way," I radioed, forgetting myself a little, and heading for the door. Come on, first mistake.

"No!" shouted one of the Alphas. Don't know which, but Alpha 4 had barged me aside by the time he'd pronounced the 't' in 'shit'. The rocket-propelled grenade slammed into his chest, sending the Marine crashing back through the makeshift banister and on through the next door. The explosion tore the room apart, floor and ceiling collapsing. Dulik pumped a round into the shaking teenage gang member framed by the doorway, young eyes seeing his own death as the muzzle flashed. From the floor, I'd have put him around sixteen. When Dulik had finished, age didn't matter.

"Fuck, Nkosi."

I dragged myself up, turning to stare at the mess I'd made. Both of them. Alphas 1 and 2 careered up the stairs, assessing the situation, choosing to head for the wrecked room while Alpha 3 stayed with us. I tried to avoid her eyes, the words 'valuable assets' ringing through my ears. And then that asset emerged, two Alphas either side, combat armour shredded and clearly in tremendous pain. But alive. I still don't know how.

Alpha 3 looked over, then at me, a brief shake of the head before she dropped into the doorway. Stepping over the meat Dulik had left, they advanced in, the WPF Officer acting as her buddy as if it was the most natural thing to do.

"Dulik," I shouted, then remembering, clicked the radio and repeated it.

"Wait there," came her terse reply, but I can be a pain in the ass when rattled.

"No, you need Marc. There's radon all through this place, we'll need to be close."

Dulik stepped back, peering over my shoulder. I assume Alpha 1 sent an affirmative, as I'm soon following with him on my rear, the other Marine tending to my mistake. Two more empty rooms, devoid of incident, caused me a little concern. If the cargo was here, then surely there would be HLA. And they wouldn't be wearing colours – and were likely to be better armed.

*"It's the same radiation signature. I have it."*

"Great work." The red glow focused in, the point clearly to the right in the warren of rooms we were working through. I let Dulik know, and Alpha 3 led us to a stark corridor flanked by plastic sheeting. We reached a stout door, the best we'd seen. Short of a 'radiation' logo and a 'bad guys are here' sign, it appeared we had found the correct place. Alpha 1 joined his compatriot at the front, cracking the door open before running through the grenade routine. He went in first, rifle up, shouting and bellowing in Spanish and English. Only a single shot rung out, followed by thumps and scuffles. By the time Dulik let me in, the smoke had cleared, and I felt Marc shuffle on my back. Stepping through, there were two dead, bespectacled older women in the far corner, their clothes and immediate appearance as far from the slums of Tijuana as you could get. Not missing out the fancy rebreather either, that lay draped across one of them – what worried me was that the other didn't. I made two immediate assumptions – one that she'd had the Drathken surgery, the other that any of her progeny had likely been gene altered. Money. That's what hung over the corpse. A big neon sign spelling trouble. Their throats had been cut, the blood relatively dry. An older man lay in the other corner, fully bearded, his rebreather not so high tech but better than most you'd find in a shanty town. Definitely T-Cartel by the tattoo stretching across his neck and the colours tied to the tubing. The rise and fall of his chest indicated he was alive, the livid bruise forming on his cheek and temple why he was out like a light.

Marc tensed, then I felt the first tentacle twitch. Four detached from my shoulders, and she slid down to the floor. I enjoyed the sight of both Alphas as they stepped back, the tentacles briefly touching each boot as she wiggled on past.

"Don't tease, they're in a bad mood."

*"You're no fun."*

The octopus eased underneath the bodies, the flesh hardly moving as she squirmed into the tiniest of spaces, only one tentacle tip left exposed.  It waggled, the tip twitching for attention.

"You're showing off."

*"I'm not. There's a ... a latch? I think there may be a removable floor here, with a door in it?"*

I relayed to Dulik, and after they gently removed the bodies with gloved hands, Marc rolled away a dirtied rug to expose the simple trapdoor. Beneath it, was an inlaid concrete box. Inside of that, an old-fashioned safe, with a tumbler lock. Dodge City indeed.

# Chapter 8

I dropped onto the bed, the soft mattress a luxury I had already taken advantage of for the past eight hours, but the temptress drew me back. After a short nap, I woke to find Marc curled up on the chair opposite, waiting. I knew what for and we took one of the greatest luxuries left – a shower. Reclaimed water, or not, it was something to savour. The caress of cold H2O on skin made my mind sing, the joy shared by the cavorting, metal cephalopod who kept clinging onto the shower head whenever I turned it onto myself. Yeah, I know, it sounds a bit weird. But luxury or not, it was time limited, and Marc wasn't taking no for an answer. Come on, I heard people used to wash their pets in fresh, clean water.

While I dried off, she bathed in the shower basin, body blocking the drain as her tentacles splashed in the receding water. A simple pleasure, for both of us, yet so needed. I left my exo-suit hung up to dry in the humidifier cupboard set aside for it, donning my URF uniform and ready (or not) to see whatever came next. Marc, rolling in a towel first, wrapped herself around me, a playful tap on my shoulder letting me know she was set ready.

The walk through the sparse, grey corridor, was punctuated by the ringing of my boots on the WNF ship's metal deck. With resources so scarce, it amazed me just how much space was given over to us. Then I remembered Rainsford's words on why we saw so few operatives – the WPF having been stretched to near breaking point over recent months. With the terrorist threat growing, they faced missions all around the world as HLA cells arose from whatever pit they'd been hiding in.

Dulik's smooth voice greeted me when I knocked on the half-open door, and duly entered. She was slouched in the chair opposite the Lead Officer, eyes on a tablet playing through the scene in the Cartel HQ. I winced when it caught me from behind heading for the doorway, before cutting off briefly in fire and smoke. Alpha 4's feed damning my actions as it witnessed the RPG flaring into life. Rainsford looked up from his own tablet screen, and I was relieved to see a hint of a welcome there.

"Ah, Joshua. Sit will you." He pointed me towards a second comfortable looking chair, which I pulled up, collecting a glass of reclaimed water on the way past. We were back to the nice WPF Lead Officer, and I was getting what I could while it lasted. "Dulik has filled me in on the raid. Apart from the ... err ..."

"Fuck up," interjected Dulik, not looking up.

"Issues with Alpha 4, who will live, if you weren't aware. Those jackets, and the distance from the release to the strike, saved him we think." I let show how pleased I was – really, I did. "Now. Ah, you've donned your old uniform. Bit early, I'm afraid. Going to need the MARC for a while longer."

"Huh?" Hey, we all knew it was coming, but the opportunity might arise where I could up the bribe a little. In life, you take what you can when you're dealt a bum hand. "I thought we were done?"

"That was the plan, and my preference," cut in Dulik. Remember her? Smooth voice, warm welcome. I did warn you.

"But Drathken Command see it different. They want to see the MARC unit in action again. They think there's potential for field use with the WPF, and Dulik here agrees, despite the surly nature."

"Hey, the unit works fine, and the operator until he gets too big for himself." This time she did glance up, and there it was. A twitch at the edge of her eye, a redness.

*"Her mate."*

Cephalopods are sensitive to that kind of thing. I stayed quiet, it was a rabbit hole I didn't need right now – nor her. But yeah, I wouldn't be surprised.

I took a drink, hiding my emotions with the glass. Guilt maybe? Hard to tell, so much was happening to me as my cushy life swerved to the left. Possibly. I did look Dulik straight in the eye, and once composed, let the glass drop, hoping my face relayed enough concern at my own actions. I nodded, as if to agree, a wordless apology.

"If I have no choice other than to carry on, then I'll do better."

"Fuck yeah, or we'll spark you out and revive you when we need your unit."

Apology accepted then.

*"Yep, definitely her mate. The air tastes of stress hormones."*

"You can taste the air? Since when?"

*"Since the exo-suit upgrade. I used to taste things with my suckers, it kind of amplifies that."*

Whoa, need to focus, not the time to get distracted by that snippet of information. Good job I showered.

"Like I said, I'll do better. How long's this for? I have a job I rather like waiting for me below. Including a lot less danger."

"Indefinite. Until the Drathken say otherwise. They want the polymetallic nodules back in our hands, and to apprehend those involved in planning the dirty bomb. They likely fear its use against any of the joint biosphere study centres."

Yep, sounds right. Targeting joint working – like the Liaison Parliaments. Trying to put a wedge between alien and human. I didn't say that out loud. I'm a kid from the favela – closed-in spaces and all. But from what I understand, outer space is as empty as our oceans, but far beyond the beckoning deep of the blue. Massive, and beyond my tiny brain. I mean these guys, well whatever they are, literally flew impossible distances, and when they saw what we'd done to our planet, stopped off to help. They could have just kept on going, shouting 'it's not our problem', but no. Their cooperation to try and solve our planet's issues is viewed by the great conspiracy theorists, the HLA, as an attempt to take over and dominate humanity. And as per usual, the crackpots in the human gene pool decide altruism is a bad thing. As if they haven't caused enough problems, fuckheads. Anyway, use a dirty bomb where we cooperate most and we could be kissing our arses goodbye while we burn in our own shit, our alien benefactors pissing off to find a people worth saving. Makes sense.

Now aliens and space aren't my fields of expertise, but I know the basics. A few of the Drathken Interstellar ships had taken root on Earth. Literally. They grow their ships in space, something inconceivable to human minds other than in a few of the weirder sci-fi vids I could find. The ships are plant based, at least that's how humans categorise the material, heavily genetically modified and able to travel from one solar system to another. The ships make it possible somehow, and most Drathken still live aboard the huge starships, rarely seen except at their plant farms, the fertiliser stations or in the joint Drathken/Human Science Labs around the planet. I mean, not even the aliens can stand what we've done to the bloody place.

Good times.

"Here," said Dulik, handing the tab over. "Those are the isotope markers for the missing nodules downloaded from MARC. What they stored in that box was a perfect match. But it'll need extracting, and they'll require more if they are targeting anything bigger than say a house."

*"That's all correct, Josh. It was definitely in there."*

I nodded, the info meaningless to me, but I need to look professional.

"Torres talked after a little *persuasion*."

And a few drugs, she missed that bit out. After law and order broke down and the WPF was formed, anything goes. Their mandate wide and forceful. Fear leads to panic.

"The polymetallics left three hours before you arrived, which matches the readouts. It needs extracting as Dulik says, and Torres's knowledge was sketchy, the Human Liberation cell not keeping him fully in the loop. The two female terrorists got separated from the HLA retrieval squad on the streets of Tijuana and returned seeking help. The bastard killed them, his paid job done – somewhere in his mumblings he stated he was after their breathing implants. The brain scan confirms he believes he's telling the truth."

"So why do you need me? You're at a dead end without knowing where it's going."

"We don't need you. We need your fucking MARC unit, and that means you come along for the ride as you're connected to its electronic brain." Yeah, not forgiven.

*"Told you I was the important one."*

Rainsford sighed, rubbing his eyes before continuing, "Because the MARC can help us check the most likely place. We ID'd the HLA women, both were based in Stockholm."

I perked up at that. Bliss. We're talking 35, maybe 38°C tops right now and from what I hear, still green. Even the weather plays ball, just a few months either end of extreme heat or floods.

Rainsford caught my look, shaking his head. "Hate to disappoint, but that's not where we're heading. The Scandi WPF have had them on comms monitoring for the past eighteen months. Until two weeks ago they thought they were clean despite some of the obvious leanings towards anti-Drathken sentiment in their posting. Then they went silent, and their personal stash of critical oxygen and resource assets sent around the bloody planet in shipping data they couldn't trace. The Scandis suspect most of the last three months of investments were a sham, hiding payments for this op, the rest financing any physical assets they could hide in the chaos of unregistered cargo. And now they both turn up in bloody Tijuana with a new smile."

Dulik stood up, "The key focus is the HLA's need to extract the radioactive material, and for that they'll need a lab and a week or so, assuming they have the knowledge to do it. With all these critical resource payments winging their way around the world, somewhere in that pattern will be a cross-reference to those who have the capability."

Now in my old vids, there'd be a long list on some database of all the scientists and their whereabouts. We'd cut away to a montage of people tapping away, or on the phone. A data analyst would rifle through their accounts, cargo chits, plane tickets and 'violin' —"

*"Voilà."*

"—voilà, you'd have the clue to the nefarious villain's hideout. That doesn't take into consideration the sheer anarchy that ensued when the Scorching really took hold. Worldwide riots, when it wasn't too hot, too wet, or people too bloody ill. Comms breaking down, connections severing as hubs nearer the extremes of the planet became unusable. And zero money spent on maintaining satellite systems.  Stuff breaks remember, not just people – especially in the heat and the wet. The rich and the powerful built walls and stored resources, while the world truly began to fall apart. Then the Drathken arrived, and one of the first things they did was set up a structured satcom system to connect those in power. I won't go into that now, but the rest of us humans, being as resourceful as we are when pressed, cobbled together all those disparate systems – the broken and the ancient – into a spaghetti mess for the common people. One my parents exploited for the gangs. And no, data's not my bag either. Try tracing anything in that tangle of hardwired, bluetoothed, Wi-Fi'd and transistor led chaos. Smoke signals would tell you more.

"We have a liaison arriving in a few hours, to enable access to satcom and make use of the Drathken monitoring system." Rainsford looked at me, his eyes hardening. "Associate Minin will work alongside us until we locate the extraction site, or where the actual bomb may be built."

Speechless. Now I know you think that's unlikely, but it's true. A Drathken was coming here, to this WNF ship. I'd never even been on the same continent as one, never mind the same room. I'm sure Rainsford enjoyed the moment of incredulity washing over me, but at least Dulik matched it. The purported saviour of humankind occupying the same space as me.

*"Us, partner. Us."*

# Chapter 9

I stood, hands gripped to the rail with eyes locked on the approaching spaceship. Yep, I said those words – space and ship – but together, as if it was real. It's okay watching vid screen recordings of their first arrival in orbit, and of those that entered our atmosphere and set root in South Africa, China and Canada. That had never felt real, almost talking of the Drathken as some distant saviour, not one you could actually meet – like an angel I suppose. Mythical. You see pictures of them and hear their promises to make things right, but physically they don't feel present. In the now.

I felt nauseous. Not quite sure if it was the motion of the sea at the rear of the WNF *Carson*, or the thought of who and what I was about to engage with. The spaceship dropped, skimming the waves, its purple hull veined with shades of blue that pulsed in a steady rhythm. It was hard to put a size on it, the transport shaped much like a pea pod I'd seen on an old ad. A smooth outer surface with two – no three humps – before tapering off at the back. As it neared, I guessed the length at around fifteen metres long and about five high where it bulged. The veins, clearer now, were exactly that, writhing out from under the ship, branches and offshoots wrapped around the leaf-like hull. I pulled my jaw back up, checking for drool, while the spaceship wheeled about so the engine faced starboard, and a rush of dust-filled air broke over me. It increased the heat, the scorch and dryness trying to force its way inside my rebreather as the wind impact shifted sideways. With eyes watering, I adjusted the mouth-ring back into place, never taking my eyes off the marvel now descending. You know that moment when you think you've seen everything? Roots – and I swear this on my parent's deathbed – roots grew downwards. I can't describe it any other way. They gripped hold of the riveted handholds that surrounded the ship's helipad, and the Drathken spaceship pulled itself towards the pad, settling onto the stern. The roar of its engines lowering before cutting out.

"Fuck me."

*"Ditto."*

Rainsford waited; head bowed with hands clasped in front of him. I sympathised; I really did. How do you meet a race that seeks no deference, which shuns physical contact and whose body language is so alien to us that they may as well be stone. When do you know you have said or done the right or the wrong thing? Human liaisons were rare, coveted, on Earth – those with the brain structure able to accept the translation mods without losing their sanity. So much so, word was the Drathken now kept them aboard their ships, safe from harm or kidnap. The HLA went as far as saying they were heavily modded and no longer human. That they couldn't be trusted. Yet another conspiracy.

The side of the hull peeled back, and I sensed the whole welcoming committee stand straighter, shoulders back, holding that last breath. A ramp rolled out – a stiff carpet of purple, fibrous plant matter – and a human woman stepped through the newly formed gap. Now I'm not one to exaggerate, well a little. Okay, I embellish. But she was beauty personified. Her skin shone, I mean like it was lit by a golden sun, and her brown eyes were wide. Her whole body moved with such grace. My nose —

*"Don't."*

"Ah. C'mon Marc. Jealous?"

*"I'm an octopus, idiot."*

"Then what's up?"

*"She doesn't taste right."*

"Taste right? I'm not taking life lessons from a cephalopod who judges people by *taste*."

*"..."*

"You raising your eyebrows at me?"

*"If I had them I would."*

The Drathken followed. Now this is where the HLA get their impetus from. You see, the old sci-fi vids had encounters in two discrete forms. There would be the humanoid ones, near humans, with a skin colour difference, or eyes and ears. The females would always be ravishing, and the male hero (yeah, I hear you) would sweep them off their alien feet. Often, with a bad alien in the background, some wrong done leading to a fight, etc. Or the alien would be the epitome of 'a monster', and that meant evil. Tentacles (sorry Marc) or slimy skin. They were frequently not biped and usually insectoid or lizard like. Earth would obviously be in peril, the aliens having travelled hundreds of light years to eat us, or blow up our cities, etc.

So, when the first Drathken appeared, you can imagine the people who went on to form the HLA choking on their corn bread. Two metres tall, purple, chitinous bodies with four legs on the bulbous lower body, jointed to an upper thorax sporting two more limbs we assumed were arms. The head presented as a combo of praying mantis and a catfish. Visualise the future HLA, sat in their lazy chairs, sharpening their pitchforks until someone announced the ultimate evil, the bastards were vegetarians! Okay, I exaggerate a little, they had a penchant for home world insects to supplement their plant diet.

I'll give the WPF their due, not one stepped back when the alien unfurled, raising its upper limbs to display a rainbow 'skin' between its limbs and thorax. A greeting reserved for the *Carson's* Captain, who responded with the elaborate salute required for a higher rank before stepping aside, casting his eyes downward. Apparently, the Drathken found the human gaze disconcerting, and every uniformed member present followed the example and stared at the deck.

A sawing sound cut through the wind, a mix of chitinous vibrations interspersed with clicks and wheezes.

"Associate Minin thanks you for your welcome and bids you to return to your ship husbandry." The liaison's voice remained flat, no lilt or accent apparent, but not the monotone of electronic systems. It sent a shiver down my spine.

*"Absence,"* said Marc. *"I don't know the right word."*

The only one that came to my mind was soulless. But how do you explain that to a cephalopod? Instead, I sent Marc a thought of sacrifice, of what the woman had given up to become the mediator between alien and human, between salvation and those in need. Her purple braided robes swished as she walked down the ramp, the rope like plant material swaying to expose the human clothes underneath. An exo-suit, similar to the WPF, though it had a silky sheen. A nudge from Marc and my eyes cast down as the sailors and Marines left, leaving just Rainsford and Dulik. Oh, and some sea-cop wondering how the hell he got himself involved in this mess.

The purple-robed woman stepped off the end of the ramp, placing herself next to Rainsford as the alien joined her, its limbs scraping against the deck. When its body came into my eyeline, I could make out the various layers of its natural exoskeleton, a thin, see-through veneer covering the swirls of growth. To my surprise, the liaison appeared to wrap a metallic blue cloth around the Drathken while we waited, an elaborate weave that the alien's limbs gripped and pinned into place.

"Apologies LO Rainsford," said the woman's voice as she worked. "Associate Minin needs some protection from the weather. My name is Clara, with no rank associated. Please, you may look up. My Associate is more used to human contact than most and can tolerate the gaze of a few."

I held in the sigh, looking up to catch a close in view of both representatives. I caught my breath, the Drathken's dual eyes appeared just as empty as the liaison's voice. But why should *I* recognise an alien's body language or nuances? Can I read the few animals I have met? Or the cockroaches that would survive way beyond any human civilisation? I needed to put a lid on assumptions. Different did not make them inherently bad as the HLA and their supporters assumed. And their actions pointed in the opposite direction. Hey, if I can like a surly, sarcastic cephalopod, I can like anything.

*"Heard that."*

Now I assumed our venerable Associate would be joining us in the frigate's WPF office, engaging the satcom systems, and generally helping with the investigation. Apparently not. And it struck me, as Clara explained that the

Drathken body was just not suitable to wander human corridors, negotiate our steps, nor squeeze through doorways, why we so rarely saw them on vid other than in adapted or pre-designed buildings. It also explained the exo-suit I had been told to wear, as we followed Clara and Minin back into the spaceship. Yeah, I said it. I am boarding an alien vehicle. How many fans would that have got me on the 'tube?

You'd have expected, walking into a plant grown ship, that the appearance would have struck me first. The peeling back of the layers, the strange controls, maybe odd seats (if they sat – every day is a learning opportunity). No, it was the sheer heat. I fumbled for the suit's control, upping the system to that akin to Tijuana, feeling Marc harrumph in my head. I sucked in a breath through the rebreather, adjusting the controls again to cool the air and ensuring the scrubber was coping with the extremes. Once we were inside, a hiss exuded, heralding a shimmering in the plant fibres before the hull folded back into place. The glow from the ceiling immediately adjusted to a more orange light, but deep, vibrant. My brain and eyes refused to work together, out of sync before adjusting.

Three tangled roots rose from the floor, forming chairs that pushed against the back of our knees. Sawing sounds punctuated the air, deadened against the hull, but Clara simply gestured to the chairs and requested we sit. The wall split and what I took for a screen emerged from the opposite side. This appeared to be polished insect shell, though the images appearing on it belied that assumption. More sawing words passed between the Associate and Clara, the woman staring at the screen as the images separated, one side a complete blur, the other clearly layer upon layer of the terrorist's ship. When these aligned with my vision, Clara clicked, a sawing sound emanating from her throat. The Drathken eased down to the floor and rested its lower body against the darker fibre there, its lower limb knee joints protruding above the thorax as it bent at rest. With front limbs clasped together, the alien's resting position heightened the similarity to a swollen praying mantis. A final shrug of the body and the wrapped clothing dislodged, ignored for now.

Sweat trickled down my neck and back, a gritty tang to the scrubbed air making it slightly uncomfortable to breathe. But who cares? I'm in a spaceship with a bloody alien. With clicks and noises flying, Clara stood patiently, eyes on us rather than the Associate until the alien finished communicating.

"Associate Minin has arranged for LO Rainsford to have access to the satcom system to coordinate operations in the equatorial regions. The use is limited to him and the assigned WPF operational officers. Should the recovery mission fail, then this may be extended to another unit if required. It is resource heavy; the conditions are worsening." Clara pointed to the alien vid display. "We have the data run from your encounter via the Deep-Sea *Socorro* Mining Operation, URF Nkosi."

I glanced from the screen to Clara, feeling Marc squeeze at my shoulders. She really didn't care for this woman.

"We need the updated analysis from the ship in comparison to what your MARC unit encountered in New Tijuana."

And then it struck me because Marc unfurled without my bidding, sliding along the chair roots and over to the new protrusion growing underneath the vid display. She had never acted without my prompt before, at least not when on duty. She slid a tentacle into a port that formed as I watched, data appearing on our side of the screen. Whatever writing appeared on the other side coalesced into a multi-layered blur of colours and imagery. I expected Marc to return, sending her a message to the modded chip. She ignored me, no response at all. A barrier that clenched at my gut. An absence that rose into a plume of panic, panic that leads to anger.

I made to get up, the Drathken rearing back at my sudden action, clicks flying through the thick air. Clara immediately stepped forward with her hand out hovering near my chest, not quite touching me, but close.

"No. Stay seated. The unit is simply running a diagnostic assessment of the isotopes' degradation. Patience. Check your chip."

I sat back down, Dulik glaring at me, Rainsford likewise aghast at embarrassing him in front of the Associate. I suddenly felt small in that hothouse, as if events were overtaking me. Marc detached, a single tentacle reaching down for the floor before seven more joined it. She dropped; an accompanying dull thud cushioned by the fibrous material. The metallic octopus dragged herself across to me, climbing up to settle against my back. There was a distance there, brief, before I felt a tickle against my neck. I took that as sorry in octopus body language, followed by a calm flooding into my chip.

Minin spoke. The sawing punctuated by clicks while Clara remained motionless, eyes dead as she apparently listened. The screen shifted with multiple satellite views briefly appearing before fading out, leaving a single image. I heard Rainsford swear. To me it was just another ruined city, systematically scorched and flooded for the last few generations. He clearly recognised something.

"Fucking Mexico City."

Now, is it me, or is swearing in front of an alien the done thing?

# Chapter 10

"Joshua."

"…"

"Josh."

"…"

"It wasn't my fault. I was connected up, all senses down."

"…"

"Please. I can't cope without your contact. This suit, it … it distances me from the world."

That did it. I couldn't let her suffer; how unfair can a human be? Don't answer that.

"Okay. Okay. Forgiven."

"…I didn't do anything to be forgiven for."

True. "Wrong word. Let's forget about it." I patted the tentacle. After the meeting had ended, my restrained emotions had come crashing in. It wasn't fair for my partner to be getting the brunt of it. "Looks like they're narrowing down the target area as best they can with all the additional interference. Rainsford is pissed about Mexico City, but he's not sharing yet. If it's that bad, we'll just be a burden. We might be going home, buddy."

"That would be good, I miss Benni and the rest. The way they make you smile. I see that happiness when you respond, like your eyes transmit the colours of emotion."

That came as a surprise. Yeah, I like them, but being away had somehow lifted a burden. A constant expectation to be Joshua Nkosi, a man who loves being the centre of attention. Another mask, and one I'd worn for the last three years. Not the real me. No one had seen that since I ran the streets of Rocinha. I forget my given name. I refuse to recall it; I have to keep it buried deep – some memories only give you pain. Hah, maybe I'll tell you when I'm less raw. I can throw you a tidbit though, reveal why I have Marc. Yes. You see, I swim like a fish. This is not a common skill anymore, the extreme weather causing many to avoid the sea with its unpredictable currents and winds. And as water became more precious, the more protective people became about it. None of that liquid gold for swimming in, even to cool off. Unless, of course, you are a fearless kid, razzing with your mate Andre. Especially if under that deep pool of seawater and dangerous currents, treasures lie. Not like in the pirate vids, you know, Long Jack Silver and all that. No, these treasures lay in the houses of the rich and famous. Even now, humans covet gold, gemstones and other shiny things. Fools willing to swap a worthless lump for clean water and food. I wasn't being altruistic here, not diving the murk for a sick dad, or a desperate sister. No. Those glittery things buy you status, and that is all in the favela. Yeah, I had the favour of my parent's gang, but is that ever enough? Now, looking back, the answer is obvious. But when you're young, not so much. And understandably, Andre and I skimmed what we could. For every trinket we brought up, we swallowed another, or shoved it somewhere no one wants to look. I was damn good at it too, my lungs keeping me under longer than most and my mind naturally reading the currents. And all that swimming kept my body lithe and strong. There was always a sense of freedom under the waves where I was finally in control, making my own decisions. So yeah, when the opportunity came to volunteer for the MARC programme, there I was front and centre. And the competition was poor – if your sub breaks two clicks under, being able to swim isn't going to help. Nor does it when your old favela friend comes knocking, asking for favours … favela favours. The type you don't get to say no to. Like I said, a lost skill, unless you are a treasure hunter.

"Come on squid," I got off the bed, glassy eyes tired from staring into the distance, rather than the cabin ceiling and its murky grey steel. "Shower time."

*"...that was uncalled for."*

"Heh, race you." She beat me purely by cheating. Those metal limbs reaching for the doorway and pulling her through before she had even finished complaining. Nine brains are definitely unfair, eight controlling the tentacles separately from the core brain. The cephalopod got to pick the water temperature, the WNF *Carson* the length of time.

** * **

I reached Rainsford's office as ordered at 08:00 sharp. None of that URF slacking, this was 'special' time. Officer Dulik, surprise, surprise, was already there, two waters in and tapping away at a tablet. My *mae* and *pai* used to talk about coffee in the morning – something Brazil was famous for. A beverage that woke you up and kept the mind sharp. Farming land is valuable now, and the remaining patches of the Amazon Forest soon to be lost. From what they said, the governmental decree banning coffee production was like holding a gun to your President's head and asking the people to pull the trigger. It wasn't the first riot, just the biggest as the Scorching took hold. From what I hear, the starships had dedicated rooms to its growth. But I think that's donkey shit. Nothing can be that addictive that you're prepared to leave people behind to die just so you can grow it.

Hovering nearby with eyes on the large wall screen, the man I only knew as Alpha 1 was studying a 3D map of what I took to be our target. I say *our*, because my brief hope of going back under was over. Apparently, the MARC unit was still needed. And URF cop Nkosi? Just call me the mule.

"Sit down, Nkosi," Yeah, Rainsford hadn't forgiven me for losing it a little aboard the Drathken spaceship. Probably not the time to mention his swearing. "We have a 'go' on the infiltration mission. It's a best guess based on Drathken satellites analysing the direction of the few vehicles leaving Tijuana in the past few days. If we'd had the access before, intercept would have been achievable." I could describe the bitterness in his tone and eyes but use your imagination. "Our new access has allowed us to pinpoint within three clicks the likely destination of the polymetallic nodules." Alpha 1 stepped away from the screen, tapping to the side to bring up the title: Instituto Nacional de Investigaciones Nucleares (ININ). "This place is slap bang in the centre of that search area, and the building appears intact. It was one of the last holdouts for the Mexican Army before the floods washed the city clean four decades ago. That's all the information we have, even the Drathken can't clean up visuals due to the radon and atmospheric interference. Any EMR scans are awash with it."

"A reason to pick the place, probably," said Dulik, not looking my way. "Hidden from their terrorist target, an intact building and enough escape routes out should they be found. They're after time, Nkosi. Time enough to extract whatever radioactive material they have. In fact, …"

Rainsford's eyes flashed her way, unmistakable. She shutdown. Perhaps this was the time to try and dig myself out of that Tijuana–sized hole.

"I don't need to know details. You just want the MARC, and I'm the operator so I get to tag along. Good with me. Less I know, the less you'll be tempted to fry my brain." I flashed my pearly whites Dulik's way and tapped Marc's tentacles.

"The MARC unit data upgrade will help – predictions on the current state of the degradation, etc." Rainsford pointed to the obligatory woman in a white coat who'd just knocked at the door. Okay, it wasn't white, more WPF blue, but it gave Marc the same nervous feeling. She twitched, then reluctantly slid off my back, wrapping herself around the arm of the waiting Richards, the Science Officer we knew too well. I could taste her apprehension in my head. Strange feeling that. Once they were out the room, Alpha 1 kicked into full Marine mode. Happy days. I was expecting 'cakewalk' to be in there somewhere. Strange what weird cliches survive the breakdown of society. Vids for you, cultural depositories.

"This is not Tijuana."

I'm going to keep my sarcasm locked up tight. Okay?

"That was a cakewalk compared to Mexico City."

(cough – trying here).

"Post the massive shift of El Nino forty years ago and the subsequent mass flooding of the Central American belt, those who endured have done so by tooth and claw. It's hot, humid, and fucking hard to breathe. Anything living in there is on pure survival mode, and we will be seen as a threat."

"And food," said Dulik. "Tell him."

"...we think some of those that survived... "

Now it's at this point I have a little more sympathy for the guy. He clearly finds this distasteful, out of his usual remit. Hell, out of mine. I was never a fan of horror flicks.

"Cannibals? This is the twenty-second century." The time of enlightenment. Yeah, says a lot about humanity that.

Rainsford recognised the Marine's distaste, helping out. "We're not saying it's common, we don't know for sure. But all the larger animals were killed in the flood. Anything in the outlands bigger than a fucking cat will die of exhaustion and the heat. The plant life is struggling to adapt – the weather is so ferocious and unpredictable – and unlikely to sustain much else. The behaviouralists predict any humans left will be opportunistic feeders. Hence, you may be potential food."

Humans at the top of the food chain, and the bottom.

"The good news is we can avoid most of the trouble. The Institute is on the outskirts, away from the main city on what was the highway to Toluca. We'll assess the mountain roads when we go in, and if they're impassable then we'll go through the outskirts of Toluca." Alpha 1 brought up an old map of the area, one of the last, he said, pre the El Nino Flood. Still a city, I struggled to see the difference other than Mexico City's apparent reputation. Maybe that was enough.

"We can't fly in?" I asked. Hey, play dumb. I'm just a sea-cop, remember.

"With those winds? No. And then there's the unpredictable thermals, storms ..."

I put up my hand, acknowledging Alpha 1's response. "I mean the Drathken ship. Will they not help?"

"No. They see this as a human affair. They are *our* terrorists to deal with," cut in Rainsford.

I nodded, pulling up my chin as if to show I understood. Rainsford wasn't fooled.

"It's our problem, Nkosi. They are here to help heal the planet, not humanity. And if they took active part, it would just add fuel to the HLA's cause. Alien interference, throwing their technological ability around to the detriment of humanity."

Fair enough, though it didn't sit right. How the hell in a mixed-up world full of entangled and intermittent comms, would anyone know? In the past, people like my 'tubers would record everything. You went for a piss, and someone probably had it on camera, sharing it on the WWWeb or something. Now? We are begging for access to the Drathken satcom just so we can connect across the bloody burnt-out equatorial ring of fire. Ah well, not my biz.

# Chapter 11

"**F**ucking helicopters," I said, rather loud, probably for around about the tenth time that day. The modified Chinook must have been a hundred years old; every part replaced or re-soldered a thousand times. We were short on time, and the beautiful shiny new version I could see ahead through the cockpit carried the WPF Fieldmaster Armour Personnel Carrier. Impressed? Well, I was, because the damn thing was bloody heavy and the wind ferocious. My head battered against the 'copters hull, the jacket I'd put behind my neck having slipped down again.

"Fucking helicopters." Make that eleven. The Fieldmaster wasn't our transport, it was the battering ram and pathfinder. The APC had shoved and clattered its way along some of the old roads leading through the mountains, hoping to circumnavigate Toluca and get us to the Institute without facing whatever lay in wait in the city. Not happening. According to the driver, there were no roads left. Just washed out or eroded ribbons along the mountainside a goat would have struggled to climb.

We were heading for Presa Ignacio Ramirez, Dulik explaining it was the former site of a major reservoir. A place where fresh water was stored for the cities, and the nearest place the helicopters could risk as the heat crept upwards of 45°C and the winds tore across the mountain range. I thought it would be hotter, but Dulik explained the reduced heat at altitude, and the increase in storms. Oh, and the minimal oxygen levels.

Apparently, people used to come to the lake for 'recreation'. Heh. Downtime. Not much of that anymore.

"Two minutes," bellowed the pilot, the Chinook dipping and swinging out to the right before a thermal swept it back up. This time, I hadn't eaten before taking off, which was a good thing considering my stomach sat inside my throat complaining about the smell from my bowels. Nice image, huh? Welcome to my reality.

We gradually dropped, the shiny modern helicopter disappearing from view while it deposited the Fieldmaster and its crew of four. Having safely made its landing, we followed, the cacophony from wind and rotors gnawing at any sense of reality left in my mind. I felt a warmth spread from the chip behind my ear and let Marc's calming words merge with the colours she pulsed gently into my brain. Our transport reached the dirt below, the co-pilot dropping its harness before swerving the complaining vehicle over to the left and bringing us down to relative peace. Despite Dulik's glare, I had removed the restraints and was at the door in a shot. With rebreather in place and the exo-suit squeezing my limbs, I was out the helicopter as soon as the Gunner had it open.

My feet hit the ground, dust swirling around them with the four-by-four waiting in its harness nearby. Unsteady, I walked past it, taking in the view behind. I'd expected a dried-up lake – one similar to the vids of drought, with half-eaten carcasses and flies buzzing around – perhaps a heat haze above. Instead, it appeared to be a vast plain of dust. A near gale whipped over the top, yet the dirt hardly shifted unlike the whirling dust devils about the vehicles. I couldn't help myself, trudging over, each step sending more dirt flying into the air before I reached what I thought was the lake edge. From here, the vast plain seemed darker than the surroundings and I was reminded of the sediment on the ocean's floor. I slipped out my baton and dug into the ground. Pulling it away, the dust-cum-soil was bound together, an effect I assumed was caused by residual water. The wind and heat swiftly took hold, the soil visibly drying out to be blown away. Fascinated, I pushed my toe into the dirt, expecting it to fill with water like on the newly forming beaches around the world. But no, it just left a toe print. One that soon collapsed when the extreme environment came calling.

"Nkosi, get your arse over here." The dulcet tones of Alpha 1 had me scurrying away from the ex-reservoir despite its pull on me. I still don't know why. One of those moments you can't categorise. Anyone watching would think it was something poignant, like a self-important arthouse vid. All wild scenery and heartbreaking stares into the distance. Fuck that. Shallow me.

*"At last, something we agree on."*

"Not all of us can survive two clicks down in the deep black."

The Fieldmaster was already gunning its engine, two crew peeking out of their respective hatches. They'd donned helmets over their exo-suit head covering, rebreathers in place, and linked by radio comms. The vehicle's green camouflage stuck out like a sore thumb close up, though I suspected once it was shrouded by the grey rock dust, it'd fade from sight in tens of metres. Low, its front end sported a slightly raised curved plough, one that I watched swing on twin pivots over the main body to rest upside down at the rear. It sported a pair of dual machine guns and a singular 20mm cannon from the small turret, firepower I hoped we didn't need.

I battered on the bulletproof window of our four-by-four, its raised chassis rocking in the grit-filled wind. Alpha 3 opened it up, greeting me with a scowl that had been semi-permanent since Tijuana. The warmth in those green/grey eyes lost since our first meeting on the ex-whaling ship. I dropped into the comfortable seat, strapping in, refusing to rise to the soldier's bait. It was going to be a long journey and I seriously couldn't face ongoing sniping – preferring a pained silence. I set my face hard and with a thought, Marc unfurled, sliding over my shoulder to curl into a ball on my lap. Go on, goad me now. Images of a pair of tentacles up each nose slipped into my mind.

*"I wouldn't do that."*

"I know, but she doesn't."

* * *

An hour later, with my back as numb as my patience, we rolled off the dust covered minor road, and the tyres dug a good half a metre down to grip the last vestige of tarmac on what was once a highway. We were surrounded by an undulating plain of dust, punctuated by broken buildings that spoke of a past long gone. The preflood map Alpha had shared showed this plain had been rich farmland, some tended by smallholdings, others by vast industrial farms that had swallowed up those lands left behind as people stopped trying. My father explained that the temperature rise had been gradual at first, the heat buildup and storms interchanging. Each yearly dip in the thermometer met with cheers, the powerful heralding that the Scorching would never come. And then the extreme weather would return, each time wetter, hotter, more violent. Humans are stubborn, and they clung on, hoping that the world would return to normal and here, on this high plain, nature's bounty would flourish again. Yeah, stubborn, but selfish. It didn't. The only fruits of our labour an atmosphere full of shit.

"Alpha 1, we have tracks. I say again, we have tracks." The radio static rippled in noisy waves, but the words were clear in that tiny space. The squad leader tapped the vidscreen inlaid into the dashboard, the APC's image jumping around, but the dual tracks were obvious where the crumbling highway wall remained intact, protecting small sections from the wind.

"Keep going, eyes peeled."

The cliches continue.

He turned to Dulik, a rueful look on his face. "Most likely the HLA, but we need to be wary. If the route's clear, we can bypass the city completely."

You see, I've watched those vids. It's like saying 'I'll be right back.' In my head, the ominous music thrummed in the background, and I checked my Glock. You might call me a fatalist; I think that's the word. But I see myself as a realist. The one behind the camera and filming the arthouse flick. Wishing someone would shove the dreary bastard into the blasted sea so we could sup potato juice and make plans some would fear to ever carry out.

"We have a barrier," crackled the radio. "It's new." The image jolted as the Fieldmaster slowed to a halt. I counted seven upturned cars, rusted and twisted, piled against each other next to a junction in the highway, steering us off and into the city. Subtle. WPF don't do subtle. At least it showed whoever was out there retained intelligence and the ability to move heavy vehicles.

Intelligent cannibals. Maybe there was hope for humankind.

"Clear it," was Alpha 1's reply. I concurred. The camera vibrated as the APC's engine roared, the jolts punctuated by the release of its squealing brakes. In the vids, you slam into the centre, the cars flying aside as the truck tears its way through. In real life, you engage the highest torque you can and shove.

And then they attacked.

The first artillery round smacked into the right-hand door of our four-by-four. Fired from outside of the city, it rammed into my side and sent the vehicle rocking upwards, teetering on two wheels before slamming back down. The wheels initially spun until the Alpha driver got the reverse gear to grip and we were suddenly roaring backwards, dust flying. The door had crumpled, the thick armour plate absorbing much of the hit and pressing in on my thigh which now likely sported a livid bruise. It didn't hurt near as much as the bloody headache Marc gave me as she screamed on impact, clambering up my torso to wrap herself as near as she could into her favoured position.

"Stop," I cried. Tears forming as her stress pulses threatened to overwhelm me, my head pressed into hands. I could feel Alpha 3 throwing me a look of disdain, but unless you have a Marc's mind in your own, you're not in the know.

The second shell hit the hood, glancing off to smash into the windscreen. The toughened glass shattered, the outer armoured edges vibrating. Heat ripped inwards, followed by dust thrown by the billowing wind. The driver wore a rebreather, following procedure, but was now near blind and combined with the shell's impact we were in the shit. The rear end smashed into the highway wall, tearing at the axle as it rose upwards. The grinding set me on edge, leaving me completely disorientated and I had no idea which way we were going. The powerful four-wheel torque drove the wheels down into the cracked tarmac and we piled backwards over the wall, a second squealing of metal greeting the front axle when it scraped over the remaining concrete. Thrown around like a turkey in a barrel, I caught sight of the camera feed, the Fieldmaster stationary with fire erupting from underneath. My first thought was they'd been hit too, but the word "mine" rose above the cacophony, shouted by Alpha 1.

Our vehicle skidded and then spun around. The driver keeping the shattered windscreen in the lee of the wind while ducking behind the half-ruin of a house at the head of a rubble-strewn street. Piles of dust lay everywhere to the sides, leaving the centre strangely bare – a winding pathway rolling away from us before the grit-filled wind hid it away again.

"Fuck," swore Dulik, thumping her hand into the seat ahead. Everything paused in a strange, paralysed silence. A rare moment of true shock.

"Pull in. Alphas 2 and 3 eyes up top – 4, check under the vehicle. Dulik, Nkosi stay inside until ordered." Alpha 1 started an animated conversation on the satcom, clearly getting a relieved response from the APC.

*"Me too."*

"Yeah, you stay inside as well."

"Got to be the HLA," said Dulik, her eyes flashing under the rebreather mask. Her fingers were pulsing as she spoke, and the rest of the body language wasn't positive either.

I tried to smooth things over, it was worth a try. "Well, it isn't mindless cannibals with artillery and mines." See. A calming influence. "Are we in Toluca?"

"The outskirts." Dulik glanced out the car window, the air whipping by; the buildings looming as they tried to hold the maelstrom back. The heat was rising in the car, and I could feel sweat overwhelming the suit where Marc lay across my back. Dulik pulled away from the glass when Alpha 1 gave the signal to wait, risking the wind's roar as he opened the door as little as possible before stepping out. Moments later, he and Alpha 4 were stretching a fabric across the windscreen, fighting the wind before managing to cover the entire hole. The brief smell of heated glue pervaded the cab, and they repeated the action with a second piece. I guessed that someone had just sacrificed their tent. Within a few minutes they were all back in the vehicle, a layer of dust over everything and everyone. The engine fired, and despite a slight grind from the rear, we turned around as the aircon kicked in. By the time we reached the highway wall, steering by the front camera and following what was left of our own tracks, we were down to an ultracool 38°C. Nearly time for a sweater.

The flapping material didn't cut out the pummelling noise from the APC's cannon, and as we rolled over a lower section of the wall, we caught the odd muzzle flash when the battered Fieldmaster came into view. The wind caught at the smoke rising from beneath. One wheel had been partially melted and was missing its tread. At the rear, upwardly aligned scorch marks were clearly from a mine and criss-crossed by another set of impacts from elsewhere. We pulled alongside, letting the APC's superior armour provide cover as Alpha 1 sent instructions over the satcom.

For the next thirty minutes we ground on, the Fieldmaster at our side, trundling as it struggled with two more damaged wheels on the far side I'd missed. Providing cover for us, its cannon and machine guns occasionally burst into life, firing into the distance at targets we couldn't make out. On reaching a second, hastily built barrier of lesser vehicles, a barrage of WPF machine gun fire sprayed into the remaining road nearby, rewarded by a dual eruption. The armoured vehicle pressed on, easily shoving aside the combo of crumbled concrete and wind-blasted metal chassis.

However, a few metres past the barricade, black smoke erupted from the rear of the APC, a distorted squeal reverberating before it ground to a halt. The swearing over the satcom link a clue to what came next.

"We're done, Alpha 1," echoed through our vehicle.

The embattled squad leader glanced over to Dulik, tight-lipped. He shook his head and acknowledged. "Stay in contact, see if you can fix it. With luck, we can get ahead of any warning they're sending the facility."

"*Unless they have satcom,*" chipped in a helpful Marc.

"If that was the case, then this goes way higher than a couple of rich do-gooders. And we'll be in more shit than a goat shed."

"*Cowshed.*"

"Yeah, one of those."

# Chapter 12

I kneaded my left thigh, the bruise making itself known and overriding my ass that only complained every ten seconds or so. I remained still, however, Alpha 3 giving me the treatment every time I moved into her 'space' to ease the aches.

We'd been climbing for the last fifteen minutes, the engine complaining as the filters struggled with the ever-reducing oxygen and clogging dust. Each metre the humidity grew, the dust wetting out to be blown in clumps against the temporary windscreen. We were stopping every few minutes to clear the camera, and it was during the third stop when the first bolt of lightning cracked across the sky. Forked, searing, it lit the mountain road and highlighted the surrounding ancient and wind-blasted trunks standing above the clogging mud. Another crackle lit the petrified forest, the sea of splintered wood rising in waves, visible as it flowed over the mountainside. My heart lurched. I could see faces among the trees, knowing they weren't there but still setting my thoughts racing. Mournful, animal eyes, accusing. Watching as Alpha 4 clinked the driver's door shut before we set off again. The thunder crashed in, rolling over the mountain, heralding our approach to the summit of the valley. The vehicle rocked, the sound wave pummelling at the tent fabric, soon followed by a second and third thunderclap. And then the wheels spun, the tyres sliding over the wet dust as it ground its way into the treads, thick and clogging.

I was not having a good day.

"Rain on the way," whispered Alpha 3 next to me, her eyes widening as a fourth bolt raced across the sky. I let a little sympathy slip by my emotional wall, wondering if she had witnessed the condemnation I'd caught amid the dead forest. A sign of humanity shrouded by her duty. Probably not. I don't think my mind works like others do, hence taking on the masks. Showing them something, anything but me to keep them at bay.

Skidding from side to side, the first drops splattered onto the roof, the noise deadened initially by the engine's complaints until the patter increased in volume. Glancing up, lightning arced across a cloudless sky, the dust absent. Yet the rain fell, rising in ferocity and battering the roof, seeping in at the edges of the tent material. The heat continued to increase inside the cab, the raindrops far from cooling with the air thick and heavy around us. My exo-suit began to struggle, leaving sweat to enshroud my torso, oozing into places we don't talk about. When the camera finally steamed up, the swearing restarted as the new Alpha 4 brought us to a halt diagonally across the now mud-laden road.

"We're fucked," said the embittered driver, hands slamming against the vehicle's wheel. He opened the door, and the wind caught it, forcing it wide with the soldier immediately drenched as the hot rain lashed in. Alpha 4 dragged himself outside, heaving it shut. It wasn't long before he clattered on the window, his gesture clear as he drew a line across his throat, pointing to the front end.

"Out," said Alpha 1, voice harsh.

I gathered myself, preparing for the weather, Marc squeezing my shoulder as I opened the door. All my senses fired at once. The splurge of mud beneath my boots, a smell of ozone seeping under my mask and coating my tongue, thunder battering my ears. But it was my sight that set me reeling. Remember the empty, winding section of the road in Toluca? It was the same here. Cracked tarmac exposed by a rivulet flowing downhill, slightly off-centre. Precognition washed over me, my mind's eye visualising what was about to happen. Maybe my other senses heard the mud or smelt its musk upon the wind. Perhaps tasted the rot released by the water. I still don't know. Octopi can taste the sea, and Marc, well who knows what the software butchers had done to her. Maybe she communicated all this through the chip, and I simply put words to the images she sent.

It surged over the rise. Not a pure, clean wash of water, but heavy, frothing mud. I've seen vids of lava flows erupting, pouring down mountain sides. The way the top half cools, or the bottom half races away, causing smooth ripples. It was like that but faster. I shoved Dulik, propelling her into the petrified forest headfirst with me on top. The mudslide slammed into the four-by-four, and I heard Alpha 4 scream as his legs ripped from under him, slapping him against the bonnet. The snap of his back pierced the roar. The cry cut off, the uncaring mud engulfing the soldier and vehicle up to its bonnet. I scrambled to my feet leaving Dulik still prone, her helmet half off with her head pressed against a hardened tree trunk.

Spinning around, I noted Alpha 3 half in and half out the vehicle, its journey to the base of the valley just starting as the weight of mud surged up and over the hood. Fear flickered in her eyes, a moment of acceptance followed – or maybe I'm being fanciful. Either way, I wasn't passing up the chance. I scrambled along the roadside, shouting at her. Calling for her to look inside and search for a rope, anything she could throw me. And to my surprise she did. Unthinking, she ducked back in, and the door slammed shut, mud smothering the lower half. That face, oh that face. It pressed against the window, mournful, accusing green/grey eyes peering my way. I let my mask slip just for a second, enough for her to see how I truly felt before she was lost under the surface of the mud.

Memories of glassy-eyed whales ran through my mind as I slowed. I never said I was perfect. She didn't have to go back in, did she?

The sludge rolled inexorably on, the four-by-four turning fully sideways as the momentum took hold, tipping it over on its side. The sheer weight of the mudslide forced itself over the vehicle, enveloping, clawing, shoving it towards the base of the valley.

"Nkosi," shouted Alpha 1, and I ripped my eyes away from the bulge amid the flood. "Nkosi! Check on Dulik."

I turned back, looking up the road's edge, only now realising how far I'd run along it. Alpha 1 waited parallel with Dulik, eyes jumping between the two of us. Alpha 2 was at his side and prepping some sort of rope pulley system. I had no idea how she came to have it, but maybe we should be thankful for small mercies. By the time I trudged up the twenty or so metres, the sludge still pouring down the tarmac, she had a coil of rope waiting for me. I checked on Dulik first, her breath steady, eyes just a little dilated, before catching the rope and tying it off as instructed. Within a few minutes they were both on my side of the road, retrieving the pulleys with a yank of a secondary cord looped over a taller, steadfast trunk.

*"You okay? Your heart's racing."*

I took a second, trying to work out if I was. The thought of Alpha 3's last look merging with an image of a single, soulless eye. Apparently, I was fine, happy even, though the fork of lightning that crashed over us tried to disagree. "Yeah, Marc. Fine. Best day ever." Hey, I was helping her apply sarcasm under stress. Needed something good to come out of it all.

The WPF Officer stirred, Alpha 2 already satisfied Dulik had a mild concussion at most, more likely just the egg and a sour attitude. A glare cast my way made me question my unselfish act before Alpha 1 explained what happened. She rose unsteadily, drinking in the mudslide, the flow hinting it was beginning to recede. I assumed they'd given up on Alpha 3 when the squad leader looked towards the nearby road summit.

"We have a mission to complete," he said.

Yeah, he pushed his chin forward. If I wasn't a cynic, I'd say he was a little choked too. But duty calls.

Dulik gathered her helmet, brushing it off with a gloved hand. Adjusting the rebreather, she checked for her Glock. The Alphas took that as a cue, running through their remaining weaponry and finding a sole assault rifle and two pistols between them. Considering the collection of grenades, we were likely still under gunned, but maybe we had the element of surprise. After all, we were alive. It was a surprise to me.

Alpha 1 took point, with Dulik next and me behind her. We trudged up the muddy edge of the road, grabbing the splintered trunks when it steepened sharply before finally levelling out. The electrical storm continued above, the hot rain lessening but still falling when we finally reached the valley lip.

We emerged to find a sea of mud stretching out before us, the entire plateau sliding over itself with gravity urging it to lap over the sides. One click ahead, a set of dishevelled buildings rose to the left, their roofs absent, metallic sides flapping in the wind. On the right, at a similar distance, stood three more with two storeys poking above the mud plain. The Marine nodded as he peered through his binoculars.

"Lights," he said. "There's some kind of power there. Three large-wheeled vehicles, and they have a boat with a huge fan on the back." He passed the glasses over to Dulik, pointing where he wanted her to look.

"The Institute. At least we have a target, but how the fuck do we get there?"

# Chapter 13

Now it's at this point you wonder just how good my home education was, right? I mean, I had two parents who 'tubers called *hackers*. Is that a good area of the curriculum to teach your kid? There is so much more I could have learned. You know, like the history of art, or post-modernistic architecture. All useful skills in the favela and a world spiralling into catastrophe.

Well, I wasn't with them long enough to learn *all* they knew. I focused on electronics and comms, the physical stuff, any further opportunities cut short when they decided I needed to disappear. I'll let you imagine it, diving with your best friend Andre in the new villa you'd found, swimming from air pocket to air pocket, scoping the place out for the choicest loot. And no, no one died. I'm sure that was your first thought. Perhaps the gang boss's son ran into difficulty, and I was the only one to get out. Or we fought beneath the waves over a trinket, and he bashed his head and drowned. No. Greed. That's why I had to leave. Some of it mine, some of it Rocinha herself when she got word I'd skimmed. Possibly even Andre. Who knows? Either way, my parents got a whiff that things were not so kosher as they had been, and that I was being watched. You get marked, the shit sticks, and them being 'creatives' and all, were already prepared. I returned from that rich villa, a few items stashed somewhere unmentionable, to be greeted by Rocinha's second-in-command. He loved his knives, called them Millie and Sasha, and proceeded to walk me through every person each blade had killed. He never once mentioned the skimming, nor that I was in trouble. Just sat me down and named each victim and the killing blow. I'd have shit myself if there hadn't been a blockage. A day later, *mae* and *pai* smuggled me out, and I took the long road to the WPF via contacts in Santiago. Of course, Millie and Sasha gained another victim each, bequeathing the world yet another orphan.

Hard to forgive myself. Or others. And I had my suspicions about who had informed on me. Betrayal is a human trait, one that it is hard to shake once it starts. And not all wear a mask to hide it, some use electronics and whispers of the favela, and retribution.

"Marc can do it," I said. "Get across the mud, hopefully steal that boat if it's electronic ignition. Maybe hardwire ..."

"*...hotwire.*"

"...hotwire it if not."

"In these conditions? The specs talk about no more than tens of metres for the chip's connection." Dulik turned to face me, dropping the binoculars from her eyes.

"You've a satcom right?" I gestured towards Alpha 1, letting my brown eyes widen and setting the pearly whites free. I didn't wrinkle my nose. "Drathken tech that cuts through all that crap. I'm betting it'll amplify the connection with my unit if you give it a chance."

I could see the reluctance in them both. Precious tech, probably the only way they could call backup or rescue if they got near enough the equatorial burn out zone's edge. And a connection to the crippled APC, though that meant they had a second satcom to hand, assuming the cannibals weren't using it for post lunch karaoke. I twitched my head, twisting my lips. "Okay, we swim for it. I volunteer to go last."

"Give it to him. What have we got to lose?" said my smooth-voiced WPF Officer. She pressed at her bump, looking my way. "But take care of it."

I so wanted to juggle with the seemingly innocuous box, feign dropping it in the muddy depths. I do question where my mind is sometimes.

"*Me too.*"

"Thanks for the support."

"*Always on call. You know where to find me.*"

I moved away from Dulik's prying eyes. She was making me nervous and adapting such precious tech with a shaky hand was going to be a fast track to hatesville. It's not as if we weren't far from a place she could hide the body. I sat with my back against a wind-blasted, petrified tree trunk and fiddled within my belt pouch to pull out a little electronic tech kit. Yeah, yeah, yeah. I know. How convenient. Of course I have one, because I'm the MARC operator. If the suit or comms connection fails, then my contract stipulates recovery of the MARC as a priority. Ironic, huh? Recovering the recovery unit. Of course, two clicks down, that involves a little skill with the robo-arms. But otherwise, they gave me a kit and training to deal with anything basic in the electronics or mechanical. But not the override, because I'm not important enough. No. A better way to put it is, grunts can't be trusted.

I looked very busy for five minutes, then began the odd glance towards Dulik. They started off as just a check in, then I dropped in the odd grimace. You know the drill.

*"What are you doing?"*

"Me? Getting the satcom connected."

*"We both know you can't do that, at least not that way. I'm beginning to wonder if I shouldn't change partners."*

"You have a choice between surly cop and GI Joe. Take your pick."

*"She packs a punch, and that chin. He could crack nuts with that."*

"Not Brazilian ones he couldn't. I'm leading up to something, drawing her in. Playing the game."

*"Camouflage?"*

"Nearly. I'm hiding my intent before grabbing the prey."

*"I think you'll end up very hungry."*

Anyone in need of a cephalopod partner?

Dulik caught my eye, a twist of her neck and a sour expression dropped hints of what was coming as she strode over. "Done?"

"Struggling," I replied. I showed her the few things I'd dared to do with Marc. There's no way I was touching the satcom. Drathken tech, there could be anything in there. Fibrous plants seething outwards after lifting the lid, wrapping their vines round my neck, and lashes from their stingers Triffid style. Loved that show.

"But doable? Alpha 1 has a backup plan to send one of us across at night. Use the rope to lash some of the wood splinters together like a raft and spread the weight." She looked as convinced as I was. If the mud was the same consistency as what rode the mountain road, once in it you were screwed. I wiped my forehead. Not for effect, it's fucking humid as hell. If the rebreather steamed up, I feared getting the full force of that revolting smell if I had to remove it. I was wishing for the dry heat of Tijuana, that's how foul it was.

"The MARC unit is saying it needs the override to connect. I don't have that, too low in the chain." I let my eyes drop, then back up to hers. "I think I overstated my abilities." I can hear my *mae* now, 'trust in your abilities son, otherwise kick them in the balls.' It was fifty-fifty, but I'd played my hand.

"Override?"

"Yeah, the key code to switch between transceivers. The MARC can't hear the satcom nor respond without that code. I tried to run a bypass." Yeah, I saw that flick. The Drathken are a very different type of alien.

Her nervous look lit a spark in me, and I felt Marc wriggle in my hands, playing to the audience. She walked away, talking to Alpha 1 before returning. Her demeanour had changed, the tired swagger a little more dejected. Likely chewing on having to rely on me after Tijuana.

"Give it here," I let my glance meet hers, surprise lighting my eyes before handing it over. She sat with Alpha 1 a while, a stilted conversation going on between them and the APC was my best guess, before handing the unit back over. "It's open."

"Yeah?" I gave her my best smile before connecting the box of wonders to my chip. This sounds really complicated. Nope. The noise associated with Marc and my connection ended the instant I dropped it on. "Ahhh, fuck, Marc. Tone it down, partner. Its too bright."

*"NO NEED TO SHOUT,"* she shouted in my head, as if it was my fault.

Dulik saw the wince, followed by the sub-vocalising and the slapping of hands to my head until Marc and I turned down our visual volume (neat, huh? Bet you can 'see' what I mean by that). Dulik didn't move, no attempt to reach out in sympathy. Zero. I was an asset. Or more accurately, Marc was.

Hopefully of more use than modded whales.

"*You okay?*"

"Am now. You?"

"*Oh yes.*" She wriggled her tentacles, curling one towards Dulik and waving it. The sour face was followed by a nod of approval.

"I take it you're connected?"

I shook my head, not letting the joy of such a clear bond appear on my face. I could get used to this.

"Yeah, I'm in. When do we go?"

# Chapter 14

Now, of course, I should let Marc describe what happened next.

Purple, mauve, violet swirls with purple streaks, mauve mixed amid blue tinges. RED (that was a mud current). Lavender strung with blue ripples and black flecks. And on we go.

Perhaps I should translate.

With Alpha 2 on sniper duty, his assault rifle sight sweeping the building, Marc slid off the mud lake's edge. Her tentacles spread wide at first, judging the tension at the surface. Once confident, she writhed in the mud until slick with the hot sludge. Then she pulled in two rear tentacles and pushed with these to propel herself forward. With her body skimming across the mud, her 'front' tentacles speared forwards, joining the ones at her side to drag herself while the rear pair pulled in to prepare the next push. For you and me, eight tentacles in perfect unison looks perfectly easy. After all, we can coordinate our legs, arms, and at times, our bodies to work in unison with training. Imagine a juggler, on a unicycle. Now add a spinning plate on a pole resting on your chin, while balancing two balls on your shoulders and whistling your least favourite song. Of course, octopi cheat by having nine brains, especially useful when it's shower time. Talking of which.

*"It tastes foul. It's too hot, and there are water sinks where the mud thins out. I have another eight hundred metres to go, and the sludge feels ..."*

You get the picture. Not a happy cephalopod. I watched through the binoculars, keeping one eye on the vehicles and the other where Marc was heading. Literally a splitting headache. Tired, her power pack depleted by forty percent, she reached the outer rim of the Institute. Closing in, it became apparent this was the top of a surrounding wall, the mud on either side balancing the pressure, preventing its collapse. It did mean if we decided on the large-wheeled trucks, we'd need to find the entrance.

"Go for the boat." I sent the image, a flash of recognition and acknowledgement coming back almost as quickly. Love satcom.

"She's there," I said into the basic radio. "We're going for the fan boat because there's a surrounding wall."

I felt Alpha 1's hand on my shoulder. It sent a shiver along my vertebrae, a ripple of wrongness that's hard to explain. Sometimes being touched ... I don't know how to describe it. When I'm ready, and I know it's coming, *and* I trust the person it can be fine. And when it's Marc, well everything is good. I know what she'll do, how she'll react. Predictable. I've always been this way. Some things affect me way deeper than people expect, like how animals are treated or how we always put humans first above all life. You hide that shit though. Camouflage it with a mask so no one can see. Put up a façade however tiring, remembering to choose the best you can for each situation. Even when being touched.

"Good job, Nkosi," he said.

"Uh-huh," was all I managed in reply.

"Alpha 2 has signalled we're clear. But as soon as that boat starts up, they'll know something's wrong. The mud slide will buy us time if their ambush squad is behind us."

"Unless they have another route," added Dulik. "But I can't see anywhere that opens out onto the mud lake."

Alpha 1 signalled over to his buddy and turned to look out towards the Institute buildings. "Do it."

"Okay, Marc. I'm watching. When you reach the boat, you'll need to access the control panel inside the small cab unit. I'll need every visual detail you can send me."

*"On it."*

On it? Next, she'll be sending me hand signals and telling me it's 'all-clear'.

A long way from pretending to be a rock and grabbing passing shellfish.

I watched through Marc's system as she slid over the wall, pushing and pulling herself over the slimy mud until she reached the boat's low hull. It was shaped like a tray with curved edges, grooves moulded underneath, and just a huge fan at the rear. There was a cab unit in front of the fan, which appeared odd, like an add-on to the original design with a driver's seat built high inside. A moment of panic washed over me, wondering how an octopus was going to steer a boat. In my mind she was just going to switch the damn thing on and over she'd trundle, the computer taking care of the rest. Yeah. Now with a closer look, I think 'computer' might be pushing things a little. More like an on/off switch and some form of steering mechanism associated with the fan. The panic turned to a sliver of anxiety – seems to be a running theme above the ocean waves.

Marc dropped over the low edge of the hull, dragging herself along the floor, body still slick with mud. A tentacle reached upwards and pulled at the cab's handle. I mentally breathed my first sigh of relief when it opened, and Marc wrapped limbs around the chair legs, pulling herself upwards. On reaching the seat, she stared intently at the control panel to give me a full view. The keys were in it. Yeah, I know. But then you are in the middle of a hot mud lake at least two clicks wide. It looked simple, a twist of the key and a press of the button. To the left side of the chair was a single lever, my mind associating it with some form of rudder.

"Waggle the lever," I said, watching as a tentacle reached over and took hold of the grip. It moved back and forth accompanied by a squeal of unoiled metal on metal emanating from behind the octopus. Of course, she translated the air vibrations, but you know what I mean. "Okay, that's for steering. If you turn it one way, the boat will go the opposite way, yes? Counterintuitive."

"Yep." The tentacle waggled the stick. *"Like my siphon. Easy when you have nine brains. Count them. Nine."*

"Don't get cocky. Turn the key to your right a quarter turn, so the top faces the right-hand wall. That's it, now press the button." The button lit green, but no noise rose from the fan. I'd been expecting the motor to be electric, silent. But also, to work. That always helps. Shit.

*"Nothing's happening."*

"I know, I know. Let me think." No response, no motor firing up, no … it's old. "What can you taste? In the air?"

*"Oil, like on that old submersible on the ship."*

Fucking hydrocarbons.

"Go around the back and stare at everything until I tell you to stop." Marc complied, and there it was, an old diesel engine. Marc pulled off the cover to expose a pull cord. This time I was thinking clearly, getting Marc to turn on the fuel switch ready. favelas have variable to zero electricity, in clean or dirty form. However, Rocinha's gang block had three different generators scavenged from the city, possibly more hidden away, all of which I learned to fire up. With the mind's eye view of an octopus yanking the cord (it was funny to me), she started the engine, scurrying for the cab as it kicked in on the second pull. I signalled the Alphas, but I'm sure the smoke was enough to tell them, that and the careering boat charging forwards. Another image for you, an octopus sat in a chair, one tentacle on the rudder, another pressing down on the manual accelerator. Probably balancing a plate on their head and whistling a tune too.

"Show off."

*"Someone has to be professional around here."*

By the time the first shot rang out, Marc was halfway across the lake. A responding bullet winged its way back towards the building, soon followed by an Alpha's tight burst designed to force the terrorist to keep their head down. Clearly, they were deaf to it, as another bullet crashed into the boat's fan, pinging off and clattering against the cab. A few more exchanges and the gunfire stopped, Marc driving the boat up the muddied edge of the lake.

It's all I could do to resist giving her a round of applause. She simply slid off the chair, and on over the hull, climbing along my legs to settle against my back. I risked a glance over at Dulik, expecting a smile or a thumbs up at least. She wasn't even looking, her mind elsewhere. Now it was our turn.

# Chapter 15

"Satcom," said Alpha 1, his hand out waiting while the rest piled aboard the boat.

"What if we need the MARC again?" said Dulik as she dropped in beside Alpha 2, the Marine's rifle pointing at the building.

He looked from me to the WPF Officer, cogs whirring. I shrugged.

"The sun will be down in an hour or so, we could ..." started Dulik.

"Thermal imaging will be shit up here. Too hot with the heat, humidity and the fucking lake. They're bound to have NV like us and we're on a clear night. If the storm kicks back up, a very clear night."

I got the feeling he was thinking aloud, trying to reason through the strangeness. Good luck with that, an octopus just drove a boat. Luckily, his mind was made up for him, Alpha 2 shouting us across and pointing towards the building while peering down his rifle sight. The squad leader raised his binoculars and swore.

"In the boat, now. They're breaking out for the truck."

Right. One truck, one boat. It could be a ruse, or they could have assumed we were the first assault of many and decided to go on the run. To me, it meant they didn't have any satcom level comms and were cut off from whoever attacked us below. We were still outgunned though.

"Nkosi, you're up." Alpha 1 pointed towards the cab. Lovely. A nice, prominent position with the driver an obvious target to stop our charge. I was about to shout about equal working rights for our cephalopod pals, when I bit back a little. No time for sarcasm. At least, not out loud. The Marine leader shoved us off the beach, while Alpha 2 started the engine, and the sea-cop took charge of his first surface vehicle.

*"That's it, just ease your foot down, now the lever."*

Yeah, the apprentice teaches the master. At least, I think I'm the master.

*"In your dreams. I'll settle for partner."*

Once my singular brain orientated, my steering experiences on a level sub helping, we picked up speed. I aimed for a circular approach towards the truck that had begun to churn its way through the mud. It sounds like a flanking manoeuvre, right? Not one designed to keep my ass from the direct line of fire. Alpha 2 began shooting using short, controlled bursts. Each aimed towards the truck's cab whenever he could. I assumed the tyres were solid, otherwise they would have been my choice. With the boat surging as it hit water, or rising and turbulent when riding humps of sludge, doubts crept in about the Marine's ability to achieve much more than keeping the terrorists' heads down. A single shot rang out from the building's direction, the bullet cracking into the right window of my cab and out through the left. It snagged a bit of my cockiness on the way. Dulik opened up; her Glock range limited, but I appreciated the sentiment. A second bullet slammed into her shoulder, sending her wheeling to the floor and I yanked the fan controls over.

"No," bellowed Dulik, pulling herself up using the lip of the hull.

I followed instructions, glad to see Alpha 2 switch targets. It was a single shot, a window shattering off to my right. I imagined the short cry and a human falling to be enveloped by the mud, because the soldier soon switched focus back on the truck's cab.

We were two hundred metres from the vehicle when it accelerated, the wheels sitting a little less deep in the sludge as it neared the lake edge. Alpha 1 signalled me over to the truck's left-hand side, and all hell broke loose. Three terrorists dropped into position at the rear of the truck, using the tailgate for cover, being far from frugal with their heavy machine gun ammunition. Bullets rained in on my cab and I threw myself to the side, feeling a yank across my back as Marc wrenched away. More rounds tore into the wood and glass, shattering the structure and bringing it down on top of me. Somehow, we kept going, the airboat skimming towards the shore as the Alphas and Dulik kept firing back.  Fire and smoke erupted in my vision and the boat tipped, slamming into something that refused to give way. I found myself flying along the boat deck, legs entangled with Dulik as we tumbled over the bow. Ramming into a splintered trunk, I cursed as my head slapped the solid wood. My mind swam. It hurt, and pain leads to anger.

* * *

A gunshot echoed through the dark. My eyes flickered open but were unable to see. Only the musk of rotten vegetation entered my mind, masking all senses in a maelstrom of panic. It coated lungs, plugged my nose, and sickened a thick tongue. My eardrums pressed inwards, muffled, pained.

*"Josh."*

*"..."*

*"Josh, you need to wake up. Wake up now. Please."*

My eyes opened, this time to reality, breaking the seal of drying mud caked on the lids. I lay face down, arms tangled painfully underneath, and my right eye filled with a hulking woman standing over someone nearby. The gun in her hand twitched, the heavy round crashing into something below. I heard a sickening crack, and something wet splattered against my cheek. I groaned as I pulled out my right hand, touching what I initially took for more rain. Pulling the fingers near to my eye, the mud upon them streaked with blood, my addled brain started to put my new reality together. I pushed myself onto my side, half my mind knowing they would work out I was alive and likely do something to rectify that, the other half wanting to see the end coming.

The woman looked my way, a gap-toothed grin forming behind her rebreather, and she kicked the corpse below her. I couldn't make out which Alpha it was, but their lack of response let me know it didn't really matter. The revolver rose, aiming my way and I peered straight down the barrel. It's the type of thing that sharpens your thinking, that moment when everything you planned to do with your life fades into the distance. I twitched my nose. You never know.

"Not that one," someone drawled behind, the voice male and the accent one I recognised. Haitian, the first of the Caribbean gangs to land in the favelas as the hurricane season decided to last all fucking year. Give them their due, they survived three months according to my *pai* before their leaders got a crab-eye view of the drowned villas. Rocinha absorbed the remaining members including Sasha and Millie's wielder. "Questioning," he continued, "then Andre decides."

Andre. Fuck no. If things weren't bad enough already.

The meaty hand let the revolver fall to her side, the grin twisting into a grimace accompanied by a wink. I kid you not, three years of trying and I think I might have scored face down in the fucking mud with my would-be executioner. That, or she was letting me know next time she aimed a gun my way, she wouldn't be taking no for an answer.

*"Pheromones say it's the last one."*

"Cheer me up, why don't you."

The terrorist strode over, pushing my head back down into the mud. She twisted my hands behind my back before slipping over a cable tie and pulling hard. If this was foreplay, I was changing my mind. She kicked my bad leg, grunting before walking back towards the truck.

*"See."*

"Where are you?"

*"Under the boat."*

"Any chance of a heroic cephalopod rescue?"

*"No. There's five of them."*

"You have eight tentacles, nine brains and three hearts."

*"And one life."*

I didn't correct her. That would be too painful right now.

"Some partner you are." I heard the truck restart, raising my head to see Dulik thrown onto the flatbed, legs flailing only to receive a crack to the head. The male terrorist, definitely Haitian by his appearance, flung her legs inside before looking over my way.

"Hide yourself under the truck and cling onto something that doesn't look like it's going to spin. Watch out for the ground in case it hits mud again."

I sensed Marc's agreement, rolling onto my side as the Haitian walked my way, languid arms covered with intricate gang tattoos by his side. He reached out, grabbing my upper arm and started pulling me up.

"Yes, you saw. Do it right and it won't hurt ne'r as much," he drawled.

On reaching my feet, I stumbled a little, the bruising on my leg saying *hi*. He made no attempt to help, letting me fall before pulling me back up. We passed Alpha 2 on the way, the back of his skull shattered, brains and blood covering the ground and likely my cheek. He'd been stripped of anything useful, causing me to panic a little before realising the line to Marc had been static free. The satcom only had to be with one of us, and as I stretched my mind back over the firefight, I remembered tearing myself away from the cab but Marc remaining. Had I ordered that? Did I ask her to look after it? There was a memory gap, and it scared me a little.

I waited at the rear of the truck with my eyes on Dulik's still form. A hand grabbed my ass and shoulder, throwing me aboard like a rag doll. I took it calmly; my body numb enough to handle it. Another hand pulled my head up by the hair from the truck's muddy floor, her eyes locking with mine. She pressed the revolver hard under my swallowing jaw. Her smile was back, and I think whatever language was her native tongue, she displayed a natural aptitude for communication.

"He gets it," said the Haitian, another voice grunting in effort next to him as the tailgate slammed shut. The truck began to move, its initial slide across the mud rolling me against the bench to finish face up. And sitting opposite me was fucking Andre, a shit-eating grin behind his rebreather, one I'd last seen ten metres down in a particularly opulent villa. At first, I thought he didn't recognise me. That smile of his a permanent fixture whether holding a jewelled necklace or at the end of one of Rocinha's beatings. A street kid through and through, and one I'd trusted until Millie and Sasha came into my life. Every fibre of my being suspected the bastard had squealed, but then he didn't have well-regarded parents to provide a little shelter. What would the knife twins have sliced out of me without their protection? Maybe a betrayal.

His eyes were the biggest clue, that slight widening, the slide over to my new girlfriend before returning to meet my gaze. Yeah, made. Shit. Now he had a decision to make, and so did I.

98

# Chapter 16

The back of the truck's cab echoed with a double bang. "Mexico City," was the muffled shout that followed. My internal clock said we'd been travelling forty minutes, my cephalopod timepiece reset that to thirty-two minutes and fourteen seconds. A pedant, but thankfully a safe one under the truck. I'll take that. With my chest hurting, I stared at my rebreather where it sat next to Andre, wrapped together with Dulik's.

"Emmanuel, on top," said Andre, lifting his chin towards the rear. "Fabienne, the tailgate. Fuck 'em up if they come near."

I raised an eyebrow Andre's way, not daring to speak until the others had complied with his orders. With the clatter of the truck as it swayed and jumped along whatever tarmac remained, he carried on smiling my way. "Flesh eaters. No bokor raised zombies, these. What man has become under the foot of the Drathken. Not seen them for a while, but the last few weeks the floods have driven them out of their holes." He spoke in standard English, the Brazilian twang underneath unmistakable.

I glanced over to Fabienne, her eyes clearly on the road behind. It was the first time I noticed they'd dragged Alpha 2 onboard, a stirring in my gut linking with Andre's first words. Did it mean Alpha 1 was still out there? Or under the mud lake. If it was the former, what would duty drive him to do?

Andre, eyes remaining on Fabienne, spoke to me low and quick. "What the fuck you doin' here man?" There was the favela, loud and clear.

"Got reassigned. That, or a brain fry. Made my choice."

Andre nodded; I could see the cogs whirring. "You're dead, you know that? Either way, the HLA are not pissing about." He kicked at a crate tied to the front of the flatbed. "Not at all."

The thought had occurred to me.

*"And to me."*

"Maybe there's a way, M—"

I shook my head, eyes hard. "Not my name. You got me the fuck into this."

"Join us here. Yes? Prove yourself," he glanced towards Dulik. "Maybe if I vouch for you."

I let that sink in. Why would he do that? Guilt? Surprisingly, I needed an out from this situation. I had the satcom, at least Marc did, and it was a prize the HLA would pay well for. But they, like all terrorists and gangs, valued silence. My silence. The satcom would only give them an edge if the Drathken and WPF were unaware they had it. Images of a Tijuana smile crept in.

Gunfire echoed from above, the rattle of an assault rifle in random bursts. Fabienne swore and raised her rifle over the tailgate lip, squeezing the trigger one bullet at a time. I tried to peer over her shoulder, the street near empty save for wind-lashed cars either side and a crumpled, ragged mess bleeding nearby. More bursts reverberated from above.

"When we first came, they set us on edge. Now, I think their death is a gift from a forsaken god. Each one a sign of humanity's folly." I eyed my old friend, pursing my lips as he spoke. He'd clearly come a long way from the streets we used to run. Fabienne huffed, dropping the rifle and pulling Alpha 2 onto the tailgate before shoving him over. There were no roars, or snarls. No hordes descending on the Marine with the camera panning back as humanity's fate is sealed by the zombie apocalypse. A couple of pathetic bundles hidden near a wrecked jeep shambled out towards the long dead soldier, wind whipping around them with the crackle of a new electrical storm stirring above.

"Why are we alive?" I asked.

That smile again. "Because I've not ordered your death." He nodded towards the front of the truck. "The Professor wants to know what the WPF know, simple. When we're clear of this shithole, and any other WPF pursuit, it'll be a reckoning."

* * *

I knew we were past the city limits when the truck slowed a little, the rush to get through putting Fabienne and Andre on edge. She visibly relaxed as the last, broken buildings passed by. Lost in a rising dust storm laced with lightning in the sky above. The humidity remained high, and the exo-suit threatened to give up on me, Marc throwing in a temperature reading near 45°C on the outside in the shade of the chassis. I felt like shit, the oxygen depletion beginning to get to me, wondering if Dulik and I would live long enough to die at the end of Fabienne's ire.

"I'm struggling," I coughed out. "And if we go any further south, I'm screwed. Won't be turning canary if I'm dead." I added a couple of extra coughs for effect, sucking in a large, rasping breath. That bit wasn't faked. Oxygen depletion is no joke. On my long list of ways I didn't want to die, it sat in the top five, right behind drowning in fetid mud or riding in a fucking helicopter.

Fabienne waggled her breathing pipe, eyebrows raised. I'm not sure what she was hinting, but I swore off my nose twitch for life at that second. Okay, it may only be for a short time, but my oath was solid. Andre grabbed one of the rebreathers, reaching over and sliding the mask over my nose and mouth, much to Fabienne's disgust.

He got up and banged a fist twice against the front panel. "How long?"

"Ten minutes until the safe house."

He collected the other breathing kit and lifting Dulik's head, fitted it carefully. She didn't stir. I busied myself counting the time down until the truck made two quick turns before coming to rest. Emmanuel clambered off the roof, his face fully masked and overlaid with a dust-laden scarf, his tattooed arms covered in a thick, heavy jacket that would have left me exhausted in this heat. Fabienne dropped the tailgate, dragging Dulik towards the edge only to be stopped by the Haitian. Shaking his head, he grabbed the WPF Officer's shoulders, preventing the female terrorist from dumping her on the ground.

"Up," said Andre, an automatic now in his hand, gesturing towards the rear. I complied, jumping down to a cracked concrete floor, dust devils stirring around the garage entrance. I glanced back over my shoulder and picked out a huge mountain lit by a crescendo of lightning despite the dust. A classic volcano, almost so perfect you were looking for the giant, clay-covered hands that had just shaped it.

We walked into a garage. The walls were bare except for shelves adorned with an assortment of old parts, grease cans and diesel barrels.  I had to question their use of the word 'house'. There appeared to be a second room at the back, maybe an old office. Other than that, the rest of the building was a ruin. Wind-blasted, bricks worn clean of their facia, and steel lintels scraped with a million overlaying scratches barely holding a thousand-time repaired corrugated roof up. I heard the roller door pulled down behind me, the last ambient light fading before a generator kicked in from the back room. As a single bulb flickered on, I finally caught sight of the two who'd rode in the cab. One, a burly-looking man with close cropped, pepper greyed hair carried a set of sleeping bags into the other room. The other, a woman in her fifties, grey streaked blonde hair and frown lines everywhere you looked, stood, legs wide, one hand on her hip as she stared back at me.  That look was full of steel. This woman took no shit, whether she was right or wrong. The closest I could come to a comparison was Rocinha, and she'd run our favela for a good twenty years. Unheard of.

"Not wasting air and fucking water on these two," she spat, "unless we get some answers. String the bitch up." Her voice grated, halfway between gravel and monotone.  Up to now, I'd been in my own movie, dodging and weaving but getting by. Now, the camera had suddenly cut away, panning back after the director had his throat slit and a new one sat in the chair.

*"She tastes wrong."*

Oh shit.

I repeat, oh shit.

Think I need a new theme tune.

# Chapter 17

D ulik's cable-tied hands hung over a chained hook suspended from the ceiling. She slouched forward, feet not bearing her weight as she swung gently side to side. I had visions of frozen meat in an abattoir, the analogy heightened by the two slashes used to cut through her exo-suit at the front. Water dripped slowly from the rubber edges, mingled with scarlet where the razor-edged knife had bit into the flesh beneath.

By now I'd worked out the woman was the Professor, and not a scientist. Catchy, huh?

*"Still tastes wrong. Like the translator, Clara."*

Okay, I was avoiding thinking about that. Crap. So, there were two possibilities running through my mind. Either she'd kicked her programming somehow, overcome the mods and gone full bloodlust over finding how much they'd packed into her brain. Or she'd been discarded by the Drathken. Used up or a botch job. Both would mean a great big fucking grudge against our alien benefactors, and a role in the HLA with her insight into their world. A valuable asset, and right now someone *big* in the dirty bomb programme. Hey, who else would know how to get aboard a Drathken ship other than one of their own?

The heavy-set man, however, was another kettle of crabs. Definitely the air of someone educated, and looking around at the choices, he was number one on my list to be the scientist unless Fabienne had hidden talents. Of course, they could have left them back at the Institute, in which case we'd have put the 'wild' into Dulik's 'wild goose chase'.

Andre kept glancing over to me, a nervous twitch that put me on edge amid four other terrorists who were planning on me being next on Fabienne's salad bar. It set an itch going near my chip. If he didn't stop, I was facing being peeled. Possibly chopped up with a salt and vinegar dressing.

Dulik spat in Fabienne's face. I had to admit from a swinging position, it was an impressive shot. Not so effective if you're wearing a rebreather and googles, but the terrorist had chosen to remove them as she took pleasure in administering pain to the WPF operative. I winced as the knife flew out, slicing Dulik's cheek, the slit starting off clean before the blood chose to pour. Dulik laughed and I could see teeth through the widening gap. Fuck me, she was tough. I'd have given them my sister's beating heart after that one – not that I've got a sister or anything. The tip of a tentacle waved my way from under the truck, and I let out a sigh.

"Hey," I shouted. Brave? Foolish? Write them on someone else's tombstone. "I'll talk."

Andre peered my way, a quizzical look in his eyes. I genuinely thought he was on my side at that moment, ready to pitch in. Perhaps he had been the one to expose me to Rocinha, organised my meeting with Sasha and Millie and the guilt was too much. Or he hadn't and retained a sense of honour towards a brother from the favela. Who knows? The fucker had got me into this, either way.

"But you need to listen carefully because I'm only going to say this once."

Fabienne glanced the Professor's way, receiving a nod, and the would-be torturer walked on over, a look of unrequited glee upon her face.

"If she touches me with that knife, I'll be out like a light for a month. I ain't no brave WPF lackey, hardened to torture and all that shit." See, I started with the truth. Fabienne yanked me to my feet, ramming my back against the wall. My precious head getting a second clatter as she slapped her hand down to press it against the bricks. Like I said, no more nose twitches.

"Gentle Fabienne," said the Professor.

*"I can't read her like others, but I think she wanted to add 'for now' on the end of that."*

"Not helping."

*"Just letting you know I'm here for you."*

The Professor walked a little closer, one hand clasped behind her back. "Explain about not being a WPF Officer."

Now I glanced over at Andre, letting him know it was his turn very soon. If I hadn't, I'm sure he'd have blurted it all out in the wrong order.

"I'm URF, a Sea Ranger. I'm the treasonous fucker who helped you obtain the pure grade. The nodules."

It was a moment of jaw dropping fun. You know, watching Fabienne back off a second as the words hit home, and the Professor widen her range beyond the nefarious villain expression she'd been sporting. Oh yeah. Then there's you, my audience. Sorry, I may have adjusted the truth a little, you know, left gaps. Did I mention I have memory drops occasionally? Yeah? This is not one of those. I need you to watch until the end, and if I started out telling you I was the bad guy all along, more than likely you'd have switched off by now. Am I right? Of course, I am. Besides, I might *appear* to be the wicked traitor right now, when in reality there's something much deeper going on. We all love a mystery, right?

*"I don't. You helped them? I don't understand. I recovered half of the nodules. It's what I do."*

"Half, Marc. It wasn't supposed to have been any. I didn't want you involved at all."

*"I don't …"*

"Later."

Sheesh. I'm up to my neck in crap and now my cephalopod partner hates me. Can this day get any worse?

Don't answer that one either.

"You are going to have to excuse my vernacular, but bullshit." The Professor stepped a little closer, and I could sense Marc curl further under the truck. This woman was creeping her out, which was a good thing. Marc was finally getting a grip on human nature, including mine.

"It's true," said Andre (can you hear the bugles, etc? The cavalry has arrived). "M—"

"—Joshua."

"Joshua was one of mine. I turned him."

"I'd like to correct that a little." Even in the face of a salt and vinegar bath, my mouth keeps on running. I stared straight at the Professor. "I am not HLA. I'm a greedy sonofabitch from the Rio favelas. That's it. No agenda. Personally, I just want my best life until we all burn in Earth's hellfire. You want to slaughter a few Drathken and their sympathisers, just keep it the fuck away from me." I watched her carefully, willing her to react. Nothing. Just a faked twitch of the mouth. "Andre knew I had disappeared from Rocinha, and there was no truth in the lies spread about my throat being slit for skimming. Rocinha couldn't look weak, but he was there, he knew. He dug, found me, found out what I do."

"And that he wasn't for turning," added Andre, looking to the Professor.

"I don't give a shit," she said. "You've put the operation at fucking risk. All of it."

*"She does. She gives a real big defecation."*

"Bastard," shouted Dulik, the words slurred as her tongue slipped between the gap in her cheek. "You f—" Emmanuel clattered his rifle into her temple, Dulik's eyes fluttering before she passed out. A sliver of concern wheedled its way into my mind for her. Tough, yes, but there's only so much she could take. And for that matter, they would tolerate.

I glanced back over to Andre, the smile definitely back in place. I'd been on medical shore leave for trauma when a message dropped onto my tablet. How he'd bribed his way to get it, he'll have to explain. But it was the whole shebang, my new name, my address ashore, my training dates and my past. That was it. *I see you.* I watched my whole world for the past three years disintegrate before my eyes. Decent air, food you could actually chew and swallow, clean water. And a safe bed away from the mentality of the gangs and their named blades. The price had been my parents' lives, giving of themselves so I could be free. And that fucker turned up and belittled it with one message. Yeah, I know. I push, and when it came down to it, I hiked the price, sucked as much as I could out of Andre and the HLA. How else could I afford the eye-mod? It can't be seen to come out of my pay packet, such as it is, because they'd be asking questions of a sea-cop and his pay cheque. Shadowy creds transferred direct, along with their ridiculous and obvious camera gadget that the WPF confiscated in five minutes. I'm a master of the sleight of hand, yeah? That's why I'm sat here waiting for my throat to be cut.

And for the record, you are still looking at the cop who came second at least five times out of a hundred. Only the eye-mod makes my shooting even worse. I was supposed to miss and have it witnessed by the sub's camera. And if I had, I would be sat cuddling a metallic octopus, watching arthouse cinema and wistfully staring out into the black.

Life. Fuck me.

"This for real, Andre?" said Emmanuel, rifle now by his side, looking at me with his head cocked to one side. "He don't look like no favela gangsta, and I've done many."

"For real, Emm. For sure. We were the swimmas, yeah? The villa scavengers, the first and the best. Until Rocinha decided otherwise, stopped her trustin' ways and tied us all to boats. Before your time, brother."

"Okay, Ranger man. Tell us who's following us, what firepower we facin'?" The Haitian raised his rifle, pretending to shoot. "I'm in the mood after our little tête-à-tête at the lake."

With the tension ratcheting up a little more, I swallowed hard, finding that my mouth was dry. If this went wrong...

"From the WPF? The APC was disabled, and our transport lost. You're looking at it. I'm not in on everything. I was reassigned because ... because of the nodules. My recovery unit got their isotope signature when we recovered part of the cargo. There were two 'copters in support with Presa Ignacio Ramirez the limit of their range. If there's anyone left to follow, that's the way they'll come."

Fabienne grinned at that point, bringing the knife point in closer. Short of licking it, I couldn't see how more menacing she could be. Yep, the canary had sung and was no longer needed. A user of air, water and food. Shouldn't have mentioned food.

"But they won't. They don't need to," I spat out as rapidly as I could.

"Eh?" said Emmanuel, stepping in closer. "What do you mean, man? You playin' a game with us?" The Professor stepped in his way.

*"The defecation is about to hit the fan. She really, really wants to know."*

And there it was. For all Marc's words, the Professor's eyes were dead. Lost in thought or comms. I hoped it wasn't the latter. If it was the next step would lead to a long, painful time with my new best friend and her condiment collection.

"Someone here has been feeding them your location. How else do you think they knew where you were? They don't have a clue I was in on it. They talked in front of me like I was just a piece of sea-cop scum. Unworthy. Once you put the polymetallic and the Professor together, it's a WPF jackpot. If that's your pet scientist over there too, then it's a double bonus prize draw. Andre here, is the one who's been fuckin' turned."

Now, I'll hold my hands up high. That was a genuine, no holds barred, lie. See, I can be honest. Erm. Well, to *you* I can be. Mostly.

# Chapter 18

Fear hit his eyes first, then panic which flickered briefly into pain before he decided on pure hate. I'll let you guess the target. Thing is, you have to add shock to that. His mouth was moving at a thousand clicks an hour, but no words were coming out.

"Bait. That's why he recruited me. Once you had the nodules, he knew you'd go for the full bomb." Making shit up now, so my fingers were crossed. "He's favela, like me. What the fuck does a gangsta want with saving the fucking world? Dulik said Andre was earning three times what the bastard paid me. It was all I could do to not spit my guts out there and then."

In one of those rare events, Andre's smile had left the building. Leaving a man so tense you could have cracked nuts with his nuts.

"No – no. He's playin' you all. Just words, man. Just words." Andre had both his hands up, eyes wide, flicking from Emmanuel to the Professor and back. "I was shootin', you saw that."

I could see the Professor nodding at that.

"You see him hit anyone? Got to keep appearances up." Weak, I know. "Check the bastard's pockets. Think about it, how, in the burnout zone, did they pinpoint you?"

*"I'm not comfortable with this."*

"My parents," was all I could manage in reply. And a betrayal, take your pick which one.

Emmanuel snorted. You know that sound of disbelief and I sensed my chances of survival ebbing away. Then came the first piece of luck on a bad day.

"You're looking pretty screwed up," said the scientist, his accent pure, clipped English. "You've been nosing in my business since I arrived in this godforsaken place. Wanting to know about the irradiated roots, then the nodule and the bomb."

I was tempted to correct him on who forsook whom. The heat, sweat and smell in that room all caused by humanity's 'someone else's problem' attitude. Maybe it wasn't the time. Besides, he was helping.

But roots?

The Professor stepped in towards Andre and I caught a tremor in that clasped hand, reinforcing my assessment of her. "If you're clean, then we shoot the bastard in the mouth. Solves the issue, yes?"

I'll give Fabienne her due, she really looked concerned for me at that point.

"Yeah, yeah," said Andre. "Do it."

*"What will happen?"*

"Watch." It's that cephalopod not seeing consequences thing again.

Emmanuel took his cue from the Professor, shouldering his rifle and patting Andre down. No surprise, he found Andre's hidden knives and the two-shot weapon he always kept in his sock. Ignoring them, he felt along the man's ancient army issue jacket, pulling out the odd magazine for his guns. Finally, he reached the outer, lower pocket. The one I'd been praying Andre wouldn't drop his hands into since Marc's little wave. Emmanuel withdrew the little box, the satcom encased in Drathken plant fibre.

The Professor took another step forward, the tremor in her clasped hand gone as she fired direct into Andre's opening mouth. The bullet crashed through his brain, sending him flying back, slamming into the truck before hitting the floor.

For *mae* and *pai*, if nothing else.

With her gun still smoking, the terrorist leader spat on the corpse and held her hand out to a shocked Emmanuel. I mean, he was from the favela, likely a family of Haitian gangstas born and bred, but the sudden violence had shaken him. A trembling hand dropped the little box into the woman's hand.

"Satcom," she said, spinning it in her fingers. "The fucker had a direct link through the burnout zone." She held it in the air, her fingers either side and for a moment I thought she was going to hold it up to the light. It was a weird gesture, like a memory was flashing though her mind, eyes distant. "Drathken tech, Emm." She glanced over to me. "He called it."

"The URF man stabbed his own in the back, Professor. No loyalty there. And like he said, he's *not* HLA." His gun rose, Fabienne's disappointed face apparent as she backed away from me.

*"Josh?"*

The Professor's hand reached out, pushing the barrel down. You know in books, when they write that someone sucks in a breath and then, when the tension breaks, they let it out? Yeah? Luckily, I had my exo-suit on, 'cos it wasn't a breath I was releasing.

"Wait. I need thinkin' time, Emm. This gadget can do wonders but I'm guessing it can also be tracked. Right now, they don't know we have it, but that fucker will have had a call-in schedule or something. This is big, Emm. It may be our way onto a Drathken ship."

I've got to admit, I hadn't thought of that. The old, grey-haired terrorist looked my way. Her gaze gave the impression she was calculating my worth, a dispassionate grading of Joshua Nkosi. My skin comes first, second and possibly third on my list of concerns. Not forgetting Marc. But on hers?

"We eat, hydrate. I need to talk to Michael about things." She spun around, walking towards the door and pulling the Englishman, Michael I assumed, with her. "Keep Fabienne away from him, Emm. For now."

They left Dulik hanging, still out cold, though her cheek finally stopped bleeding. The smell from Andre was dreadful, the temperature refusing to drop despite the complaining generator's attempts to bring it down. Emm dragged the corpse to the garage doorway, stripping Andre of anything useful, before raising the door a little and rolling the body out into the dust. The ferocity of the heat reflected a change outside, the wind having died down, dust wafting and dropping to the floor. I guessed we were receiving the last rays before night fall, but my time sense was all screwed and Marc had been silent on me since Andre's brains vacated his skull.

"Tie him to the truck, Fabienne, yeah. Don't want him getting any ideas." Emm said as the door rolled down. "And no sticking him until the Professor says."

She pulled me from the floor, her mood a little changed, dragging me across the wheels and adding a few extra cable ties to my wrist before slotting them through the wheel housing. I had my back to the stink of the encrusted tyres, the mud drying and crumbling onto my back. I avoided any eye contact; this wasn't the time to antagonise. See, I can be restrained sometimes – hey, that's almost funny.

*"Almost."*

"Welcome back, partner."

*"…"*

"I had to, Marc. I didn't know they'd kill him. He wasn't an innocent."

*"No, but you could have warned me of the consequences. It doesn't feel right."*

True, but then would Marc have done it? "We need to get out of here. Otherwise, I think me, and Dulik will be dead by morning." Okay, forgive me. Right? She has three hearts, and I was plucking them all. "Then you'll be alone."

*"I … I don't want that."*

"Then I need some help. Not yet, in a while."

* * *

The second piece of luck arrived when the Professor and her scientist crony decided they needed rest, aka sleep. How they'd manage it in the heat, I don't know. For the last three years and so many months I'd got used to the comforts of temperature-controlled rooms and timed showers. The garage had the stink of the favela, a long-forgotten stench that tried to draw memories, good and bad, from my mind as I drifted a little in and out of a half-sleep.

*"Joshua."*

I recommend a cephalopod alarm clock by the way. If you don't wake on the first ring, they tickle you awake. Or shout in your head, depending on their mood. Today it was the tickle, there being two terrorists in the room and all. I squeezed my wrists, my handy octopus pal having already sliced through multiple cable ties, and felt the last one give. I didn't move, eying the rise and fall of Fabienne's chest near the wall opposite. I had no visual on Emmanuel, but Marc did, sending a set of images along with an analysis of his breathing and heart rhythm. He wasn't faking the deep sleep.

Now, at this point, you're probably waiting for my redemption, right? I rescue Dulik, arrest the HLA members and salvage the box which I'm guessing has some form of dirty bomb inside, or at the very least, the extracted isotopes. The anti-hero saves the day with a sardonic, 'I told you so' grin as he hands over the bad people to the WPF. Got to remember where I'm from, right? Not all things are black and white, nor do all heroes always undertake heroic acts. For instance, *risk*. Success is not judged by the process, but by the outcome. You can be the hero, and dead, or the survivor who gets to tell of heroic deeds in their version of the story.

What doesn't help is an eight-legged conscience. But hey-ho, needs must. *"I don't know if I can."*

"Can you see Dulik? That slit in her cheek, the sag where her facial muscles are severed? That was for fun, Marc. She'll be feeding me my testicles before she's done."

The silence was punctuated by the gentle scrape of her metal tentacles as she dropped into the dust, and I watched as Marc slid across the floor, silent, riding the dust with her flowing movements. When she reached within tentacle distance, I moved, body stiff and awkward at first. Keeping each shift of limb and torso slow and steady, breathing in tune with my movements, I crept across to Fabienne. My mind focused on the knife in its sheath at her side, and the movements of her body. In the vids, she'd have muttered in her sleep, rolled over as I neared. Maybe an inner instinct would kick in, and Fabienne would wake instantly, knife in hand. Watch enough flicks and you prep your partner to cut off any cry. But I hadn't gone completely soft, my days running with the Rocinha crew flooding back. I had the knife in hand by the time the first flutter and moan emanated, and bless her, Marc smothered those as I slit her throat. Go team Nkosi.

I glanced over to the office door, conscious that I had zero control once it opened. I slipped out Fabienne's pistol, pocketing a spare magazine and a grenade before gently rolling her into a position to let the blood pour away from the door.

Marc sent me a wave of emotion, one that almost floored me until I silenced her. I stopped and stared at the octopus, my face pleading, and she scuttled off towards the lorry. Yeah, this was going to scar my partner. But that's how life was for us now. Blame the new director.

She slithered up the lorry wheel I'd been tied to, before clambering over the tailgate. By the time she'd slid onto the flatbed, I was at the back of the lorry, Marc's chip allowing a view of what she was doing. It had been a difficult choice, to risk the flatbed and possibly waking Emmanual with the increased potential for noise or attempt the office with dual occupants. Both would leave me exposed should the others wake. Marc arrived in a similar position to that for Fabienne, only for the Haitian's eyes to flicker open. I'm sure the last thing he was expecting was a metal octopus staring back at him, tentacles raised in alarm, waving in front of herself for protection. Experience teaches you that in those moments your next decision is riddled with adrenaline and may not be the best thought out. The terrorist lashed out, fist smashing into Marc's body. The octopus wrapped herself around the blow, tentacles squeezing, and sliced the man's hand from his arm as the sharp edges bit. I could see the scream coming and sent my panic searing into Marc. A mistake, it paralysed her systems, and I fired, the bullet crashing into Emmanuelle's neck a good fifteen centimetres below were I aimed. Eye-mods have their uses, but it seriously screwed my long-distance perception. His throat exploded, blood splattering Marc who dropped the hand and scuttled away from the thrashing terrorist.

I had already dropped to the garage floor, the pistol aimed towards the office door. The last thing I expected was the scientist to come crashing through headfirst and onto the dusty concrete. My finger twitched, but I had enough control to keep from firing. An assault rifle poked around the door, bullets spraying above Fabienne's body.

Fuck that.

Low risk, yeah?

The grenade slapped into the door, bouncing inwards and after what felt like a lifetime, exploded. The flash filled the garage with burning white light, the accompanying cacophony faded out by the hands I'd clamped to my head. I hoped Marc would be okay, the flash warning I'd sent of more importance than the sound. Without the time to check, I was up on my feet, bypassing the scientist and rushing for the doorway as a wail echoed back over the residual explosion. I glanced around the door, catching sight of the Professor curled into a ball, hands over her ears. Taking a step in and placing the gun against her head, I fired. Like I said, no risk.

I was desperate to check whether anything was wired into that once human brain, but I still had two unresolved issues. Spinning back outside, I caught the burly scientist trying to get to his feet, the crack I dealt him on the back of the head resolving issue number one. Marc's tentacles overhung the rear trailer, unmoving, and fear bit at me, rising into anger at myself. I lifted the pistol over the metal panel and emptied the magazine into the space beyond. No return fire came, nor cry of pain or challenge. I risked a glance over, Emmanuel's eyes wide open but clearly dead. I chose to take that burden on myself, despite knowing the severed hand was as likely a death sentence as the bullets I'd poured into him. I reached out, grasping Marc, bringing her close. She didn't respond and my heart skipped as I sent message after message. Her chip finally glowed, the energy bar so far in the red it remained barely a sliver. The mechanism had shut down, preserving Marc's memories at least, awaiting a recharge.

After all, she couldn't die.

That had happened a while a go.

# Chapter 19

I awoke, sore as hell. Heart pounding as my mind activated the chip, scanning for Marc. With a brain addled by sleep, memories poured in amid the stifling heat and I pushed myself off the scavenged blanket. I walked over to Dulik who lay on her side, eyes still closed after the sedative I'd appropriated from the Professor's medical kit. With her cheek cleaned and neatly sewn, the other scars glistened as glue and tape caught the weak light. Nothing more I could do, so I lifted her eyelid, the haze slowly fading. I gave it an hour before she would awaken and then checked her bonds. There was no way I was letting her loose, at least not yet. You heard her when Andre started talking, and she heard little after that with Emm's intervention.

Passing the scientist tied to the same wheel I had been, I didn't bother to check his eyes. Needing the sleep and his silence, I had introduced him to the same sedative. Only a bit later than Dulik, Michael helping me with a few modifications and requests first, and the last thing I needed was him babbling away in front of the WPF. By the time I'd entered the office, my mind had wandered back to the potential of the satcom again. The Professor's response hinting at the possibilities and dangers, it presented. I needed an edge, and that was one. Next to it, laid another.

Marc lay straddled across the diesel motor, the combination of cannibalised wires and electrical plugs charging my partner's energy cell far slower than my integration suit, but needs must. I gathered together my electrical kit and spare parts. A tentacle waved my way, and after checking her power bar had entered the green, engaged full contact. Relief washed over us both as the connection renewed and a tear dribbled across my dust-laden cheek. I'd worried that all my tinkering may have fully wiped her memory, made her forget me and not just the encounter with Andre.

Yeah, I'm one of those 'modern men' from the vids. All connected to my feelings, okay? At least I am where a cephalopod is concerned. As far as most humans go, not so much.

The negative side was the whole garage had turned into an oven box, a little olive oil and I would be cooked in about an hour – suit or not. Ten minutes after hooking Marc up, I'd been forced to roll the bodies outside of the garage door, the smell choking, my mind unable to disassociate from the state of Mexico City. What must it have been like when the Scorching rose in its full ferocity? When the first heatwave took hold and never broke, ratcheting the temperature, stifling life. Day after relentless day. And then you break, leaving the house you strived for, or the land you tilled, giving up in search of water and relief from the relentless heat. Only to find it stretches and stretches, vehicles dying from the choking dust and heat, people turning on each other in a desperate need to escape. And knowing human nature, the gangs preying on the weak and feeble, or scamming their desperation and leaving them in the dirt to die. Five years ago, I could have been one of those. Prepared to do anything.

I filled the truck with whatever I could scavenge. Food, water, diesel and weapons. The four essentials of life. I threw in the cables I'd cobbled together to charge Marc and after wolfing down whatever the dried meat and grain meal was stored in the office, I looked over to the truck again, swearing gently to myself.

"It's time, Marc. We need to check that crate." And time for a test.

*"We? You mean your beloved partner gets a taste of the bad stuff?"*

Well, she's certainly acting like her old self this morning. Tentacles wrestled with my hand a while, playfully teasing at my fingers, before sliding up my forearm and wrapping around my neck. It felt good to have her back despite the added weight, and we wandered over to the truck, taking comfort in being together. I had sopped most of Emmanuel's blood with his clothes, though the stains were still evident. Marc appeared unconcerned, my handiwork hopefully working, but I'll talk more on that later. She dropped to the floor and dragged herself across to the crate while I clambered aboard. By the time I was there, she'd insinuated a tentacle or two under the lid, prying the loosely nailed crate open. The inner was split into two, one side holding a cylinder of about thirty centimetres thickness and around fifty centimetres long. It had been roughly welded together initially, poor workmanship by Michael that made me wince, then later resealed with a defter hand. Mine. At its side, two containers which I assumed were all lead based on the little I know about such things.

"Well?"

*"There's no way I can tell if our node's isotopes are in there. This has all been modded. And the outside of all three is shielded, but I reckon there's a lot of radiation present the way they're set up."*

Clearly Marc couldn't sense Michael's previous nights work. His welding might be crap, but he knew his radiation. If Marc couldn't tell, then nor would the WPF. Hopefully, I had my rabbit up my sleeve. Or was it in the hole? Sheesh, old stuff.

"So best guess, one dirty bomb and two containers to make more."

*"Probably. What is a dirty bomb?"*

"To be honest, I'm not definite. It's not as powerful as the old nukes, remembering much of that tech and capability left with the starships. I think its based on spreading radiation, and with that fear. Considering how fucked up most of the world is, I was wondering why the HLA see it as such a good thing. Seems a lot of trouble, when they could just have made a bigger bomb from what's lying around."

*"I don't think I'll ever understand humans."*

I dropped the crate lid, nodding to myself. "You and me both."

The muffled noise arising from outside the truck drew my mind back, and I dropped off the rear to find Dulik wriggling painfully against her bonds. I walked over, dropping on my haunches out of kicking range. Her eyes were wide and perfectly readable. The traitorous sea-cop walking around free as a bird. What else was I supposed to do?

"You need to listen. I want to take the rag out. It's not in there to stop you screaming or calling me every dirty name you know. It's there because after I sewed you up, the blood would have drained down your throat over night. Okay?" Dulik gave me that wide eyed *'I'll rip your heart out and have it with ketchup look.'* I showed her Fabienne's knife and Emmanuel's assault rifle, as well as drawing her attention to the trussed scientist at her side.

"I could tell you lots of lies about how I now happen to be in control, but you'll see through them all. I did sell out, yes. Andre threatened to reveal that my credentials were falsified to the URF, ruin my life. My parents sacrificed themselves to give me a chance, and he was going to take that away from me." See, I can tell the truth. "But it was on the agreement that nothing and nobody got hurt. I had no idea they were after stuff for a bomb, I just thought it was greed at first. Then, when I was in too fucking deep, he said he was HLA, and it was too late."

All true. See, you thought I was a really bad person. That's why you can't know everything immediately. Life isn't a simple path with few complexities. It is all interconnected, a web of circumstance that can overwhelm you if you let it. Stay shallow, and there's never enough shit to drown you. I hope.

Dulik stopped struggling. She sat up straight and eyeballed me, looking for cracks. There were many, plastered over with a sheen of cocky resolve, but that you can keep to yourself. I put the knife on the flatbed of the truck, returning with the pistol in my hand.

"I've seen enough old vids to know this is the point I'm supposed to give you the gun and say, 'trust me'. Not happening. You have no reason to do that or to believe anything I've told you. I can only see two ways out of this. Either I kill you and take the truck, drive south and head home with something worth selling. Or I take you and the scientist back to the WPF and beg for a pardon. Without me and Marc, you would already be dead. You need to think on that. On your knees." She complied, though clearly unsure of my intent. Experience pays. Once she was up, I got her to lean forward. With her arms tied behind her back there was no way to lever herself for an attack. Once she realised this, she opened her mouth, and I drew out the bloodied rag, taking care not to snag my stitching.

I expected a tirade, what I got was sullen silence. Marc wriggled onto my calf, then up my back as I stood. I patted the tentacles she latched onto my shoulders. It took a few seconds of orientation for Dulik to work things out. The front of her suit was next to useless for water retention, but I'd taped it up for heat protection. On her back was a backpack, its water bag full, the bite clip strapped against her shoulder. At her feet was a nearly clean plate full of the dried meat and watered grain meal. Eating would be difficult, her hands still tied behind. I hadn't factored that in, but I'm far from perfect. Marc scraped down my back, scurrying over and waved a tentacle at the plate. With a glance towards me, Dulik nodded, and very carefully began to eat with a cephalopod's help.

* * *

The garage door trundled up. My octopus clock had one tentacle pointing at the four and the other at the twelve, and we were nearing the coolest part of the day. I estimated a stifling 41°C, predicting an easterly wind with a tinge of dust. By midday, add at least six degrees to that, possibly a lot more.

By the time the door had risen, a small fox's head popped up from its human feast, wild eyes latching onto mine. Its fur was mangy, patched with scars across the haunches. Behind, I could make out two smaller ones gnawing on the Professor's exposed head. It was the first life I'd seen, except for the ragged wisps of humanity in Mexico City. I walked closer to find the mostly eaten bodies were swarming with ants and beetles, each cutting, sawing or burrowing their way in. Life adapting, feeding off humanity. Almost poetic, you might say.

I caught the scrape of feet behind me, turning as Dulik charged at me, screaming. I sidestepped, kicking her leg away so she collapsed to the ground. Unable to get up with her hands cuffed, she started shouting while staring at the human mess I'd created. The foxes refused to move, snarling back at the Officer as a new threat, protecting a precious meal.

I could see where this was going and so I lied. "You can't risk a bite. They could be rabid." Hey, I like animals, people not so much – sue me if you can find a judge within a hundred miles of the Scorching.

She clammed up, staring at me from the ground. My first thought was of her distaste at the killing I'd had to do. A necessity to my mind, and it was possible there would be more if I didn't get her on my side somehow. "Stay by the truck."

I turned away, waiting for the swearing but she must have realised just how mad her actions appeared, and skulked away. These people were her enemies, would have cut her down without remorse. Yet to my mind, she could not accept their part in the food chain. Odd. It was then that I noticed one of the smaller foxes spitting something out and a little realisation hit – a memory lapse. I risked the dog fox's wrath by wandering over, spying the array of plant roots and tendrils drawn out from the Professor's skull. These I had half-expected, but not the satcom the female fox had spat out. In the rush to sort Marc and get some rest, I'd forgotten to check on the Professor's mods as I'd intended. Risking things further, I gently made my way across and recovered the Drathken comms device, mind reeling at the possibilities. I was more convinced than ever that the woman had been a Drathken plant (excuse the pun), and that there was a strong possibility they already knew about my traitorous acts. Maybe not what happened after, including the cause of their spy's demise, but that something drastic had happened. I couldn't help myself, peering straight up into the sky, half-expecting a spaceship to be watching over my shoulder.

*"What you looking for?"*

I opened my hand, letting Marc see the satcom. "Someone could be watching. But it doesn't make sense, unless she could bypass the link, or it's a dud. Was she working with, or against, the Drathken?"

*"They made a bomb. Doesn't seem she'd be working with them."*

"Unless it's bait, attracting the big fish."

*"Whoa, you mean like a lure?"*

It made my mind up. Running south would put the crosshairs on my neck, with the only two people who witnessed the events between leaving Toluca and now about to leave on a truck full of their radioactive material. Please forgive me at this point, I wonder where my mind is sometimes, possibly the stress making decisions for me.  Let's just say I encouraged the dog fox to chomp down the Professor's satcom with a choice morsel or two and leave it there.

Marc didn't speak to me until we were halfway to Mexico City.

# Chapter 20

Driving a truck isn't easy, driving one with one hand cable tied to the wheel even less so, but Dulik made a fair fist of it for the first twenty kilometres. The road swirled with the usual grey dust, most of the abandoned vehicles shredded by the wind, their bodies shining as if new when the sun penetrated the thickening clouds. We only had to weave in and out a few times, where a storm or three had shifted the vehicular skeletons, pushing them along on the remaining steel wheels that resisted the weather's attempts to strip them down to their molecules. We were five clicks out when Dulik finally spoke.

"What do you think the WPF will do with you? And the Drathken?"

I eased my legs, stretching them out. Feeling the bruise from that first encounter with the HLA. You could say I was biding my time, formulating my words, but in reality, I didn't know how to answer. I gave it a minute.

"It depends on you, really. You were there. You heard Andre, and me. Then woke to find Marc and I had taken the entire HLA cell out and recovered the terrorist's bomb. I mean, you could claim the glory for yourself, if you had the mind. Bury me in my own shit."

"My word against yours? If you kill me, who else is there to rat on you? You're not stupid, why am I still alive?"

It was a good question, and the more astute of you will have been wondering the same thing. I probably am too.

"Who's going to believe that a sea-cop took out an entire HLA cell? If I'd left them inside the garage, then maybe someone would put the evidence together. But there'll be nothing left once the bugs and foxes are done. The Professor, the lot, all the evidence gone."

She didn't react to that, passing my less than subtle test. Not a flinch in response to the Professor, convincing me she had little idea of the cell leader's Drathken links. One bright light amid the dark pressing in on me.

"Might give you that," she said, partially slurred as her tongue touched the inside of her cheek. "But I don't fucking trust you."

"Feelings mutual. I would prefer you alive, Dulik. It makes everything easier, maybe smooths my conscience a little. But there's far more irradiated shit back there than my nodules."

We bounced around in silence for a while, my mind pinging over the connotations of the Drathken's involvement and Dulik's apparent ignorance.

"They obtained a lot of crap from old labs, like minor medical isotopes, some that were used in industry and parts missed from the nuclear stations in the scorched wastelands. Wherever, and whenever they could. And they keep moving, always in the burnout zone and so out of sight. A gram or two here and there adding up. We never thought they'd risk anything bigger, but the *Socorro* nodules are comparatively rich in nuclear byproducts from waste dumping. It must have proved too tempting, or they needed more in a rush." Her eyes stayed on the road, which is a good job as I put the pieces of a story together. If I swapped out Andre for the Professor, it would still look like someone had been waiting for everything, or everyone, to come together. I could still recover this. Come out alive and maybe a tainted hero. If that's what I wanted.

"Still leaves me guilty on the first charge, even if it's under the duress of blackmail. But right now, without me, you'd be a human jigsaw lying on a dirty garage floor, and the HLA halfway to whatever place they'd planned on using the bomb at." There was a barely perceptible nod in response to that, one that shone in my head. A hope that maybe things would get a little easier.

*"You might be right. Her heart rate has decreased a little, her rebreather is working less hard."*

We hit the outskirts of Mexico City around 6am, the sun's heat searing in the cab despite the aircon stripping as much as it could. The minor dune on the road ahead stretched out between tumbled down houses, constantly shifting under the wind's insistence. Down the quickly drying centre, remnants of past floods flaked away as the wind exposed them to the sun. The rumble of the truck penetrated the silence, echoing back off the ruined streets as we searched for the pathway the HLA must have taken. Part of me wanted to be up top, keeping an eye out for the fever and hunger ravaged humanity that clung on to the city streets. I said part, I'm not completely stupid. We'd passed through close to dusk first time, only encountering very few remnants whose families had clung on long enough that their children knew of nothing else but their territory and daily survival. That any lived on demonstrated that even under the harshest of conditions life could find a way. Yet Mexico City was as sparsely populated as the seas, near empty, a void that life could no longer fill. You see, the Scorching had a secondary effect. At first, as the temperatures rose, reproduction of many species fell into chaos. Broods became gender specific at first among the reptiles and turtles, and for many fish and bird species too. Then, as it increased, heat stress caused multiple still births and miscarriages, pregnant animals failing to maintain body regulation during pregnancy. With birth rates falling, and food becoming scarcer for many, it was only when this impacted humanity that they began to worry. Farming continually shifted further north or south, forever seeking newer ways for animal production to be more efficient and to help with heat regulation. At first it was attempts to gene mod the animals, then electronic modding became the rage to help regulate biochemical processes. Later, they grew meat in vats, and when the Drathken arrived, they had processes to develop more protein rich fungi and algae strains. All the while nature died around them. Indifference to their fate put down to human survival. Better than it just being someone else's problem, like before, I suppose.

A blood-curdling scream cut through my thoughts. One where irony may play a part, if that's your thing. We had entered a blocked street, the rubble from a fallen tower block wind-stripped and raw across the road. Dulik had ground her way into reverse when the cry tore through the metal panel behind my head. Dulik slammed on the brakes as I checked the side mirror. Seeing nothing, I dropped out of the cab with pistol in hand. The cries continued, sobs that were quickly cut off. When I reached the tailgate, Marc pulled herself off my shoulders and grabbed hold of the roof frame, her images of what lay inside the truck graphic. I pulled myself up, aiming for a ragged mess of clothing that writhed over the scientist, estimating where the head might be. I fired twice, the first probably missing as it buried itself into the strips of billowing cloth. The second hit something solid, the crunch of bone and a feral grunt followed by the human creature spinning to the floor. Sharpened and partially bloodied fingernails protruded from the ragged clothing, with the scientist's soulless gaze evidence that his terrorist ways were over. The cannibal moved, rags spinning and swaying in such a way I couldn't grasp where its body started and finished. My third shot tore into something as it threw itself at me, nails extended, wild eyes surrounded by dirt above a blood-filled mouth. I fell back from the tailgate, shock preventing a fourth shot when Marc lashed out, dual tentacles wrapping around the cannibal's neck, yanking back as her others gripped onto the truck. I landed on my back, the crack of a broken neck crossing the void between us. The body swung to the left, Marc releasing and letting momentum send it spiralling out into the street.

"Nkosi!" shouted Dulik. I scrambled to my feet and ran for the door I'd left open. A body flew out, the crunch of boot on chin accompanied by snarls of pain and anger. The cannibal hit the floor, their swathe of clothing rolling in the dust before the woman came to her feet. A glower at me, and then at the dead body, set her howling, convincing a sea-cop lost in Mexico City that an attack was coming. I raised the handgun. The woman spat, rotten teeth flying and ran, jumping over debris and fallen walls, her ragged clothing whirling around her. The bark of an assault rifle cut through the near silence, a single round, fired one-handed, smashing into the back of the running wild woman. Too far to hear, my mind filled in the blanks, assuming her agony reverberated across the street before collapsing onto the rubble.

Why?

I expected the assault rifle to point my way next, a trigger pull to answer my own question, but I heard it drop to the seat. When I glanced over, Dulik had her eyes forward, chin on the wheel. Walking over to the cab I dragged the rifle out of the way, placing it in the footwell and handed her Fabienne's knife. Right now, I couldn't untangle right from wrong, from a moral or personal point of view.

"Hang on," I said, then walked around the back. Once over the tailgate, I checked what I already knew, that the scientist was now cooking dirty bombs for the devil himself. I'd drugged the bastard with a little too much sedative, and well, let's say he'd been out a while, only for the first thing he saw when he woke to be a pair of sharpened teeth. Shit. I wanted to know about the irradiated roots. Of all the goings on in the garage, that had to be the weirdest of the weird. It couldn't have been about the Professor – no way the HLA were dealing with her if they knew she'd been modded.

Avoiding the blood, I checked I had the man's personal items and a set of tools with his fingerprints all over them. We had lost the tablets back at the mud lake, but I got Marc to check he had stored a facial image. On his confirmation I rolled the man out, dumping him next to the dead wild man who took his life. Yeah, I'm avoiding 'cannibal'. In my mind they were hunters, and we were simply on a list of potential quarry. It's something humans do, prey on each other. If you have what I want, then I have the right to take it from you. Whether your creds attained by violence or greed, or the food and water you have that I don't. And we're good at it, *taking*, until we too fall prey to another. I do wonder, at times, whether we spend so much time watching our backs, that we fail to see what is in front of us. Stood in that eroded street, buildings lying broken and torn, the sun beating down as the temperature clicked over into the high 40s, how could I possibly believe that?

"Nkosi," came the slurred shout. "We need to get fucking moving."

# Chapter 21

Dulik pulled the truck up at the mud lake's entry point, the old tracks having either hardened or turned to dust. The wind had dropped, and dust hovered eerily in the air, a false mist that gently swayed its way downwards. The calm felt strange, my ears echoing the rage of the wind in my head as if its memory wavered there, unable to believe it had ended. I adjusted my rebreather, risking a breath of not so fresh air and immediately regretting it as the dust caught in my throat and lungs suffered, scouring the air for oxygen. By the time I'd put it back on, Dulik had gone in search of the boat wreckage. We found little of Alpha 2. Scraps of uniform here and there, a myriad of small footprints preserved in the mud and dust, even a snake trail amid them. Still life prevailed.

*"There,"* said Marc, dropping an enhanced image into my chip.

I squeezed Dulik on a sore shoulder and pointed twenty metres down the lake edge. When we reached it, Dulik dropped to her haunches, staring at Alpha 1's remains. The squad leader lay three quarters in the lake, his upper half ravaged by the same scavengers and the ever-present wind. A sleeve bore his insignia, the helmet his localised radio. Then it happened. You know that moment, when your brain runs over old memories, ones that under moments of stress, your brain had filed for perusal later. It always happens at such inopportune moments.

"The satcom," said Dulik.

See.

There and then, it struck me that I could have kept the Professor's. Palmed it off to Dulik. But then, was it traceable? And would the then current owner find him or herself enjoying the fertiliser farms as the HLA claimed happened to all dissenters? I was praying my satcom couldn't be hacked, that the connection I had with it was exclusive. Playing the odds, and I so love risk.

"In the lake somewhere, I assume. Or the terrorists have it, though I searched them all. If it's as important as you say, would they have bothered with the charade at the garage?"

I could feel Dulik's eyes on me, calculating, assessing. I made to dig down into the lake, using Alpha 1's knife that had ended up on the lake shore. The residual marks in the mud around it showing his attempts to escape or defend himself.

"Possibly. You—"

"—Yeah. I had it last, I know. But we crashed, I woke up. No satcom." I didn't embellish or plead, nor let my eyes slide high and to the left as I looked back at her. I let Marc slip off me, glad to get some relief from the weight as the sun rose higher. She dropped between us both, spinning slowly round. Dulik reached out a hand and Marc wrapped herself about it, turning over and allowing the WPF operative to see her underbelly – no satcom in sight.

It was then I glanced back at Alpha 1's body, the part I'd been unconsciously uncovering. The knife had slit through a multitude of fibrous tubes, each plunging into Alpha 1's corpse. They recoiled nearly as quickly as I did, nausea rising, my throat full of acid.

"Shit. You see that?"

Dulik was up by my side, glancing down, and though there was denial in her gaze, somewhere in her mind she knew.

"What in hell was it? They were in him, like he was the mud ..."

"Or feeding." Dulik grabbed a withered branch from behind her, digging out a hole. Each stroke met resistance as the tuber like growths pulled back after being exposed, their tips splaying wide, as if tasting the air or sensing the light before withdrawing. "They're all over."

"They're not natural, right? I haven't seen any of those on my vids before."

"Nor I." Dulik gazed towards the Institute, eyes distant, looking but not seeing. I wanted to scream; the world was screwed up enough already without more human-made crap infecting it. I was betting on gene modding – revenge of the plant monster, etc.

"It's not important. We need to get moving. If we're in luck the APC will be on its way or at least waiting for us."

I didn't say anything about cannibal karaoke, probably not the time.

I offered to take the wheel, but Dulik remained as stubborn as she was strong, and drove the truck straight into the hardening mud. Without the rain a crust was forming on top. Not yet hard enough to withstand the truck's weight, it made the going tough, the rear end sliding out and the engine labouring as she revved hard. It took three times as long, but eventually we arrived at the Institute, parking up and entering through the first floor where the terrorists had adapted a window. Despite her injuries, and an armed traitor at her back, Dulik went in first, assault rifle high as she crept inwards. It became apparent the HLA had only used half the space, most for ramshackle living quarters, the rest utilising the labs for the extraction and bomb building. We knew our attack had forced them to leave in a hurry and expected wrecked labs and all the traditional signs of covering their backs. But none of that was evident, the lab appeared to be still functional. Automated processes had been stopped in their tracks when the power had been cut, and some of the more ancient computers appeared to have missing parts torn out. But all else lay still and intact. The only damage lay on the upper floor, where Alpha 4's single shot had shattered a window. This storey now in the hands of a colony of aggressive ants, ones we left shut in on first sight.

Not being an expert on radiation, we turned to Marc whose scoping of the rooms highlighted little but the distant memory of their passing. After an hour, hopes of finding anything definitive about the HLA and their plans faded, Dulik disheartened and resorting to searching their sleeping quarters until Marc flagged a message into my brain.

"You sure?"

*"No, I thought I'd waste your time. No rush to be anywhere, have we?"*

"Dulik," I said, waving her over as she opened the door, pointing back towards the room she exited. Strewn with sleeping bags and boxes, old gas stoves and their cannisters stacked behind, it sure appeared to be a sleep space. "Marc's saying there's a residual signature where you've just been. When you opened the door, it flagged up."

"There's nothing in there," she replied, swivelling to peer back into the room. "Just a repurposed lab." Curious, she went back in, the door not quite shutting as Marc scuttled behind, grasping its edge. Dulik used the muzzle of her rifle to lift the sleeping bags, scanning beneath and finding the floor empty. Following in, I watched as she repeated the process on two others. "No mats. If they've been here more than a day, there's no way they'd be sleeping directly on the floor."

"Anything Marc?"

The squeak of metal upon the linoleum floor greeted my words as she pulled herself over to the pile of cannisters, tentacles grasping and throwing blue tins aside as she dug down. With a start, she swept back, the area before her empty.

*"Wow, weird. There's a signature that stops abruptly at the wall."*

I relayed to Dulik, approaching the apparently smooth wall only for Marc to curl out a tentacle and pull at my finger. Another tentacle indicated a spot directly above where she'd dug down.

*"I think there's something there. It shows up on my UV sight."*

I slid my hand into the collection of Michael's personal equipment in my jacket pocket, pulling out the toolkit, and selecting the aluminium torch. Though not as powerful as those in my sub, I hoped it'd do the business. Flicking it through the spectrum and hitting UV, smudged fingerprints appeared, and as I adjusted the wavelength, they clustered around a single spot.

"Do it," said Dulik, standing back, rifle raised.

"Since when do I go first?" Ignoring the lopsided sneer, I pressed the exact spot, backing away to let Dulik see (honest) as the door recessed, then swung away on smooth hydraulics. Inside was a dark space, a musky scent wafting our way. The only thing separating it from a horror movie was the lack of lights pinging on to reveal Dracula in his bloody coffin. Dulik took the torch from me, shifting to white light and holding it beneath the gun's barrel as she stepped inside.

Dank, moist heat emanated from the short corridor. On the smooth floor streams of husked tendrils wafted into eddies as her boots trod through. Keeping back, sliding a remnant of sleeping bag over my mouth, I followed behind with pistol in hand. A secondary door lay half open, its rubber edges dust covered. Dulik eased it back, releasing more of the ash-like substance, to enter a small lab space. Tanks lay on three sides. Two were three quarters full of very wet mud, the third open, a scoop driven into the soil with husked roots wrapped around its handle. Sacks of a salt like crystal lay everywhere, and empty tubs with a residual liquid drying inside.

"Whisky Tango Foxtrot," said Dulik. "What the fuck?"

*"The roots appear dead,"* said Marc. *"Killed."*

"In a rush," Dulik glanced over to me. "Did you check that crate?"

"In the lorry? A bomb and some radioactive containers, at a guess."

"A guess?"

"Huh. Sea-cop remember," I replied, pointing to myself.

Dulik's eyes flicked to the ceiling, the tut slurred, the sentiment not. "Grab a sample. We need to get the fuck out of here. And we need to check those containers as soon as possible."

"Hey," I said as she pulled the scoop out, slapping it onto my chest. "Since when did I start taking orders again?"

"The moment you set me the fuck free." Dulik strode out the door, dropping her rifle towards her hip, muttering as she exited.

*"You should hear what she's saying. Only some of it's true."*

"Thanks, *partner*."

* * *

With Dulik clearly in a hurry, we returned to the truck, though she was obviously tiring. The debate was short and despite her discovery that I couldn't drive, I managed to have picked up enough to get us across the lake. My fears over being forced to stop lay unfounded, the thoughts of alien roots in the mud lake taking their due from my corpse kept my foot on the gas and eyes locked on the route. I blew a whistle of relief as I drove onto the caked road lip on the other side, only for the engine to splutter. It choked again, foot pumping having no effect, and then the engine misfired. Marc's tentacle tips dug into my shoulder and hips just as lights flashed on the console, and the truck completely stalled. Panicked, and with the steep road down to Toluca ahead, I slammed on the brakes, Dulik supplementing them with the handbrake as we slid sideways, spinning, Marc's grip ever tightening.

A sense of the inevitable struck, mixed with a dread that'd sat at the back of my mind since discovering the Professor's satcom. At first, I thought it was a change in the atmosphere, an alteration signalling the return of the wind. But Marc whimpered in my mind, grating nerves, leaving a raw fear that settled in and wouldn't leave. As we swivelled, the Institute came back into view, the rear of the truck clattering into something hard and coming to a complete stop with the mud lake laid out in front of us.

"I—" was all I managed before heat washed over the lake, shimmering, drawing the moisture upward into a fine mist. Alpha 1's recovered radio roared with static, swiftly followed by an arc of electricity sparking its way across the dashboard. Dulik's jaw dropped, her hair standing on end as I glanced over. Me, being the brave hero, opened the cab door and threw myself out, forgetting just how high we were. Hitting the ground with an oomph, the combined mud and dust luckily absorbed much of the impact. Marc scrambled after me and used her tentacles to help me up. I dragged my pistol from its holster, scanning behind us, my own body tingling as Marc flopped to the ground.

"*It hurts.*" I had to agree. The thought waves she sent my way certainly felt like pain though I knew she couldn't really feel any.

"What in hell is it?"

"*I'm on fire. All my sensors ... I don't know. Josh, help me please.*"

Marc curled up by my feet, tentacles tangling inwards, a protective posture maligned by tremors running along the tips. I kept quiet and low, edging around the truck to peer back across the mud lake. To this day I am unable to describe the shadow. Was it in my mind? For no stills or vid pictures show it through my eye-mod. But I swear it was there, a weight in the air, hovering above the mist and the Institute. The air crackled with energy, whether electrical or not, who am I to know? And Marc was busy writhing on the ground behind me, her agony sweeping into my head, short-circuiting any clear thoughts. Forgive the blank screen at this point but the world seemed to blacken, the day coming to an instant end as if someone found Earth's light switch. A blink, and we were back. Well, nearly. Where the Institute building had been, a smoking hole remained, rapidly filling with the sludge that lay beneath the mud's thickening crust. Gone, and scouring the lake, I spotted a number of indents where the remains of its stone blocks peeked above the surface before slowly sinking. The truck door slammed and Dulik, her hair still crackling, walked past me, rifle loose in her hand. Bending down, she appeared preoccupied by the drying mud, pulling out a raft of withered tendrils, grey and husked.

The atmospheric shift returned, inevitability suddenly weighing down upon my shoulders. And now I could name it – dread. The same rising fear Marc shouted into my head.

*"Josh—"*

I scooped Marc up, her tentacles pulsing but holding on, and I ran for the stone forest. Dulik's boots pounded behind me, whether chasing the escaped traitor or recognising our fear, I couldn't say. Weaving between the broken columns of once trees, a heat haze (yeah, imagine how hot that has to be) fell across my back. Instinctively, I threw myself down, Marc beneath me, Dulik managing another stride before a thermal wind picked her up and threw her bodily against the next trunk. Alpha 1's helmet clunked against the hardened tree, Dulik landing face down amid the truck debris that clattered around us. I can't recall how long we lay there, even Dulik remained still, the echo of the explosion reverberating across the mountainside as dust clouds roiled around us. I waited, needing the dread that sat heavy upon me to lift before I faced moving.

*"Radiation."*

Or that word. I have to admit, it sure does get you moving.

Back on my feet, ensuring my rebreather was attached, I grabbed Dulik's arm. Big mistake. She rolled and lashed out, catching me on the ear.

"Radiation," I bellowed in her face, hitting the ground with my head ringing. Apologetic hands pulled me up, and groggily Dulik had me moving, aiming away from what I assumed was the blast radius of the dirty bomb.

"Keep moving," she shouted, struggling on, the wind still high. "Best to be out in the open. The radioactive dust should disperse and with the rebreathers we are unlikely to inhale any despite the exertion."

Grateful for her words, enabling me to focus on the chance of survival, I pulled myself away from her grip, my head clearing. After a few minutes and with Marc's tremors subsiding, we eventually came to a stop, peering back towards the ex-truck and the explosion cloud riding the mountain gusts. The dread had passed, though I couldn't remember it leaving.

*"S-sorry, Josh. Everything went wild. Did I hurt you?"*

"No," I lied. Come on, she'd had it rough.

*"Sensors are returning. The radiation levels are still relatively high but dropping."*

"Any thoughts?" I said, breathing hard, peering at Dulik.

"None that are grounded in fact," Dulik answered, staring back at the distant remnants of the truck. "Other than some fucker blew up the institute and triggered the bomb. You think it was on a timer?"

"Honestly? You asking me that? You felt what I did, and the static. And you saw the bloody Institute."

Dulik flattened herself against a trunk, eyes dropping, then turning back to me. "I don't want to say it out loud. I don't dare put it all together."

"There are only two possibilities. Choose one, because when we get back, we're both going to be in the shit. Not a lot of evidence left, a dead squad of Marines and a sea-cop with an exposed secret. Either the HLA have a way to cover their tracks, and that begs why they don't use it on the Drathken, or ..." I felt Dulik tense, not wanting to contemplate Drathken interference, and in so doing, choosing to sacrifice her. If the dirty bomb was such a threat, and they decided to act personally instead of through human proxies, it could well be a turning point. One with long-term repercussions and with two witnesses.

"I need to think."

Really? Sheesh. I need to live past tomorrow.

*"Me too, partner. Me too."*
"..."

# Chapter 22

R ough.

The only word to describe it. Each step down the mountainside jarring my aching knees. Dulik fared better, but she didn't have an octopus hitching a ride.

*"Hey, you wouldn't be here without me."*

"True. And that works both ways."

*"Do you really think that was the Drathken?"*

"No comment, buddy. No comment."

Hey, I love the tentacled hero, but nothing is going down on record about our interplanetary pals. They're here to save humanity and hopefully the Earth. Like the old adage goes – sometimes your eggs get scrambled. And yeah, I know the original version of it. Right now, Dulik and I may well have a target on our backs. I'm just hoping her loyalty and sense of duty win through over her honesty, otherwise we may well end up on toast. Benevolence was not on show when they filled the Professor's head with all that shit, and right now my creds were on them baiting a net to catch the HLA and whatever resources they'd gathered. I'm also betting there's a certain garage in the same condition as the institute. And I'm feeling very guilty about a hungry fox family right now.

After a few hours, we hobbled our way diagonally to meet with the road a couple of clicks below our ex-truck. Marc was still letting us know about the radiation levels, but overall, we'd come off light considering. Maybe I'd grow a tentacle or two.

*"Ugh."*

The mud from the previous day had mainly slid by with what remained dried and flaking in the heat. It made the going slippery, but smoother and more consistent than the valley side. Even so, the going was laborious, our pace slow. Tiredness, coupled with our rapidly reducing water became increasing factors. Dulik's torn suit lacked all efficiency, most of our water heading her way, and mine was struggling with the excess heat caused by the constant walking. How anything lived out here in the day, beat me, despite still being in the lee of the mountain. Once the sun peaked in the next hour, we would have to seek shelter or be feeding nature's survival heroes. We really needed to reach the valley bottom before then.

The wind picked back up, rushing down the road, and with it the dust returned. Marc let me know this was a good thing, my fears over the radioactive dust helped by her consistent referral to 'dispersal rates'. It was soon accompanied by the sun rising above the plateau with the heat increasing in response, and we were soon fully immersed in the Scorching once again. The Burnout Zone, well named.

"There," shouted Dulik, about ten paces ahead of me, eagerness prevalent in her voice. "There's a building."

I stopped myself from commenting on her exaggeration. With the valley floor in sight, the sludge rose towards us like layered lava baked over by the sun, and to one side Dulik waving me over to the corner of a building that stood bravely against the elements. I hobbled over, dropping into the wall's shadow and out of the wind, the noise in my ears dropping to the rush of it streaking over the shattered brick edges. The temperature dropped about five degrees, but I decided against a hat.

I flopped. Marc unfurling and draping herself across my lap, relieving the ache in my back. Dulik, however, remained active. In the second half of the building, she'd found a section where the mud had pooled, water forming across its top. She busied herself scooping this through a bandage from her suit. I did wonder if she'd leave it out in the sun, you know, boil it for free, but instead she unclipped something inside her exo-suit leg, drawing out an empty bag with an odd spout. Within minutes, she'd squeezed the liquid in and was drinking brown water. We soon shared, despite knowing full well what had run through the filtration system over the last few days. Survival is not for the squeamish. The whole thing put my rigorous sea-cop training to shame. I could, however, switch on a shower and find my way to the canteen before you reached my limits.

Talking of which, I extracted the various dried meats and cereals I'd secreted in my jacket. You can take the boy out the favela, etc, etc. It was almost a feast.

"Well?" I asked, chewing slowly on the tough, likely vat grown meat bar.

Dulik peered back, holding the water bag in front of her mouth, hiding her thoughts like I sometimes did. "You're fucked, is what I'm thinking, and you want me to drag you out of it."

"No. Think it through. We're supposed to be dead, either in the eyes of the HLA or ..." Add your own words, there are octopi eyes and ears around.

"It doesn't sit right."

I glanced down to Marc, sending a sleep request and the metal tentacles unfurled, the chip shutting systems down to preserve power. I checked again, and satisfied, looked back across to a stressed-looking WPF operative.

"Then tell them how it is. But you know your people, they'll probe and question until they strip your brain of what you saw. If they sanction drugs on WPF Officers, then you'll be singing. And then they'll report it to their alien bosses. We don't know the consequences, but considering we were supposed to be on that truck ..."

"They may well drug me, anyway. And especially you."

"We reduce the risk, Dulik." I took the bag from her, trying to draw her eyes to mine and for a fleeting second, succeeding. "We have the same story, on repeat. If it checks out against Marc's records, then your chances of survival go up."

"Survival?"

Lights fully on, someone was finally at home in Dulik's brain. If they were prepared to take us out in the zone for whatever reason, what would stop them from finding a way to do it when they had the trust of the world?

She caught my eye again, a nervousness to the look not helped by the stitching across her face, "You think they'd take me out?"

"Until they set the bomb off, I would never have thought it. But if they perceive a threat to their work on saving humanity, what's one operative and a sea-cop against that? Look at how you act carrying out their remit, no quarter taken. Wielding the gun as if you have the right to be judge and executioner. You are their tool, and from where I sit, they look pretty merciless to me. Saving the world has to have a cost along the way."

"But for what reason? Was the bomb so important?"

"If you don't know, how can I answer that? But to my eyes, they were prepared to kill their own proxy to get rid of it. And besides, it wasn't just the bomb they destroyed, was it?"

"The lab, the means to make more."

"I was thinking more of the lake full of irradiated fucking roots."

# Chapter 23

We slept.

I have no idea how, the heat even in the shade and the howl of the wind cut through everything. Yet we did. We won't discuss the dreams. However light my conversation, you don't need the darkness that shrouds my slumbering mind.

On awakening, Dulik quietly filled her bag, handing it to me so I could top up my reservoir before going through the same rigmarole. By the time we were ready, the sun had dropped, and we began the trudge around the mud slide in the cooler temperatures. Hah, who am I kidding? It was still fucking hot, just less so. The wind had risen in ferocity, however, with Dulik mumbling something about a thermal cooling at the top and differentials. She probably wasn't mumbling, but when you're holding on to your rebreather mask because the raging air wants to rip it off, everything sounds muffled. We staggered towards the mud slide's edge, finding the last hundred metres had solidified and started our way across, the wind now battering our right sides. It wasn't until we'd travelled five hundred metres or so that my brain started replaying Alpha 1's fate on repeat, my eyes drinking in the cracks and fractures in the crust after each step. Don't you love that? Sometimes it's an 'earworm' where you repeat the same song lyric, or phrase from a vid, other times, it's a visual – an eyeworm? Probably quite ironic, considering what may or may not have been boring its way into the ex-squad leader.

To say I was relieved to reach the other side is an understatement, it was all I could do to not throw myself on the floor and kiss the dust. Of all the ways to go, I have to say being eaten slowly by something was now at the bottom of my list, nudging out death by helicopter and oxygen depletion A quick death I'll take, then feed me to whatever you like. Let me become part of the food chain. In many ways I'd lived with those thoughts once I became aware of what life was truly worth to other humans on the favela. We were just another barrier, someone to step over or on as you made your way to the top of the pile, or the cemetery. Not much time between either for some, if I was honest.

Life is cheap. No longer precious, if it ever truly was. Its true worth lay in the beauty under the ocean elevator platform. What it could be. What it had once been before.

Dulik staggered, screaming out, dropping to the ground ahead of me. By the time I reached her she had bit back the cries, hands busy winding the last of her bandages around a quickly swelling ankle. Each bind met with a different swear word until they merged into one long tirade. On moving to help, the responding stare warned me off, and I started scouring the few metres I could see for anything she could use as a crutch or stick. You won't be surprised to know that somewhere as blasted, heat-baked and utterly miserable as we were contained nothing useful.

Dulik replaced her boot, the tirade continuing as the wind-blown grit ground into her feet. She rose, wincing on the first step, staring back at me. It's hard to describe that look. The emotional mix too complex for words, pained would suffice if there weren't so many causes for it. I settled for desperate and offered my arm. The WPF operative took it with a reluctance that soon morphed into acceptance. Together we hobbled our way to a series of buildings I didn't remember on the way out of Toluca, but I prayed we were on the right track. It was a valley for fuck's sake, how far off could we be?

After an hour covering what we'd made previously in ten minutes, we entered the first of the buildings. Everything had been stripped bare, whether by families finally giving up and taking their world with them, or by the heat and storms taking their due.

At least it couldn't get any worse, right?

I propped Dulik gently against an inner wall, double protection from the wind with a partial but sound looking roof above keeping out the worst of the dust. We chewed half a meat stick each, her eyes never leaving the ankle that likely pulsed its pain back at her. We were out of painkillers and sedatives; I'd used the last on the scientist while deciding whether I could trust the terrorist shit or not. The wild man sorted that conundrum out for me.

"I'm fucked," Dulik said. She had a way with words. Her eyes caught mine. "You need to go on to Toluca, make contact with the APC." Alpha 1's helmet flew my way, the radio mic attached still flashing orange internally when I checked the battery life. "Take the assault rifle."

"No. I've not trained with it; I'll stick to the pistol." You can tell I'd accepted her decision, what else was there to do? Stay and be the hero? "How much water you got?"

After she checked and admittedly only retained a fair amount considering she'd be static, I split the remaining food. Again, I took the main share, but Dulik understood. I scoured the room, heaving a few fallen blocks and other detritus to block her in a little. I'd seen those vids where they make tin can alarms. You know the ones, strung along entrances. No such luck, but hey, I tried.

I nodded to her and made for the door.

"Nkosi. Don't fucking forget me when you get there, right? Without me, your story may hold up."

It won't surprise you to know, I'd thought of that. But maybe I'm not as bad as you think.

Maybe.

I had walked another click before I felt the atmosphere change. The wind rumbled, its pattern of battering my right side disturbed. Goosebumps arose across my back and arms, and then the hairs on my neck tingled like in any good horror vid. Then came that moment when you just know you're being watched from behind. It'd been an exhausting few days, physically and mentally trying to keep my head above the dust as my life was exposed. All I could think of was my shower, comfortable bed and that seat at the canteen table. Gone, taken from me by a man who now fed foxes and beetles on the other side of Mexico City.

"What the fuck now?" I shouted, bellowing into my rebreather, anger coursing through every sinew. A waste of precious energy, I know, and I spun around.

My last thought was of Marc.

### Interlude One

I know what you want.

A montage where you get to see everything that happened between scenes. Something to fill this mysterious time gap.

Not happening.

If I do that now, well, you won't reach the end. You'll think I'm some sort of nutcase, my brain melted by my time in the burnout zone or irradiated by a mysterious shadow and a dirty bomb. Maybe sent a little crazy by the wind and dust.

Perhaps you're right.

But the real reason is that I didn't remember shit until later. So, you're getting this in *my* chronological order. My story, my rules.

*"Cough."*

"Did you just say 'cough'?"

*"Yeah well, it's what you do when you want attention. Except I can't actually cough in colour."*

"Okay."

*"How about I just change it, because you obviously can't take a hint? It should be our story, our rules."*

"Sheesh."

### Interlude Ends

# Chapter 24

I woke up, my face wet. Yeah, you heard, wet. And it wasn't getting any less wet. Hot, distinctly smelly breath washed into my cracked rebreather. A heavy tongue rasped across my unshaven cheek despite the dust, and I opened one eye to be greeted by another, an orange one with a hopeful black pupil peering back. The muzzle slobbered a little, and the tongue licked out between hot, panting breaths. My brain woke up, and I rolled away, thoughts of foxes and chewed bodies streaming in when the dog barked in response. My head swam, attempts at sitting up or scrabbling away mired in muddy thoughts. I flopped over, only to feel Marc press into my back. She'd been switched off a while now and an urge for her company washed over me as I imagined the dog deciding I was tasty enough to risk an attack.

The dog bounded over, releasing another bark as it bowed low, then nipped at my heel. When I didn't respond, it bounced back in and that's when I caught sight of the harness strapped around its body, clasped at the back of its neck where an aerial protruded into the air.

"Ah come on, give me a moment," I said, pushing myself onto my knees and the grey-brown mutt ran in, the bark barely threatening, more a greeting. I held out my hand, low, not having a clue how to greet such an animal. Very few were seen in the favela, they were, after all, a walking barbeque. Rocinha, however, had several. I hardly ever saw her near them, convinced they were simply a sign of her status. Flaunting the ability to feed a pet, an animal of little purpose in her eyes, and now so rare. Luckily, the dog knew more than me, approaching to sniff then lick the hand. I swallowed hard, noting the scars along the back of the creature's neck, the aerial dug deep though the transceiver appeared to be external. Modded. It was then that I reached back to check on a pain in my neck, my fingers brushing against hardened skin. A new scar.

Shit.

A second bark resounded ahead of me and emerging from the morning dust storm a battle-scarred Fieldmaster rolled towards me. At its side, an armoured four-wheeled drive, and in front of that a squad of four WPF Marines with another modded dog that barked, only to be slapped on its haunches by one of the soldiers. My new best friend stopped, deathly still, eyes momentarily glazing before it whined. It dropped to the ground and stared at the approaching rescue party, a small tremor running through its back legs.

Staggering to my feet, I reached around my back to switch my partner back on. I felt the chip fill with warmth, the connection solidifying my resolve and place in the world. I had missed it so much and felt guilt at the necessity to cut her out from my conversations with Dulik. At least now, we faced what was to come together.

The dog whined again, then rose, awaiting some form of command as the Marines made their way across to me, guns held high, bellowing for me to get down on my knees. Part of me resisted. The bit that had complained at getting up in the first place, maybe. Or that stubborn streak moulded in the favela. An old mask, one I was going to need. A second shout led to my hands rising, placed at the back of my head before I dropped to my knees, every joint complaining. Cable ties slid around my wrists, the holstered pistol removed and Fabienne's knife confiscated. They wrenched at Marc.

"Hey, that's an expensive piece of URF equipment," I shouted, my new attitude kicking in. "Above your fucking pay grade."

The Marine backed off, raising his rifle as Marc unfurled her tentacles from around my shoulders. Pulling her body around, she latched onto my arm, waving a tentacle towards the soldier – the one with a URF insignia etched into the base.

"What the fuck?" came the choked reply. Marc, I'm sure, was enjoying the moment.

"There's a WPF Officer injured, some ways back in the last building. Name of Dulik.  She's got a swollen ankle, torture wounds and a mean fucking attitude." You've got to admit I was right on all three counts.

*"Yep."*

See.

The Fieldmaster pulled up, the hatches springing open to reveal a couple of faces I recognised despite the rebreathers. A few words back and forth and the cable ties were sheared with warm but welcome water thrown my way. Despite heavy legs, I refused the opportunity for a ride, walking alongside the Marines and enjoying the company of the dog following at my heels.

*"Harrumph."*

"Jealous?"

*"No. Well a bit. Just try swimming with it, that's all. And that breath."*

I tapped a tentacle but managed a smile towards the scruffy animal.  In another life, maybe I could have had both a Marc and a dog. What would I have to do to earn that?  After ten minutes we reached the building, and I warned the Marines off sending their modded animals in on the hunt. "Let me go in. She's got an assault rifle and an urge to exact some payback."

I shouted my way in, bellowing her name, letting Dulik know it was me. Her muffled cry came as a relief and scrambling over the rough barrier I'd made, I found her pretty much in the same place. Those great survivors, the beetles and ants had found her though.  Her face covered in bites, hands bleeding and the ground littered with the hordes she'd fought off, with a few mangy, rat-like creatures among them.

"You look a might rough," I said, holding out my hand. "The cavalry has arrived."

"How long?"

And to be honest, I had no idea.

As tough as they come, by the time Dulik had lain across the back seats of the four-wheeled drive, her wounds had been cleaned and dressed without a murmur of complaint. The respect on show when they saw her facial wound was quite inspiring, and they paid extra attention to its cleaning after what we'd been through. On the mention of the explosion, and the radiation, we were swept by the APC's electromagnetic spectrometer, appearing as an orange glow on the screen that set the crew laughing. We were in no danger but were asked to remove all external clothing. These were bundled away, I assumed to be saved for analysis, leaving us wearing the exo-suits. Marc settled herself on my lap as we headed back towards Toluca, and beyond that the pickup point. I don't remember falling back asleep, but a belly full of water and rations can do that to someone. I still longed for a shower.

"*Me too.*"

# Chapter 25

It was gentle at first.

The first shower utter bliss, with Rainsford sanctioning double the normal time, allowing an opportunity to scrub my way to cleanliness and enjoy moments where I could let the liquid bliss swathe my body. Marc frolicked, yep. No other word for it. Put an octopus in the desert, it isn't going to be happy. Let it loose in a shower, well, she sent every drop of joy my way, the chip spreading a drug-like euphoria that unbalanced me until I adjusted.

Once scrubbed and all aglow, I donned the URF uniform, determined to signal my intent to return to the Rangers and the old boring platform with the best perks in the world. Marc clambered over my shoulders, aligning her tentacles in their usual places. My body, still weak, felt the extra weight, but I tapped her tentacle and headed out for the first meeting with Rainsford. Not a debrief, he stated. Just a first chat while Dulik was under sedation.

Yeah, right. I bet you believe it as much as I do.

"Sit down, Joshua," were his first words using the light jovial tone he had employed on our first meeting way back when. I know it might have only been a couple of weeks, but to me it was a whole other life. I sat, hands in lap, waiting. I glanced over to the large blank screen, Marc informing me it was on, and the camera built into it operative. Surprise!

He continued, a few pleasantries about how I was feeling, before the first real question. "The institute." Now, to me, concern over your operative's torture injuries would have been an appropriate starting point, maybe the loss of your entire fucking Marine squad. People. Life. "Explain to me what happened when you returned there."

I sighed, mentally crossing my fingers Dulik would do the sensible thing. "It blew up." It's important I'm awkward right now, and not spill my guts in the gush of an obvious cover up. I need to be Nkosi, the surly, sarcastic sea-cop version. Not too eager to please, fuck you very much. Mask on. Rainsford raised an eyebrow. "When we returned, after Dulik was fucking tortured and her cheek sliced open for fun, it blew up." How am I doing?

"How?"

"How what? How did we survive? No fucking idea." Need to tone the swearing down. I pushed my hand through my sprouting hair, taking a moment. "We stopped off on the way back from Mexico City. Dulik doing her duty. We searched the place in case there was any more HLA or bomb making stuff. We found none. We left; it blew up."

"By the dirty bomb? The one in your truck?"

"No. That exploded some time after. On the edge of the mud lake. We barely got out alive."

"Yes," said Rainsford, peering down at the tablet on his desk. "How?" A trap of a question. Simple, one designed to allow the interviewee to ramble. Now I know the man thinks he's a professional, but he's never sat across from Millie and Sasha.

"If I'm honest, the only way I see it is that Marc warned me. The chip connection is fluid at times, you know. But I knew, and I ran. Both of us. When it blew, we were far enough away that the explosion didn't kill us. And Dulik said we were safe out in the open, you know, with the wind dispersal."

"Yes." Man, he was giving nothing away. A finger tapped at the edge of the tablet, and he swung it around, showing me the Fieldmaster's scan. "You got a dose, that's for certain, though initial tests minimise the likely aftereffects. Dulik is in recovery, she'll be fine, and clearly got the same level of exposure as yourself, Nkosi." Pick that up? Nkosi. Yeah, some disbelief in there. But maybe that's his job, rule out everything and disbelieve what's left until there's no alternative. Or he was trying to unbalance me. "The nurse will bring you some anti-radiation drugs. Don't skimp on them, we need to be sure."

Shit. I bet we're thinking the same thing right now. Anti-radiation – yeah right. More like anti-silence.

I got up to leave, only to be met by Rainsford's raised hand. "Leave the MARC unit. We want to download its records."

I felt Marc quiver, a tremble that had me worried. *"I'll be okay,"* echoed in my head, but I wasn't convinced. In fact, I thought this may well be the end for both of us if they uncovered the memory wipe I'd done back at the garage.

# Chapter 26

**M**arc had been gone an hour, returning with Richards, her white-coated nemesis, to find me checking the back of my skull in the mirror. Yeah, you may ask why I'm doing that. Well, remember the bit in the desert? When you were asking for the wibbly wobbly montage? Well, you didn't get it there because I had zero memory of it. Just a scar. One that was bothering me near as much as the hole in my memory.

Then I remembered Marc.

Her camera and its temporary auto cache.

Would Richards have checked it? Wiped it even?

I still had the toolset and sacrificed the tablet I'd been loaned by the WNF to cobble together a connection with Marc's port, who squirmed and complained throughout. Fifteen minutes and I had it downloaded, wiping everything left in the cache in case it was incriminating. It was a close-run thing, the stored recording stretching back as far as switching off Marc for the chat with Dulik.

But I couldn't watch it now. I had days of the anti-silence drugs to face. All I knew was that there were no Marines banging on my door right now, so it's more than likely Richards had not seen whatever was on there or it was nothing. Blank. It was killing me not looking, but I had my masks – I could choose who I wanted to be, get through the questioning and then I could look.

The next few days stretched interminably long and oh so wide. The 'anti-radiation' drugs were timed for a half hour before each of my debrief meetings, and I felt my tongue loosen, my mind's grip upon the events fade into a constant battle to hold on until Dulik joined us.  If I could keep my story consistent until Dulik either tore it down, or backed me up, I at least had a faint hope of getting through. What choice did I have?

It was on the third day when Rainsford declared she was awake, and having undergone surgery for her cheek, was talking freely. The bastard obviously didn't tell me any more, leaving me to sweat. By this time, I was convinced he had me nailed as guilty for something. At the very least, having the affront to survive when they lost their precious assets. But the questioning remained insistent and focused on events around the bomb and the institute. He could smell something was wrong.  But finally, the tone changed, shifting from questioning to an all-out rush. I found myself swept up in what was going on, given only a few hours notice to pack and get ready to leave the ship. Time enough.

I watched the full playback, my eye-mod recording it for prosperity before I wiped it clean. Yeah, and everything came flooding back. The reason for the scar, what had been done to me. It triggered all my memories.

I wished it hadn't.

<br>

**Interlude Two**

"You sure you can cope with this now? Can I trust the fans to stay with me, because it's some ride."

*"Stop prevaricating and show them. And me, I don't remember this bit."*

"Okay. I'm on it. Since when did you get so bossy, partner?"

*"Isn't a tentacled conscience always supposed to be in control?"*

"Maybe the 'tubers and I know each other a little better now. Fans of each other, you might say. Well, 'tubers, welcome to my world, it's going to be some ride. I hope you're ready for this next bit, 'cos as crazy as it might seem, now the shit really hits the 'tuber fan. Stuff is about to get real. It's wibbly wobbly screen time."

**Flashback Time – Wibbly Wobbly Screen and Stitch Incoming.**
**Title: 'What the Octopus Saw.'**

Out in that desert, when I turned around, I had many images in my head, the last of which was a pair of Drathken holding some kind of weapon aimed my way. Their four legs hooked into the dust, their bodies shining with a layered type of metallic red armour. I assumed their dual black eyes gazed my way, but what do I know of Drathken physiology?

One pulled the trigger, my whole body suddenly encased in fire. Every nerve end screamed, muscles spasming, my jaw slack. I remember falling, hitting the ground, and dust insinuating its way into the rebreather.

* * *

I felt my eyes flicker, but they wouldn't open despite an insistent urge to blink. Assuming they were gummed up, my brain commanded a hand to move towards them, to squeeze across the bridge of my nose. It simply flopped, falling loosely by my side. An addled thought slipped out, an impulse to make my other hand reach across and lift the other to damn well do the job I'd told it to do. That too lolled at my side, my mind too awash with strange colours and emotions to work out if it was just having a bad day or my limbs had started a revolution. I squashed my lids tight, rapidly blinking to break the expected hardened gum. Nothing happened and panic set in. But it couldn't root itself in my psyche, the tangential nature of my thoughts letting it slip out of my grasp. I tried a new tactic, parting my lips, then breathing out through my nose. Each felt odd with a stickiness around both until I associated this with some form of tape or band-aid. Everything then slotted into place. A weapon firing, an alien somewhere between a praying mantis and a catfish staring back at me as an arc of energy slammed into my chest. Falling, and now this.

I shifted my shoulders, feeling for Marc and getting nothing positive in response. Activating the chip, a sliver of emotion connected, pained concern sliding through. I realised then it was for me, not herself. I tried to strengthen the link, to see what she saw, but it kept cutting off and refusing access. Forcing my way in failed just as badly, a sulk pervading my thoughts until I realised she was connected to a machine – and that's when I accessed her camera, bypassing the CPU link. I spiralled, unable to assimilate the images with reality. My brain eventually caught up, our frequent experiences of seeing through each other's link enabling my cerebral cortex to accept the pictures. I lay strapped on my side on another machine, not one gleaming with metallic goodness, but a purple and green combination of plant and insect shell. Tendrils were in every orifice – nasal passage, mouth, ears and … ahem, use your imagination because we are not showing that. My eyes were taped shut.

But the true horror hit when I looked at the screen behind the two red robed Drathken deep in conversation, prodding at a tablet. It showed my back, and more importantly the exposed neck and base of my skull. More tendrils slid in and out, connected to solid, pulsating blocks of plant-like matter. That was my body – opened up – and they were … were … adding to it.

My body refused to respond despite increased efforts, almost as if my conscious and unconscious self were separate entities. A warmth spread through my lower back and an alien hand placed on my hip squeezed as it spread throughout my body. There was a connection there, someone trying to reassure. Of course, having your spinal column exposed without your permission kind of makes that a one-way conversation.

I remember nothing else until my face got licked. A time gap, a sense of loss perhaps. And the colours the Drathken wore. Red. Why was that important?

**Flashback Ends**

So, there you have it.

And, I might add, then dumped into the bloody hot of the desert afterwards. WTF. You forcibly make me into one of your modded translators or whatever, and then drop me in the middle of nowhere? Take me home, let me have a shower. Fresh air and food as a reward for the plant-shit you put in my brain.

I told Marc everything.

"That's gotta hurt."

"I am modded. Drathken adjusted, with extra equipment shoved in my skull. And all you can say, is *ouch*?"

*"There must have been plenty of room."*

"…"

*"Not funny? Too soon?"*

"How do I taste?"

Yeah, asking an octopus how I taste. How the world has turned.

*"If you hadn't told me, then I don't think I'd have found a difference without concerted analysis. Maybe they didn't put as much in as for the translators? There's a taint, but you don't freak me out."*

"Good to know."

*"At least, no more than usual."*

Top tip – don't teach a cephalopod humour.

I still had little idea about why it all happened, and more to the point why the aliens kept me in the dark? Am I to be an undercover spy on my own people? Would I get a choice? And then it struck me, were the Drathken aware I woke up? I assumed they had to be, after all their tech was so far ahead of ours. But I was groggy, my thoughts a little awry due to the small matter of ongoing brain surgery. I could remember bypassing Marc's central unit and accessing the camera direct via the chip. I don't know alien body language, and as far as I'm aware, their speech. But nowhere amid the fog do I remember that being noticed.

And there was Marc. Did my alien surgical pals discover the wipe of Andre declaring my guilt? Removing that memory from Marc might just keep me alive and out of WPF jail, as long as Dulik had seen sense. Right now, it seemed she had, though the sudden need to leave had to be connected with her recovery. And then there was the satcom, hidden away, my rabbit in the hole next to Michael's little addition. Did they miss those? I couldn't risk checking until we were a long way from here. Or more specifically a good distance from Richards.

I had one clear conclusion though. Marc couldn't have retained a full recording of my surgery. Surely Rainsford wouldn't let me be swanning about if they knew? Despite the questioning, I was able to move around freely. And they certainly hadn't appeared to be aware of my contact when they rescued us from Toluca. If it wasn't on there, had the Drathken wiped it and any other indication she'd been on a Drathken Ship? Even switched off her system safety protocols would have triggered with any perceived danger. So *why* would they remove that? Surely if they were working *with* the WPF they would share something?

So many questions, and no real answers except I was now modded, the WPF didn't know, and I had no idea why.

# Chapter 27

An hour later, we boarded a helicopter with a rapidly approaching tropical storm followed by a burgeoning hurricane event forcing the WNF *Carson* to sail for port. Despite the rising wind pervaded by dust stripped from the North American mainland, we took off. The first half an hour of the journey was a reminder that I still fucking hated helicopters, the fuselage not remaining static for anything longer than a second or two. For the life of me, I couldn't understand the need. We'd left a perfectly good ship to partake of a one-way trip to nausea city. Yeah, I threw up. More than once.

Did I mention where we were going? No? No surprise there, because it was a 'need to know', and I sure as hell was not in that circle. Rainsford, Dulik and a pair of Marines who looked like they'd chewed on a wasp nest sat opposite. Maybe they'd heard what happened to the last set of Marine assets. I wasn't handcuffed and my partner in crime sat on the seat next to me under the constant watch of our friendly guards. I felt like a prisoner, even if I wasn't restrained. Maybe it was being a few hundred metres up in the fucking rollercoaster from hell.

A few hours in and we crossed the mainland, passing over a mishmash of new buildings thrown up where the coastal cities and towns had drowned. Nothing new to me, so I finally managed to slip off into a fitful sleep, the dreams dark and not for sharing. I woke briefly when the helicopter dropped down to refuel, only to re-enter my dreams where they left off. I couldn't tell you how long we flew for, but my octopus pal could if I really wanted to know. To me it made little difference.

It was the last thirty minutes of the flight that you really need to see. For many of you, the Drathken starships were last filmed when they entered Earth's atmosphere. The mighty purple and green behemoths appearing to hover above the land like CGI in a Hollywood blockbuster. I'm sure many of the older generation remember waiting for the battle cry and the hordes of mini spaceships rushing out to blast our cities into dust. Well, we'd done most of that ourselves, and the three main ships simply landed in places cleared of people, to no more fanfare than the watching crowds of media and locals staring through their cameras. No tanks lining up a shot or generals declaring a need to release the dogs of war. Tangles of roots, if that's what they were, shot out from underneath, piercing the Earth. To some the vid looked like they dragged themselves down to settle on our world. Others talk as if they pulled the Earth up to them. I prefer that version.

The first of the Drathken ships stretched out before us. Ten kilometres long, its weight unfathomable, and by all rumour, never to fly again. A sacrifice, a sign of their commitment to our world and the desire to save it from us. Can you imagine humanity doing the same? Crossing whatever the void is up there, to give of themselves, to help others? You know, maybe we would, or like to think we would. We just forgot to help ourselves.

Its overall outline appeared similar to that of the smaller ship Associate Minin arrived on, though the bulges giving the peapod like appearance were multitudinous and wreathed in tendrils that drove into the soil beneath. Over the surface, huge purple and green leaved plants grew, many baring fruit, others thick vines. A mighty forest rising from the earth and surrounded by factories. Yeah – apparently the ships need to be fed a diet of nutrients in a combination different from those usually found in our soil. The fertiliser factories, churning out their own smoke, enrich the surrounding earth. Remember all those millions who have died as the oxygen depletion took hold and the seas rose? They wanted to put them to good use. As the Drathken said, we are no longer in a position to ignore our fate. We must all give. Of course, of the few billion who remain alive on Earth, many find such an action repugnant – against scripture or belief and rejected the call. But enough volunteer to supplement the ships as the Drathken adapt to our planet. And they planned ahead, remember I mentioned the starships? The ones full of the rich and the powerful. When my *pai* got hold of the manifest, trying to find a way to get him and *mae* aboard, he found a waiver form declaring that on your death you relinquished the right to burial or cremation, agreeing to give your body over to the ship. If they didn't sign, they didn't board. Interesting when you consider who did leave us to our fate.

The helicopter shook, the thermals buffeting the cockpit as it came into land. I felt a shift in mood as the pilot declared we were on approach, Rainsford stretching, Dulik's eyes falling on me. She hadn't given any clue as to what she'd revealed of our mission and it churned at me, my nerves a ragged edge that I needed to soothe or else I'd say the wrong thing to the wrong person. I felt my mask slipping, the not knowing disturbing. The sighting of the Drathken ship had set further confusion upon my thoughts – far deeper than dropping into the WPF Headquarters, or a torture chamber, would have done. Whatever they thought happened back in the burnout zone, they were cutting out the middle human, so to speak. It meant I was about to meet more of our alien benefactors, and possibly I would end up as a side dish to those scrambled eggs.

*"Is this really happening?"*

"Yeah. Why else would we be here?"

*"You think we're going aboard?"*

"I doubt it. Maybe there's a liaison office here."

*"Will a translator be here? I found them difficult."*

The helicopter landing area was rich with noise and colour, and once down I could see the whole area served as a transport hub. Much of it military, but not all. However, the huge security presence felt oppressive. Not akin to the Drathken call for friendship, more of humanity's continued need to question the helping hand. Missile batteries pointed skyward, tanks and APCs littered the ground. A huge, fortified wall, punctuated by manned towers stretched as far as I could see. It couldn't all be for the HLA, could it? Maybe there was a greater anti-Drathken sentiment than I realised. Or were they a resource to guard jealously?

We approached the terminal. By the way, I love that name. Whatever happens, your journey comes to an end somehow. Anyway, our credentials were electronically checked, scanners running over the ID chip in our wrists and Marc's Drathken/WPF linked pass analysed closely. By the time I was through the others had taken the best seats in the top-of-the-line four-by-four waiting for us. I got to ride in the back on one of those tiny drop-down seats that hurt your back. I grumbled at every jolt, but at least the aircon was running. We were in Canada and if I remember right, just east of Vancouver. Land of snow in winter. Heh, funny. It must have been in the low thirties and if my mind was right, we were in early spring. No snow for the Eskimo.

The ship loomed above us, the plants wreathing its hull shimmering in the haze. I picked out bulbous growths amid the forest, pulsing under the main canopy. The closer I looked, the clearer it became these were mounds smothered in a large beetle like creature, swarming over the ground and along the trunks of the alien trees. Their colours constantly changed, or perhaps they appeared to alter as the sun hit them. Maybe they were different species? My head swam with possibilities. So much life.

The vehicle pulled in next to a human structure, a low, flat roofed building that merged into the ship at the rear. Like an external growth or a mod. When the door opened, Dulik waited as Rainsford approached another security checkpoint. Her face grim and I felt Marc squirm.

"You told them," I said. Fishing, I know. I couldn't have been less subtle with a rod and reel. But I needed to know before any more questioning.

She looked at me straight. "Not everything."

Ahhh. Better cast my line again.

"What did you leave out?" Now she was a WPF operative, right? I was the bad guy, remember.

"Andre. They've hardly discussed the garage." She kept my gaze. "You came back for me."

Can you hear that sigh at the back? But that still left why we were here.

"But you told them about the Institute, what we felt and saw? Is that why we're here? To explain to the Drathken."

Dulik nodded, eyes briefly looking at her feet. "It's too important. And we made it here. If the Drathken had done it, for whatever reason, we'd have just been *disappeared*." She glanced over at the factories. This, of course, gave me a fresh perspective of how deeply entrenched the Drathken were in the WPF. When I called her a *tool* back at the truck, I'd been embellishing. Looks like I was under the mark, not over it.

Rainsford waved us over, a huge soldier at his side jabbering away about protocol. He wasn't wearing a rebreather, either.

"It's all they asked me." I said, trying to look subtle while talking out of the side of my mouth. "I gave them the spiel about the HLA. But I'm a simple sea-cop, no experience of the Drathken. I'm sticking to that until they lead me elsewhere. And Dulik … thanks."

I let her lead the way, Marc still squirming around my waist.

"What's up?"

"*It all feels strange, wrong. The air.*"

"You mean the soldiers? Like the translator?"

"*More like you. But everywhere. They taste wrong, and the air hums with …*"

Nothing like a cephalopod to cheer you up on a bad day. She sent me a picture of our chip connection. Yeah. Into the lion's den we go. Everything and everyone's connected.

# Chapter 28

The membrane fogged the corridor beyond but allowed enough of a view to pick out the change from metal lined human walls to the fibrous plant of the Drathken. It moved in and out, giving the impression the ship breathed. Before it, the security team had us stripped, with our clothing searched and sent through a series of scanners. I feared for Marc, but Rainsford took them through her security protocols and Drathken schematics. I had a lump in my throat when they tried to scan her, not knowing what effect it would have. But the shielding held, and she was as lively as ever when she wrapped herself around my back. I patted her tentacle, waiting for Rainsford who came through last, red faced and ruffled. I took no pleasure in it, honest.

I turned to face the membrane, overtaken by an urge to touch it and I stretched out my fingers. The tips breezed over with barely any contact, the covering pulling itself away as if rejecting my touch. When I refocused, a blue-armoured Drathken stood on the other side half-filling the corridor. In his hand a weapon, rifle like, and familiar. The black, soulless eyes gave no hint of its thoughts, but as Rainsford joined us one of its 'feet' pressed low into the corridor wall. The membrane split at the centre and peeled back. It sounded like Velcro slowly being ripped – strand by strand – apart.

By the time it was done, Clara stood by the Drathken's side. Remember her? The Drathken modded translator who freaked Marc out back on the ship? She had a neutral expression on her perfect features just like back then.

*"She no longer stands out."*

I wanted to ask what Marc meant, but Rainsford greeted Clara, their exchange of words lost amid the rising hum in my brain.

If you watch closely, you'll see the pictures jump. That's my eye-mod responding to a new input. There, see it? Just as we take a step inwards. You get the flicker; I got the full whack job. Boom. My senses blossomed, mind filled with new sounds, smells, sights. The touch of a soldier upon his beloved gun, the sweet taste of a fresh orange upon a clerk's tongue, the thick atmosphere coursing down a farmer's modded lungs, the click of the milking machine squeezing an alien beetle to release its mucus. I was everywhere all at once, and I staggered, Dulik catching me before I fell. Clara glanced back, but I rubbed my bruised thigh and adjusted the rebreather, smiling an apology her way. Dulik gave me one of those investigator's looks, and I pointed to Marc.

"Just a rush of new info. I've tuned it down."

*"Focus,"* said Marc. *"It's like when you first got the chip."*

"What is?" Nothing like being held out on when you're two steps inside an alien spaceship, with trust already at a premium.

*"There's a satcom embedded in your spine. I can sense the signal, similar to the one between us. It just fired up."*

Fuck.

Yeah, maybe I need to say that again. Shit fuck.

"Are you saying I'm connected in ..."

*"I can't see the system you're connected to, nor what you're sensing. My input is your own sight and sound converted to colours."*

Yeah, Marc's satcom, the one Dulik gave me back at the mud lake and the device that sealed Andre's fate. But now my personal surgical mod appears to have its own version, and it's singing a different tune.

It was then that my world tipped a little (more). The corridor kind of changed, or at least my interpretation of it. The walls now glowed, streaming interwoven pulses and patterns, lines of information that I couldn't translate, but I knew had *meaning*. Amid this maelstrom, we passed door outlines and off corridors, each masked by a thin but opaque layer of the membrane. With my new connection I could sense Drathken operated inside and beyond the eyes of humanity. Probably in parts of the ship no human had previously seen, the usually stiff and distant Drathken presenting in ways I couldn't interpret but my mind framed as 'relaxed'. Natural. Maybe it was the satcom, I don't know, but this wasn't the feeling of ominous threat. Just creatures alien to us, living their lives away from our human need to know.

The strange, spongy floor split in two directions. Not linear but splicing off like a root or a vein. One slightly to the left and up, the other more to the right and slightly downwards. To a human eye it appeared non-uniform, out of kilter. I found myself staring at a schematic in my head, one that adjusted in real time. New corridors grew slowly on the upper section, while below us others gently closed off. A living ship, growing and adjusting.

A pulse burst inside my neck, raging, searing along my spine. My joints stiffened, driven by a compulsion, a need sizzling through every nerve. In my mind, one element of the ship's plan pulsed, wreathed in the same spark of power spewing through my body. I *had* to be there. My walk changed, not like my masks when I deliberately alter how I present to others. No, here I was not in control, my movements odd as I fought against the compulsion, joints hardly bending. Dulik took my arm, an odd look on her face. I nodded towards Marc again and reached out a hand as if to calm the metallic octopus.

In response, I asked Marc to flood my brain. Colours poured through the chip, gentle, soothing, like the caress of eight tentacles, each working to leech my brain of the coursing adrenaline. Struggling to balance what was happening, I lost track of where we were, my mind interweaving two realities over the top of each other. One the corridor as seen via the satcom link, the other the shimmering wave of calm washing over my brain. Divorced from reality, I kept walking, an automaton slaved between two worlds.

Clara stopped; Rainsford's incongruous look soon lost to a gawp as the corridor peeled back. Waiting there was a crystalline car, or train carriage. Its smooth surface bubbled with octagonal flutes decrying their origin, polished and giving the impression of a carved honeycomb. The door rose, and inside was a collection of hollows designed for Drathken bodies to rest. Piled around these were soft looking pod cases arranged like human cushions.

"This will take us to the Associates," said Clara, arm extended towards the door. Rainsford glanced back at us both, before entering the vehicle and prodding at the pod cases. By the time he'd settled, Dulik had joined him.

My brain sparked, inputs surging into a confusion I could no longer contain. Marc's thoughts slid out, and the satcom slammed the door shut behind. A prisoner of my own mind and body, I looked down at my hands, ones I no longer controlled. Pulses sheathed my spine, the compulsion to comply overriding everything. And something grew inside me. It's hard to describe, perhaps I lost my mind. All I could visualise were tendrils insinuating their way along my spine, wheedling into my brain. Roots. I grabbed Clara, or at least my body did, and threw her into the carriage, ramming the door shut. As soon as it engaged, a wave of membrane encased fluid pushed against the rear, shoving the car out of sight.

I don't know what I expected to happen next, maybe I'd run, or tear through the corridors, wreaking havoc among the Drathken. Instead, my hands drove low into the floor, sliding into something akin to a root cluster. The schematic pulsed in my mind's eye. That one spot, low and central growing larger. Connections flowed in and out, some thick, others slim with multiple branches. The hand withdrew, and seconds later another crystalline car emerged from the vein. I felt myself open the door and step in.

*"What are you doing, Joshua?"*

"…"

*"Josh? What's happening?"*

"…"

I felt her panic, tasting so much like my own, but I was wrapped in the corner of my own mind. Lost. Watching what was left of a comfortable life tear apart before my eyes.

# Chapter 29

Now I've seen lots of vids. The ones where the spaceships are all geared up for intruders, yeah? Alarms going off, alerts spread throughout the ship. Sensors scanning for the non-Drathken lifeform and all that kind of stuff. Heh. Speculation, you might say. So, let me ask this question, why? It's like a submarine prepping for boarders two clicks down. It isn't going to happen. Or, put another way, if it's something you've never speculated might happen, why would you prepare for it? Strange what you think about when encased in your own body.

What I knew, was that the satcom was buzzing with confusion. At least, that's how my brain assimilated it. I wondered, as we rode the veins of the Drathken Ship, just how the aliens were connected. Did they all have satcoms? Or would the ship be laced with communication systems? How would they kill me once I was found? And above all else, why the fuck my body was acting as it was when it had been Drathken who operated on me. Whatever I was doing, it didn't appear as if the aliens on board this ship expected it. Perhaps there were inter-ship rivalries? Or factions, aliens who worked with the HLA, not against them. A splash of colour came to mind. Red.

And that begs a question about one of my assumptions. The Professor? What if she wasn't the bait, but genuinely wanted to activate a dirty bomb? She'd had a satcom, one likely to have worked its way through a fox's system by now, unless it had been sent to the great fox hole in the sky.

Am I the new Professor, perhaps?

But I don't have the bomb.

The carriage stopped, pulling up sharp as the fluid broke and gushed away either side of it. The vein wall peeled back, my crystal door opening to a corridor flooded with a panicked glow. Communication, but by light, not satcom. My head turned, scanning the stream of information flowing along the wall, and acted. Breaking into a run, I heard the first sounds I associated with the aliens, a sawing of chitin upon chitin vibrating through the thick air. I ran towards it. Ahead, turned to the side and apparently reading the corridor, was a small Drathken. Its purple body mottled and slightly cracked where it peeped from beneath the blue robe. I didn't know what to expect next, perhaps not the sharp elbow I directed to its thorax or the crack of chitin that accompanied it. My hand plunged into the newly created fracture, squeezing and ripping out something wet and beating. The Drathken dropped, legs briefly twitching as I leapt over and continued to run.

Can you hear me swearing? If I was in the shit before, I was now fully neck deep in the fertiliser factory.

More chitinous sawing echoed above the padding of my feet, and this time I slowed down, heart racing as the corridor curved S-like ahead. My hand plunged into the floor, gripping and snapping a fibrous root tendril from a connection joint, a second disconnecting the other end, pulling out the metre long rope fibre. I flexed it, and seeming satisfied, peered around the corner. I could see the Drathken, this one a familiar size with a weapon clearly holstered at its side. I interpreted its movements as agitated, four feet skittering along the floor and its eyes independently sweeping left and right.

Exploding into action, my body drove low along the corridor. The Drathken seemed ponderous, slow to respond, as if it moved through mud or treacle until it struck out – one arm lashing towards me, the other drawing its gun. The hooked hand scraped across my back, snagging and tearing the fabric. My shoulder slammed into its knee joint, the snap echoing off the hardened door nearby. With my hands spread wide, the plant rope wrapped a second and third leg, pulling tight as I dropped to roll beneath the torso. I heard another crack, and my momentum was arrested by the rope, coming up facing back towards the collapsed Drathken. A sharp kick to its underbelly caused fractures to spread from its epicentre and once again a hand plunged inward.

My mind reeled. A virtual nausea rising as I dealt death to creatures who'd come to save the dregs of humanity. I couldn't understand what my body was doing, nor why. I fought the demands, the violence fuelling my need to escape, to stop. Whomever had control was here to kill, and the only target I could comprehend would be more of the Drathken. I stuttered briefly, falling to the corridor floor. The compulsion grew, its resurgence encasing my thoughts, pushing back any resistance. Rising, forced to drag the rifle from beneath the leaking body, I wiped off the mucus and checked the firing button. I dropped then, hand plunging under blue cloth, snapping off the Drathken's arm and plunging it into the wall beside the door. When it slid back, I fired.

A circular room lay beyond the door, domed, humming with rhythmic patterns that intertwined into a raucous cacophony. My ears hurt, pain drilling inwards, but forcibly ignored as the rifle barked a bolt of energy. It sizzled across the room and drove into the first Drathken, ramming into its upper body. A second alien sawed and clicked, communicating a sense of fear I found myself recognising. With my emotions suppressed, I fired again, the bolt crashing into their head. Eyes exploded, and the body writhed and twitched as it fell. I swivelled, apparently uncaring, finger pressed down upon the firing button, burning a hole into the wall next to the entrance. Smoke rose and the light patterns surrounding the door frame died away.

A pause, a breath.

Death lay scattered around me – of which I took no part – yet my hands were blood-stained. Locked away, I screamed, railing against what my body had done. Yet the satcom buzzed, unheeding of the emotional pain, orders spurring limbs into motion.

Clear of any threat, my head turned to scan the room. A ten-metre domed glass case sat in the centre, covering a purple, heaving mass. On closer inspection, fibrous tubes plunged in and wrapped around a pulsing, muscular organ that reminded me of a giant heart. Each ripple riding its surface magnified in intensity as they crashed into the plant-like conduits, the sinuous hulls heaving, pushing. The heavy beats separated in my head, each matching an inward or outward wave along the protrusions. As I moved to look closer, the nest of tubes drove into the floor as they left the dome, only to curve up, re-emerging and hugging the outer walls, driving upwards through the ceiling.

To my mind we were in the heart of a living, breathing ship. And my body and brain were here to do no good.

I was the patsy, and somewhere was a weapon, and I could only think of one place it might be wired.

The compulsion struck me, slapping my mind in its attempts to quell the rising panic. Despite the dread, my head snapped around to look directly at the purple heart.

I reached out to Marc, my call pained, in desperate need.

And Marc answered.

I drove my mind into her satcom. It cut through the noise and pain – gave me a moment of clarity in the maelstrom. And control. The link overrode the satcom threaded into my spinal cord. It still pressed, the ship's urgent call demanding reconnection, and in turn, inadvertently triggering whatever compelled me to act. I staggered to the fibrous floor, knees sinking into the spongy surface. Metal tentacles lightly touched my knees before pulling themselves up and Marc rolled over, exposing her beak and underbelly. Is this because I compel her? Or because she feels my need? Have I imbued the machine with her spirit or inhabited it with my mind? Am I one, or both?

I feel my hand move to my tool belt, I know I instruct it, a subconscious thought, another moment of desperation. The link between us is weakening, the ship's override insistent and energised by something more powerful than my little cephalopod's battery.

If I had been strong enough, I could have ordered her to kill me. Perhaps I should have. Or to rip out the link device and whatever else was laced into my spine, threading its way into my brain. Surely that would end the pain?

But I'm a coward, like much of humanity. I can't let go, not while there was a moment of hope. I want to live, fight on.

Now to think.

Attached to my spine was a satcom desperately trying to link with the ship, to renew the connection and finish its triggered programming. The only chance I had was to fool the unit that it had completed its mission. I could use what I'd learned about the satcom to attempt an override using Marc's, but if that went wrong, likely we'd have Joshua-flavoured jam spread across the walls, assuming there was a weapon sewn into my spine. The alternative was to destroy the ship's satcom link itself, but right now every Drathken on board had my name etched in their mind. And you know, I might stand out a little, though I may be able to pull off the accent.

*"Localised satcom."*

"What?"

*"Destroy the room's link, then attempt the override."*

"You think that'll work?"

*"No. But hey, got to give it a try. Otherwise, we'll have Joshua-flavoured jam across the walls."*

"Not helping. You been listening to my thoughts again?"

*"Me? But the gun won't do it."*

"I know."

I slid the screwdriver into Marc's armour, seeking the magnetic markers between her tentacles and the torso. Each of the eight had to be pressed in sequence, otherwise all attempts would fail for the next 24hrs. Get them wrong three times and her internal CPU would self-destruct alongside her memory chips. But I'd had a little recent practice, repeating my actions back at the garage. To my relief, the hatch popped open.

*"That tickles."*

A wet tentacle slipped out, wrapped itself around my fingers, tickled at the membrane between them. Marc climbed along my arm, teased at my ears before dropping into her tank.

What tank?

Mind slips, memory lapses. The brain surgery perhaps.

Except, reality is a bitch.

And I've been hiding from it for so long.

I'm on a Drathken ship.

There is no tank.

There is no Marc.

Marc died. Richards killed her. My only friend.

Oh God.

### Interlude Three

*"Is it time?"*

"I think they're ready."

*"Am I?"*

"Maybe more than me."

You don't know what it's like to lose something so precious ... so alive ... or do you? Are you in danger of losing it now? That's for you to decide, but take a look around, just in case you missed it.

But don't judge me – judge your *opinion* of me on the lies and decisions I made.

When you have something so cherished, so wonderful that the joy of it hurts every moment you experience it, yet it is ripped from you, what is left? What chasm do you spiral into? And if that time was taken away by another, a callous, unthinking act with no awareness or emotive connection as to why it so affects you, are they truly to blame? Or is it you, letting your *self* be swallowed by the ecstasy, allowing that experience to be so fulfilling that nothing can match it?

I have tussled with these thoughts so long that I have lost my *self* among them. I must ... I fear to ... but I have to *show* you. Forgive me now, for when you know everything, just allow one small part of you to understand and this ... this vid will have been worth it. My only fan perhaps, but a precious one.

*"Cue wibbly wobbly special effects and a caption that says six months earlier. Stitching flashback vid now."*

### Stitch Incoming – Six Months Earlier

I dove from the elevator platform edge, my skin both relieved and stung by the saltwater. But it felt natural, an environment I had feared in the first few days due to the sheer depths below me, but aware now of the wonders waiting for me. Surfacing, feeling the sun bite down on my face, and the scum irritate my hair, I drew in a breath through the filtered snorkel.

*"Come on. I'm hungry and we don't get long enough."*

The sound of those words ringing in my head were a thrill, not like the initial fear-filled times when my brain first registered I was actually communicating with an octopus. Marc floated ahead, her orange body aglow against the dull blue of the water near the sea's surface. A single eye looked my way as she flicked her tentacles, the mound between her eyes bulging like a nose, though I knew it wasn't, twitching as she did so. It always made me smile, an almost human gesture. The suckers made no attempt to cling on, just a gentle caress that meant come and play, way before her colours spoke to me. Diving under, we spun amid the coral below the platform. One moment Marc would speed through, propelled by her siphon, cutting a pulsing wave jet after jet. The next behind me, clinging to the elkhorn, a tentacle stroking the back of my leg as I whirled around on the hunt. Hide and seek, cephalopod style. These were attuning sessions, the chips working in unison, calibrating themselves to the stupid human and his cephalopod sidekick immersed in the glory of life that lay beneath the elevator platform.

And that moment, when the sunlight caught the nudibranch's glory, a moment decreeing the sheer beauty of life on Earth.

**End Stitch**

I can't. I'm sorry. I j – just can't watch any more. Jump to the end, please.

**Stitch Incoming – Five Months Earlier**

Pain slammed into my mind, and I spiralled. A hammer to my senses, the rebreather slipping from between my blue lips, throat choking on the dry air as it rushed in. Falling to the deck, a second wave raced through my brain, the chip on fire and pulsing panicked messages of dread and fear.

*"Josh!"*

I stumbled. If only I hadn't, maybe I would have got there first, dragged myself along the wet floor instead of being curled up in a ball like a pathetic coward. A life lost in a moment. Science Officer Richards threw open the door, taking in the writhing mass of metal that screamed silently, tearing at my mind. She grabbed the sync unit, the one I'd dropped on the first agonising wave, and retina scanned access.

"No, *No!*"

She hit the kill switch.

One press. The end. Connection severed.

The pain inside my head ended, but it never left my heart.  Medtechs followed, fussing, probing. But they didn't check my eyes, not once. And they should have, for burned on there was a single image. The MARC unit cracked open, a wriggling, fighting octopus desperate to check on its beloved human partner. Suckers tearing surface skin from the frantic scientist. A moment that encapsulates humanity – for fear causes panic, and panic leads to pain. Pain turns to anger, and the source of that anger, that moment of hate, was crushed under a scientist's boot. Merely a discarded test subject. A nothing.

We destroy in this cycle we call life or allow others to destroy what we love with indifference. Take your pick, the end is always the same.

**End Stitch**

That perfect moment in time, taken from me without a thought. Do I blame Richards? Humans are beyond fault, or disgrace. We had a world of beauty and wonders in our hands and killed it with fear or apathy. We do not deserve blame, for if we did, we would have never allowed such moments to be the fleeting epitaph to a scorched world. We deserve indifference instead, for the Drathken to let us die, for the world to heal without us. We are a stain, and from others we deserve ... nothing.

From ourselves, only pain.

And Marc? Multi-purpose All-terrain Recovery Cephalopod. Yeah. Except that was Marc 1, a failed experiment lying lifeless upon a wet deck. MARC 2? Just swap the All-terrain for Automated. They murdered my only true friend and replaced her with a fucking robot – can metal and gears truly replace sapience? Love?

I struggle, I know. There are gaps in my mind amid my true memories. At times I accept the loss. But the dark dreams, the moments of joy, and pain, have me in their grip. I need that love and I'm sorry, but I no longer know where I end and Marc begins any more. Whether the voices are real or echoes.

I need them, however. Her voice remains a conscience, perhaps. Otherwise, I fear what I would do.

I only know you need to listen.

Life is precious.

Or indifferent. Take your pick.

But there are *consequences*.

I'll let the vid run. To the end, to the now.

Where were we? Ah, yes:

*I reached out to Marc, my call pained, in desperate need.*

# Chapter 30

My mind whirled, the floor warping in and out of focus. No tank, no tentacles, no Marc. She was dead, crushed under the boot of an uncaring scientist – a failed experiment and nothing more. Watching her die yet again sent a shudder running through my soul. The satcom in my spine squeezed, its demands rising. I stared back at the MARC in my lap, the panel open, the satcom latched to her motherboard. And there, in the space that contained the remnants of my sanity, sat a tiny bomb. It wasn't for the Drathken.

I know what I said about Richards. That I could lay no blame on her shoulders, that her sheer indifference to a life and what it meant to me, and to Marc, was the truth behind the act. But that anger, well it turns to hate, and I have never been able to rid myself of that. It inhabits my dreams, those moments where I swim free amid the coral, wreathed in sunlight, eyes and heart filled with wonder. Blame? No – but hate – oh yes, I can hate.

I can not let it go.

I will not let it go.

I refuse.

How can the beauty of such a moment be a nightmare? How can you dread reliving those joyous moments? Because when you wake up, there is an absence, a hollow in your heart and mind so empty it crushes your soul.

And all that fills the void is others' apathy. And my hate.

Remember the HLA scientist, Michael? I saw my opportunity while Dulik slumbered under the sedative, persuading my newfound friend, with the help of Fabienne's knife, to make a little dirty bomb of my own. Nothing powerful, but you don't need much when a building's system is designed to cycle air for you. The isotopes would do their job. End Richards' fucking indifference, make people care. Nothing gets a human's heart racing like radiation and make them appreciate life.

Lifting the bomb out of the MARC, my mind recalled the scientist's last instructions before I gave him the sedative. At least when he was bitten, he only had a moment amid the drugged dreams to realise his death. A service, really. Though I never did find out any more about those bloody roots. Maybe I was getting first hand experience.

I knew where the ship's link was, the whole schematics for the Drathken plantship seared into my brain. It was inevitable, my fate sealed the moment I listened to Andre's voice message. The MARC unit fired back up as I closed the hatch, tentacles twitching, wrapping themselves around my forearm.

And it's my mind, I do as I will. I need Marc. Not the MARC unit, but my Marc. Everyone needs a conscience, don't they?

*"Whoa. I'm back."*

Marc clambered up my elbow, wrapping herself around my waist and shoulders, easing her satcom link next to mine.

*"I'm ready. At least this way, if you turn into paste, I find out what it's like to fly."*

"Remember the emotional retraining you suggested *I* undergo? You may have to sit in with me."

Patting her tentacles, I rose to my feet as the door reverberated, heavy thumps clattering into the hardened shell. I placed the bomb next to the pulsing, swirling light of the satcom system that sat under the thunderous purple heart – surprised? Fate? More likely it controlled the flow on demand, but there are times when you think everything is against you. The timer was simple, a press and run countdown, but we weren't going to use that. Marc restructured her link, conjoining her satcom with the one desperately trying to override my body. She let it flow and the need to comply rose, joints stiffening, and a heat spread along my neck. I staggered back, my own mind filled with red numbers counting down – my morbid imagination playing tricks. Perhaps, on the verge of death, you need something to focus on. I fell behind a control panel wreathed in light patterns when the door crashed open, energy bolts flying.

A tentacle squeezed my shoulder. Marc triggered.

And a bomb erupted.

Light, smoke and heat filled the room.

A horrendous scream pierced the air.

No. It wasn't in the air, it was Marc's satcom in my head. It sang of fear and agony, screeches and clicks uttered in panic, filling my mind. A ship's pain encapsulated in the sheer terror of a connected people. It shut off. But I can still hear it now. I will always hear it.

*"The room's local satcom is now offline, I've overridden your receiver and rerouted it through mine."*

"I'm alive?"

*"That, or I'm talking to myself."*

I'll let you think on that one.

Rising from the floor, a distinct wave of unease rolled over me. A confusion – the unknown sweeping me before it. I just needed out of that room, with a needling worry about the radiation setting my nerves on edge. The floor felt wrong as I took a step towards the exit, the sponginess gone, and it didn't push back against me like it had before. Inert. Amid the smoke and flame, the dome had shattered with pieces scattered about the room, many piercing deep into the purple-veined tubes. The muscle shivered, its rhythm disjointed and the membrane turning grey before my eyes. The infection spread outwards – as if I was watching a plant on a time-lapse vid being overwhelmed by disease or fungi. Shudders rippled through the tubes before they too were engulfed in the raging grey wave, throwing ash into the air. My heart ached. I had brought death to the ship regardless of what lay woven about my spine.

I waited for my fate. Sickened and paralysed by my selfish act. But no energy bolts flew, and I pulled my eyes away from the dying heart to let them fall upon the Drathken writhing on the floor. They had caught much of the blast, chitin penetrated by the dome's shell, limbs sheared, unseeing eyes still accusing.

*"We need to go, Joshua. We paid the price of living."*

From the mouths of mechanical cephalopods.

I stepped amid the arms and legs of the aliens who had come to save our planet, reaching amid the gore to collect one of their weapons. Feet pounded along the once silent corridor, stick thin arms bracing the doorway as a Drathken head peered around.

In the vids, the aliens are constantly armed, always ready for a fight. They walk about their ships as if they are fortresses, forever on alert. Can you imagine that? This is real, not a flick, or a death-dealing game. The ship is a home. This body had already killed the defenceless, and in truth, on triggering the bomb I may have murdered many more. Do I stop now? Give myself up? Where does it end?

*"We paid the price."*

"But it doesn't mean we carry on paying." I fired, the bolt searing into the door frame, forcing the Drathken to rear back out of the way. Screaming obscenities, I charged, throwing myself through the door. I dodged right and away from the quivering, blue robed alien. A skittering filled the air, sounds full of fear and hurt. Ignoring them, I rushed on, the greying floor beneath me hard and unyielding.

As I ran, my memory of the schematic faded, possibly lost with the disconnect. Marc tried to help, attempting to realign with the ship's systems only to cut off as its agony echoed over the comms. With no concept of direction, or possibility of safety, panic took hold, and I found myself running for running's sake. How far would I go if I piled into a group of Drathken? What would I do? It struck me then, a fleeting memory of where we were. The *compelling* had taken us downward, in fact so far down we were close to the base of the ship where it rooted into the ground. The heart, if that's what it was, must pump up and around the vessel from there. Nausea rose, my throat acid at the thought of the grey death being transported across the entire ship. A radiation sickness perhaps, a cancer. The payment for my survival.

*"Our survival."*

Ahead, the intermittent membranes along the walls were drying, flaking and cracked. No longer opaque, more of the offshoots from the main arterial corridor were opening for me. The few distant Drathken I saw were hurrying along these, the air alive with their panicked, skittering speech I'd first heard outside the heart room. The fifth of these appeared empty, flowing downwards. A decision made, I battered into the taut membrane, the partition shattering rather than tearing under my assault. The atmosphere was thicker inside, the heat overwhelming, yet dry. Bypassing more offshoots, a first glance inside registered them as cabins, or more likely homes. Personal spaces, ones I had no right to be staring into.

My feet slid, scraping an ash-like substance from the upper surface of the dying floor, digging out a few centimetres where the cancer continued to penetrate. I stopped, staring at what was happening when a family rounded the corner. I know, aliens, right? Why should they have families? And how would I know they're a family? Yet the signs were obvious. The two smaller, brightly hued Drathken pushed backwards behind their taller parents who deliberately faced me – the danger, the killer – astride the corridor. Protecting.

"What have I done?"

# Chapter 31

Heart pounding, with the thick atmosphere choking in aching lungs, distress rolled over me. The gun rose, a need to live surging in my gut, sickening me but pushing to act. I didn't aim their way, some credit in the bank there, but I wafted it to the side in the hope they'd understand. The parents moved, legs deftly shifting their bulbous body at an angle between the murderous human and their progeny, and I ran at the first hint of a gap. I prayed they wouldn't lash out, attempt to pull me down. Selfish reasons, perhaps, but I knew I'd fire.

Once through, the sawing noises rose amid the skittering I associated with fear. Ahead, the corridor darkened, lights flickering as the grey death spread along the walls. My eyes struggled to adjust.

*"See through me,"* said Marc, her head appearing over my shoulder. She couldn't see too far, but the CPU adjusted for light across the spectrum and gave a ghostly view of the space ahead. *"The corridor to the right slopes down, if we're still going for the bottom."*

I jinked right with no other plan in my head. A Drathken walked in front, away from us and towards the next junction. I pulled up, slowing as they continued on their way. I had no concept of what they could hear or sense, though by the satcom's visual input on our entry onto the ship, I assumed their eyesight operated in a different way to ours. Could it hear me? Apparently not, the alien turning to the right and thankfully upwards by the angle their body shifted to. I gave it another second, before checking they had continued on. Peering left, the air appeared to thicken, and in Marc's eyesight, glimmer with dust motes unseen elsewhere. In the hope we were close, I drove on to enter an otherwise pitch-black room full of entangled pipes and fibrous tubes.

*"Perhaps it's the root system? They look healthy."*

"But now what?"

*"Hey, this was your idea, not mine. I'm just the sarcastic sidekick, remember."*

"Can you work out anything from the root patterns, oh reader of light? You know, like direction. I'm assuming nutrients will be sucked in towards a central point to feed the heart thing we blew up."

*"We? I was just acting on orders."*

"You can tell the Drathken that when they pull off one tentacle at a time. Direction?"

*"Assuming it works like most Earth plants, there are a few thicker sections that feed in all over. Best guess, turn left and walk straight ahead and I'll tell you which one to pick out."*

I followed Marc's instructions, adjusting our direction as we followed the 'root' or 'vein' she'd identified. We altered the pathway a few times, constantly worrying about when the Drathken would find us. Whatever we'd done to the satcom had disrupted their normal comms at a guess, along with the cancer spreading along their lower corridor light feeds. But that family would soon be talking and surely it couldn't be much longer.

We must have walked a couple of hundred metres, passing a few up slopes to our left heading back into the main ship again, when we finally reached what I assumed to be the ship's hull, or inner husk maybe? I had little idea whether we were above or below ground, but with the adrenaline dropping, and my body crashing in response, we needed to try something soon. Around the thick, fibrous covering of the main arterial root, the husk appeared thinner – a weak point I hoped, like on any joining of two distinct materials.

"You're up."

*"Eh?"*

"Eight limbs, remember. Time to dig through. Many tentacles make light work."

*"And what are you going to be doing? Having a snack?"*

"Thought I'd watch a vid, chill out a bit. Watching your bloody back, now hurry up."

I dropped my sulking metallic partner onto the root, and she swiftly lashed out, driving her tips into the join. Now I know this is a long shot, in so many ways, but my reasoning was sound and not the least bit out there, right?

Take a coconut. Rare, in your experience, but trees are still cultivated in the lower parts of Brazil. The outer husk and shell are a self-contained system. What you may not know is that a coconut floats – remember I was a swimma, yes? Now, when that floating nut reaches land, it splits open ... *gestates.*"

*"Germinates."*

Like I said, germinates. This splits the outer shell and the husk. Weakens it while it lays down roots and starts a new tree. Are you seeing it now? The Drathken ship has flown through space while needing to be self-contained, like a submarine. But now, after landing, it has germinated. I'm hoping that the inner shell and outer husk are much weaker at those points. At least from the inside.

*"You're basing our survival on a coconut?"*

"And a stroppy cephalopod. Not sure which part is more insane."

*"Could you at least have told me this beforehand, so I could have surrendered with my dignity intact. Oh ..."*

"What's up?"

*"I've reached an outer shell, it's really tough though, split away from the root a little. I'm on sixty percent energy. If ..."*

I could hear the echoes of many feet on a hardening floor, as well as the odd click and sawing. They weren't close, but it wouldn't be long.

"Come out," I said, and as Marc exited, I peered down the hole. She'd dug a good two metres in, the excavated fibre partially dissolving as she'd thrown it backwards. Ahead, was a pitch-black shell, fractures and one wider crack at its base where the root pierced. Lining up the Drathken weapon, Marc crossing her tentacles by my side, I pressed the button. The energy bolt flashed out, smashing into the shell and lighting up the entire hole. What I took for the hull appeared scorched and unharmed, but the reflected energy had burned into the root itself.

With my mind's eye seeing through Marc, watching our back, I fired again and again, burning through the meat of the root and out on to the other side. By the time it was wide enough for Marc, I felt her tentacles stiffen and, looking out from her view, caught the first sight of a Drathken head.

"Marc, dig us out."

*"Aye aye, partner."*

Turning back, I took aim and fired. My first bolt lashed into one of the main roots, causing a screech to rise from the four Drathken lit by the energy and swiftly burning fibrous matter. I fully expected a volley my way, dropping behind a nest of tangled smaller branches for protection.  Instead, they stopped, unsure, then started backing away. Their speech echoed through the room, harsh and angry, with the skittering interlaced.

Assuming they feared further damage to the roots, I rose, only to hear the first human words for a while in the depths of the Drathken ship.

"Nkosi," it was Clara, the monotone voice strong and bouncing off the walls. "You have done enough damage. Stop. Give yourself up."

I didn't answer, a squeal in my head from Marc cutting through her last words.

"Nkosi, you have hurt our ship, is that not enough?" She appeared out of the gloom, the beauty of her features a stark contrast to the ugliness in my heart. Guilt and survival.

Backing off, I spun and dove into the hole, pulling myself along and down into the hollowed root. Grasping the fibres, I squeezed my way through the hardened hull, emerging to find Marc had driven upwards – calling me to follow – her last tentacles exiting into a darkening sky above. More shouts reverberated my way, but ignored, and I pushed my way clear of the root and soil, allowing no thought for what the factories enriched it with.  Spitting away the last vestiges of the mud, I rolled and kicked at the edges of the hole, filling it as best I could before looking for our next move. We were on the near side of the ship, facing the transport hub surrounded by the multi-towered wall designed to keep the alliance's enemies out. Apparently, they had missed one.

# Chapter 32

I'm alive.

It came as a shock to me as well, expecting whatever compelled me inside the ship to be waiting outside to finish the job. Eradicate the evidence, perhaps. But now we needed an out, and as my friendly neighbourhood cephalopod couldn't pilot a helicopter despite demonstrating great technique with an airboat, it left two options.

*"Three. Climb, drive or die."*

But then again, I was wearing a WPF uniform and under the confusion caused maybe that was the way – brazen it out.

*"You know that works in the vids, right? Not in the real world. Dulik and Rainsford, remember."*

"Possibly." I glanced around, the area seemingly in far less panic than I expected. There were no rampaging jeeps rushing to the Drathken ship, nor soldiers running at the double towards the transition gate a few hundred metres to my right. Nothing. For whatever reason, the alarm hadn't been sounded.

I stood, brushing myself down, and let Marc climb over my back. There was no hiding who I was. Whatever else was about to happen, we faced it as one.

Striding out, keeping eyes ahead with hope that my bearing exuded the confidence of someone expected to be there, we walked towards the centre of the hub. In my mind, we needed to be where it was busy, not alone approaching the walls or an obscure area where we'd stand out. My heart hammered and Marc let the occasional pulse of anxiety tremor along her limbs. Being generous with the occasional pat to her tentacle tips, I kept striding on, knowing those touches were as reassuring for me as for her. We reached the primary thoroughfare that approached the Drathken liaison building when the mood shifted, tension crackling as soldiers held their fingers against their ears to block out the hubbub of vehicles and factories. A warning must have gone out, or an alarm. The response was swift but chaotic. Units forming, cars and APCs speeding towards whatever station they'd been designated. Everyone with a preassigned purpose or one dolled out over the radio. Except for me.

I feigned putting my hand to my ear, stopping and sweeping the surrounding area. Still nobody paid attention, and I carried on, heading for the motor pool with zero plan in mind.

*"We're screwed."*

Had to agree.

An engine gunned behind me, the wheels squealing. I forced myself not to turn, keeping my pace steady, but it closed, a creeping dread running up my neck. At least it didn't explode there and then. With my hand pressed again to my ear and near the curve of the rebreather, I glanced behind to see a familiar four-wheel drive heading my way. Dulik was at the wheel, Rainsford riding shotgun, and I could see torture and death written across both their faces. I swore, wishing I hadn't dumped the Drathken rifle back near the ship, and panicked. I ran, briefly, before Dulik pulled the vehicle across my path, and I slammed into the bonnet.

"Nkosi," shouted Rainsford, half out the vehicle and unarmed after entering the Drathken ship – a chink of light until the Marine in the back poked his assault rifle through the door. A dull thud sent a shiver down my spine, hands searching for Marc, lungs drawing in a final breath until a second deadened shot reached my ears. Opening my eyes, Rainsford lay sprawled across his seat, Dulik dragging him back aboard. The Marine stared glassy eyed from the rear, a blood flower in his skull dripping.

"Get the fuck in," mouthed Dulik at the dumbfounded ex-sea cop. Yeah, me.

Shit, what now?

*"Hurry up, Josh. Now."*

I stepped forward, my head numb. I clambered in the back, pushing the Marine upright with his helmet down over the bullet hole – I have no idea why. Dulik had shifted Rainsford, strapping him in, and Marc slipped off my shoulders, grasping the dead man's neck as the WPF agent drove on. I stared straight ahead, unable to think of anything appropriate to say. And there it was, the same thing I'd seen in the mirror back on the *Carson.* The same scar Marc had imaged for me, but this one lay across the nape of Dulik's neck, exposed by her sweat-laden hair pressing against the headrest.

We'd both been taken, operated on, unable or unwilling in the madness that ensued to share our experiences. Unless she didn't know. And what about not revealing my association with Andre? Was that deliberate, a ploy? Was I her patsy, or she my handler?

Whatever happened to simplicity?

Dulik drove calmly towards a building, seemingly a mess hall, steering the vehicle to the back and exiting. She quickly had Rainsford propped behind a pair of waste bins, staring back at me, waiting for me to act.

Decision time.

*"We paid the price. I want to live, Josh."*

Irony, huh? Of course I must have put the words into her head. You see, we both know she's an automated unit, at least now you do. Sorry about that. But I'm the one that *needs* her to be alive, to be there *for me.* To help make sense of my world. Without Marc, what would I become? I'll let you work that out, while I drag the Marine from the car and dump him into a food bin. I took his equipment and dropped in behind Dulik again, waiting to be driven to freedom. I can hope.

The car pulled away, re-entering the maelstrom of vehicles toing and froing from the ailing plantship. Still no siren or indication the soldiers regarded the base as under attack. Dulik joined the stream of vehicles heading towards the base exit, eyes forward, fiddling with her WPF ID. It felt like hours, each stopped car inching us slowly forwards to our certain doom. I pressed back into the seat, a hand caressing Marc as she waved tentacles in apprehension.

Dulik pulled us forward, smiling at the soldier, handing over her ID badge and proffering her wrist. The scanner pinged, the green light seemingly taking an age to appear. The guard pointed to the back, at me.

"And him?" he said, glancing back at Dulik. She brushed the hair away from her facial scar, causing the guard to swallow hard and then nod her way. Rainsford's ID was in her hand, but the guard waved her on, sympathetic words lost amid the engines tone.

"Fuck me," I said.

*"Go procreate,"* added Marc.

# Chapter 33

I don't know how long we drove, hours most likely, the darkness descending as we mounted the buttressed highway towards New Vancouver. I expected choppers at any moment to come rushing overhead, lights blaring, Marines rappelling down in front of us. Perhaps an old Humvee crashing into our side, sending us rolling down into the invading sea either side of us.

None of that happened, and we sped along, one of the rare vehicles on the walled coastal road that so few chose to drive along. It had been built up, an extra five metres or so, but as the storms rose in frequency, it often crumbled and washed out. At least, that's what the signs warned us of along the way. Parts had been walled in, those running between the old valley walls where the sea squeezed in, whipped up by whatever storm had your number on it. There were multiple signs warning to tune into a specific radio station, all ignored by Dulik as she stared straight ahead, silent. The wind was non-existent, dropped, weird how the absence of something can be more ominous than its presence. It had become a part of daily life, yet it was only now with space to think, that I realised just how much. And instead of dust on the wind, scum-covered foam bubbled over the edges of the road, or up the valley sides to waft above the highway walls.

As we approached Burlington, we turned inland, the sea having claimed much of Seattle. The city declared a no-go zone before I was born. With the highway beyond saving, we drove into the hills above the Skagit River

Inlet. Picking up a newly widened road system we then wound our way to a steel bridge and on into the forests beyond. These were sickly, ancient trees I presumed unable to cope with the constant cycle of drought and flood now prevalent this far north. The landscape caught in the four-by-four's lights a mix of the fallen and the felled as humankind couldn't afford to let anything go to waste.

Eventually we reached the highway above Seattle itself, watching, as the sun rose above the hills, the crumbled tower blocks caught amid the glistening ocean lapping at their fractured windows. Word was, unlike Rio where the rich beat a hasty retreat, there were those in the US that refused to leave their drowned cities and ran the authorities ragged until they held their hands up and just let them be. Lawless places, somewhere an ex-sea cop could hide. But one look at Dulik told me our journey was not done, and after a few more hours she spun the wheel to find ourselves on a rough trail that could hardly be called a road anymore. Thirty minutes in, and she brought the truck to a halt, slamming her hands on the wheel, face set tight. She didn't move, a rictus in her neck and a tremor coursing along her spine.

I knew she battled the satcom, the compulsion that had taken over me in the ship. Dulik appeared to be affected outside, possibly tuned into a specific channel I was thankfully not privy too.

*"I can help."*

"If you stop blocking my bomb, they may well take me down, Marc. I'm supposed to be dead."

*"Yet she saved you. And we presume was compelled to do so."*

"To get rid of the evidence, perhaps? Remove me from the scene when I should already have died. Maybe Dulik's role is to prevent the Drathken from finding the implants and discovering it was one of their own who caused the … the cancer." It hurt to say it. Images of the alien family filling my mind.

"I need it out," Dulik's words were spat between grinding teeth. "Out."

She fumbled in her pocket, shaking fingers dropping a knife into the footwell. I glanced down, Fabienne's blade catching the sunlight.

"Cut it out. Please."

Something gripped my heart then. A streak of sympathy I rarely feel. I lashed out, punching Dulik in the ear, then slamming her head into the door, twice.

* * *

I paced in the darkness, the wet stone surrounding us gleaming in the light of the single torch I'd found in the rear of the truck. Dulik lay on her side, hands cable-tied behind, an emergency blanket between her and the rock floor. I'd even removed the rebreather to keep her out of breath. The old mineshaft smelt of mildew and rot, something must have recently crawled in there to die. The walk had been easier than expected, Dulik having stopped next to the head of an old trail that led to the mine. Marc lent a tentacle or two as we carried the unconscious operative, despite my fretting over her power levels.

The ex-WPF Officer stirred, the bruising on her cheek and temple testament to the sympathy and concern I had for her future. The pistol in my hand wavered a little before I holstered it. A fear of what I might do coursing through me. I was out of masks and the energy needed to maintain their pretence. This was me, the favela kid.

"Wake up, Dulik," I said, low and steady. "Marc says the satcom signal can't penetrate the mineral layer. Is that why you brought us here?"

A barely perceptible nod greeted my question, she shifted her weight, trying to rise and sit up. I didn't help. Currently free of the satcom, would she regret the compelling's demand to save me? Or to lie for me? I was no match for her if she freed herself, and more than a little worried even with hands bound. Using the shaft wall, she eventually righted herself. The stare hard as she wheezed.

"Cut it out," she said, half-pleading, half in hatred. "I can't stand it, Nkosi. I need to be in control."

It rang with a truth I related to. Not everyone had a Marc in their life.

*More's the pity, the world would be a better place. Less screwed up.*

"I'll sort it," I meant it too. "But I need to know what's happening. Why you saved me. Who the fuck put these things inside us?"

"I don't know all the answers. Just the pain and the demand to do as I'm directed. I was freed of it inside the Drathken ship for the first time since you left me in the desert. I fell asleep out there, had some shit weird dreams, and woke with a stiff neck and a fucking headache from hell. Five minutes later I'm trapped in my own body, watching through my eyes as they made me do things, say whatever they wanted. I can feel their anger, Nkosi. Hate for those on the Drathken ship and what they're doing. But it's not HLA. I think they're Drathken themselves."

"A faction maybe," I mused aloud. "Someone who wants them to stop helping us. It would explain the Professor."

"You think this is the HLA?" she cut in. "Why go through all that crap with the raid, and Mexico City? And the tech level. It doesn't fit."

"No. It's like us, Drathken who believe there's another way. Look at all the terrorism before the Scorching. Even the HLA themselves, resorting to violence when someone disagrees or suppresses. Why should aliens be any different?"

Dulik nodded her head, wincing. "Maybe."

*"Doesn't answer the big question, does it? What do they disagree with?"*

Ignoring Marc, I drove on, "And Andre? And the Institute?"

"Come on Nkosi. I'm WPF," she said it as if that was enough. But she picked up my body language. "I would have reported what Andre said, you traitorous bastard. The institute? I was muddled on that. I have no idea what the fuck really happened."

I walked away from Dulik, rubbing the back of my neck and fiddling with the scar that squirmed under my touch. I stared at the mineshaft walls. Another arthouse moment.

*"At least she's truthful."*

"Yeah, she takes no shit. Even when asking me to cut out a potential bomb. But it's her talking, we agree on that."

Sighing, and scratching one last time at my scar, I turned back to the prone agent. "But you were made to say those things? To get us on board."

She nodded, eyes glancing over to me as she answered, "That's my best guess. What did you do? The Drathken went near insane, their behaviour erratic compared to what we've witnessed before. When we reached the far end of that transport tunnel, the place was in chaos. Drathken scuttling everywhere. Associate Minin took one look at us and just upped and left. In the end, Clara directed us out. No word on why, and then they activated a defence protocol. Battened down the hatches. Disengaged from the liaison building and all human interaction. Rainsford was fuming. With your actions towards Clara, he assumed you'd broken the diplomatic protocols the Drathken demanded."

"And you?"

"That you'd done whatever you were compelled to do, like me. What was it?"

Staring at the ground, I squeezed my feet into the fetid mud. "I blew up the plant ship's giant heart. Not deliberately, compelled like you. And I killed."

"How the fuck did you get a bomb on … oh shit." I could see it hit home.

"Yeah. Inside me but Marc extracted it. We ended up blowing the ship's satcom link in there. We think it was my trigger." Yeah, I know. I'm ashamed and I lied, okay? How do you admit you caused the death of a ship, and maybe killed hundreds of Drathken, to save your own skin? "But the explosion took out this giant heart thing that was pumping stuff around the ship. Then I ran, found my way out."

"You think that I…?"

"Have a bomb too? It would make sense. Destroy the evidence." Harsh but true. favela style.

*"She doesn't know any more, Josh. For all we know, she could be taking us somewhere for more alien mods."*

I nodded and raised the gun, emptying the clip into Dulik's head. Like I said, I'm not used to sympathy. Or risk. She needed an end, and I provided one. I ducked down behind a set of rocks awaiting an explosion that never came.

*"Oh,"* was all Marc managed when she looked over my shoulder. The tips of protruding roots writhed, sensing the air, before driving inward and back inside Dulik's shattered skull. As she sagged, more swirled beneath her clothes, wriggling along her spine, sliding out to ram against the rocky ground near her hip.

*"They're mildly radioactive,"* said Marc. *"The same isotope signature as the nodules."*

I ran, convincing myself it was primal fear driving my legs out through the side shaft and not the thought of those things being inside me. The crack and fizz of rock behind spurred me on and we charged through the wooden fencing Marc had pulled open earlier.

I know what you're thinking. Cold.

Where is the Nkosi we cared for?

The jovial, fun-loving man with the pearly whites and cute nose twitch?

Did he die under a scientist's boot?

I could say he was never me. A mask. But almost...

Perhaps he was the man I always wanted to be. The man I dreamed of when surviving the streets of the favela. Gone now.

Don't judge us.

We don't deserve it.

# Chapter 34

**Interlude Four**

I promised the remainder of this vid would be in chronological order, and I've kept to my word. Mostly. However, we searched for a purpose, Marc and I. Something to make all the pain and the price I'd paid worthwhile. I won't bore you with the mundane life of terrorists on the run, for that's how I became labelled. My face on every channel, the slow healing of relations between the Canadian-based Drathken and their human counterparts. I assumed there was a price for humanity to pay, for surely our benefactor's gifts did not come for free. I just didn't know what the cost may be, yet.

But we knew our cost. Marc no longer left my side, constantly near with her satcom blocking the one wrapped around my spine. Did you know dreams of alien roots bursting from your eyes, the tips waving in the night before plunging back through mouth and nostril can be a distinct cause of sleep deprivation? Surprising, huh? And the dread that rises at every rumble, stomach upset or headache – waiting for the squirming to start.

If you thought conversing with an automated conscience was crazy enough, just think where my mind was then. Murderer of aliens, humans and their hybrids, carrying my own set of irradiated tendrils ready to go full *Alien* on my ass like the old sci-fi vid. So, I'm sure you can understand our decisions from this point. We had little time left and made a list of potential friends:

Drathken – hmm. Yep. I gave cancer to their ship and murdered their kin. Don't think I'm on their front door guest list. And if my thinking is straight, this faction, the one I think wear red, would like us either dead or to use us as a weapon that'll also make us dead. Like full chest-burster mode but probably out of somewhere equally unpleasant. Not friends, not even close.

WPF – why are we even listing them? One dead boss, an agent I murdered (though I'd argue she was an 'it' by then) and apparently it looks like I duped them to get aboard the Drathken Ship so I could give it cancer.

The URF – cough. Yeah. See WPF, filed under subsidiary.

Rocinha and the favela – I have nothing to sell but Marc (imagine the squeals in my head right now) or the satcom wired into my spine which I'm sure they'd be glad to remove. Millie and Sasha would be oh so careful with their surgery. Not happening.

So that left the HLA, the Human Liberation Army and possible puppet of the Drathken Red Faction (cool name, huh? It's probably something involving a lot of sawing and rumbles, but we prefer ours). Maybe. At the very least they could help me with our *other* list before the Reds decide to use me as fertiliser. Yeah, *our bucket list.* And it's a doozy.

Easy, then. Just rock up to the local terrorist recruitment agency, put my name down and wait for the email. How the hell do you contact the most wanted organisation outside of yourself? Well. When you're the Human Liberation darling, apparently, they find you. That, and staying in every lowlife, rundown shithole I could find. The HLA grapevine wrapped me in their arms and welcomed me in. Were there more Professor's in their mix? Red Faction agents? Probably, but for now we had mutual goals.

And no, we do not share their beliefs. Just their goals and their resources, in return for being the new HLA figurehead until our death and another steps in. Nkosi, Drathken Killer. I accept the label, for that is what I have done. But not the cause. Maybe it is better Marc and I show, not tell, though by now you should understand our motives. However, humans are inherently programmed to avoid the obvious, dismissing our expectations as unreal, unhuman like. Instead of empty words, Marc and I believe in the courage of our convictions.

Life should be sacred. Well, nearly all life. Like we said, we have the HLA resources at our disposal, and we have a list to fulfil.

## **Stitch Incoming: Somewhere in Canada**

*"It's coming."*

I agreed with Marc, the night vision goggles picking out the small convoy of trucks and the single WPF Marine four-wheeled drive at the front. They were driving without lights, only the moon's ambience intermittently appearing in the dark as the dust whirled amid the rising storm.

"They have night vision capability," I said, stating the obvious. "Team Delta, you have a go, I say again, a go. Do not hit the fucking trucks."

Rising from the dust-laden floor, I leaned into the cracked trunk of the Douglas Fir, eyes on the road, waiting for the night vision flare that would signal the engagement. Static crackled over the radio-link and then the telltale fire trail burnt out the NV. I pushed the goggles up and took the first few steps down the slope while my eyes adjusted. Gunfire echoed over the ensuing explosion, the WPF vehicle erupting with orange and red flame as the RPG hit. It spun, rocking and rolling, before a second, face-on hit, struck the engine and the hood blew up and over the windscreen. More gunfire bursts struck the glass, until finally the armour penetrating sniper round smashed through the screen, rupturing the driver's head. The car spun to a stop, and the assault rifles of Team Beta cut through the fire and smoke to end any potential resistance.

By the time I'd hit the road, Marc hanging on tightly, Team Echo had the truck drivers out and spreadeagled face down on the ground. Clean. How it should be.

Swallowing hard, I approached the still burning WPF truck, eyes watering but accepting the discomfort. With my compatriots from Beta at our side, I levered open the rear door, peering inside, heart pained. The pair of modded dogs lay stricken, bones shattered and eyes bloodied. They were Australian cattle dogs, something we'd learned over the last few months. Able to withstand tremendous heat and hardship, they were ideal work animals for the WPF. Though clearly not perfect enough. I drew out the pistol, placing one bullet between those soft, imploring eyes, just below the aerial unit. The other watched on. I'm sure she was aware, so I stroked her just behind the ears. Marc's tentacle caressed my neck when I fired a second time.

Now, at this point, you're probably harking back to the modded whales. The ones the HLA used at the beginning of our vid, yes? The one they blew up with the others in that raid unaccounted for. Then there's those dispatched by Alpha 3. Remember her? Hopefully drowned in that mudslide or preferably suffocating under the hardening mud at the bottom of the valley. I hope she suffered. Not because those agonised and mistreated creatures didn't crave for an ending, but because to her destroying them was just a job. One to laugh about. I doubt she even considered them truly alive. Indifferent? No, un-fucking-caring. Anyway, let's just say everyone on board that ex-whaling ship, or those HLA sanctioning the whales use, are on the list. Fuckers. Give a modded madman and his cephalopod partner the weapons to fight back, it's what they do. But first we need to prove to our new friends what we are capable of.

I walked down the line of the three trucks, each driver shaking under the gun barrels of our terrorist band. I whispered in each ear, anger lacing my words, wrenching their heads back so they could see the weapons and Marc's weaving tentacles. Within minutes they were back in the trucks, weapons pressed against their kidneys and our newly painted WPF copy of a four-by-four out front. With the WPF transponder and IDs acquired from the defunct vehicle we replaced, we drove on, another hour passing before approaching the Animal Research Institute's main gate.

The transponder woke the guard, their yawn and stretch accompanied by a request for ID. A cursory glance, and the institute's night delivery rolled into the grounds. The yammering of the dogs in the rear-most truck greeted by a grin from the security guard. Team Delta exited first from our WPF vehicle, covering Echo and Beta while they clambered out of the animal transports. Twelve terrorists, plus me, Marc, and our cause.

*"Knock, knock."*

"We are a go, Team Delta." They powered in through the main entrance, rifles raised, firing on those inside whether their hands were up or running for their lives. No quarter given. Beta watched our backs, while Marc and I joined Team Echo to enter from the rear. The squad of four shattering the roof windows, before crashing through the main sea lab roof. With gunfire raging, I harnessed up, Marc controlling our descent until we reached the wet lab floor. We were there because Echo had the trickiest task – securing the tanks and ensuring the sea pens were safe while awaiting Delta's controlled rampage through the building. By the time my pistol was out the floor had pooled with blood-filled water. One of the tanks had blown, its contents spilled upon the tiles among the deceased workers. A dolphin flapped against the ceramic floor, one black eye facing towards us. Its head was scarred, though no aerial protruded, and then it simply lay there. Was it waiting for orders? Or perhaps accepting a welcomed end?

*"The pens,"* said Marc, an urgency in her voice. *"Can we roll the dolphin in there?"*

I peered across to the sea pens. We'd debated long and hard about whether to use them as our entrance to Frankenstein's lab before passing. They were all occupied, and after a check, I worked with two of Team Echo to heave the dolphin the ten metres into the water. A brief lull was followed by a flurry of thrashing water, fins and tails crashing, the two occupants battering against the passive creature we'd introduced.

*"No!"*

"It's inevitable, Marc. Like Clara. They see it as something unacceptable, wrong. An aberration."

Ushering the two members of Team Echo away from the pen, I collected the blood-covered data tablet laid across one of the dead technicians. It was locked, but with a little of Nkosi know-how (the scientist's retina scan and fingerprints) and a cephalopod's comms we had it open.

"Mod Lab secure, sir," echoed in our ears from Delta 1. "Working our way to storage."

"Understood. Echo 1, 2 and 3, stay here. Open the sea pens. I want tanks A through D destroyed, their contents euthanised like we showed you. Tanks F through J can be released, use the sluice. Echo 4 with me." I strode past Tank E, sighing at its shattered state and headed for the wet lab's exit. Ignoring the remaining dead techs, I opened the doors out onto the corridor, following the plans Marc had uploaded with our personal guard walking ahead. We checked each office. Those clear we left alone, ready for the exit when we'd burn every data log and server we found. Those with cowering people ... I'll let you assume where our wrath lay.

On reaching the Mod Lab door, I swallowed hard, a dread sitting in my stomach. On entering, Marc's chip shrieked, her shared mind filling mine with scenes of torture and death. A bloodied sight, I ... words and pictures are not enough. How have we come to believe that playing God like this is right? That we can crack skulls, drive our tech into an animal's brain or spine, and still declare ourselves as the higher lifeform? Many of these poor creatures will have been gene modded. Their biological structures prepared to receive something as *alien* as a transceiver or CPU wired into their spinal column or wrapped about their brain stem.

*"This has to end."*

I walked past row upon row, with death amid the aisles – the modders themselves bloodied by my newly provided HLA resources. Their famous figurehead identifying the animal splicing and WPF actions as a barrier between the HLA and the successful disruption of Drathken/human relations. Simple. Especially when you are the feared Drathken Killer.

I entered the storage area and worked through the tablet spreadsheet, releasing those prejudged to be able to survive on their own, and those we could rescue. The rest? I think you know. A release.

We left soon after, incendiaries finishing our work.

But it is perhaps in that moment, that I saw real clarity. Against the roar of flame, I knew it would be impossible to bring down every Drathken sponsored gene and modding lab, or every government that saw life as a resource to use up at their whim. No. As the research lab burned, and with it the people who regarded such science as their calling, I understood what had to be done. And perhaps, for once, I was in the right place, at the right time.

*"This can't continue."*

"No. We paid a price, now we need to collect."

**End Stitch**

# Chapter 35

"Fuck me."

"*Why do you keep using that word?*"

"Because 'procreate me' doesn't have the same impact." The speedboat slammed into another wave top, ramming my shoulder, and the metal tentacle clinging on to it, into the rugged seat belt. "Fuck, the fuck me."

"*I sense you are gaining a hatred for speedboats.*"

"They're second on the list after devil-spawned helicopters. Give me a sub any day."

"*I miss those days. Simple. Quiet.*"

"Yeah. Saner, maybe."

"Up ahead," said Delta 1, the radio cutting through the engine noise and sea wind lashing our face. "Hundred metres."

Lights highlighted the ship's outline against the darkening clouds as dusk fell. It had only been a few months since we'd last been here, but little had changed since then. The ex-whaler still had the same outline, and from my HLA sources, had acquired a new crew and assignation, but plied the same trade. Irony. The real kind.

Shouts from above heralded our arrival. Ladders were thrown down and Delta team clambered aboard. More engines echoed off the ship's metal hull as the other two assault teams arrived. Sending Beta over to the starboard side, we climbed the rope, Delta primed as the new ship's crew gathered around, waiting.

Marc, as usual, caused a stir. That, or they recognised the Nkosi chin and his cute nose from the pictures below the Drathken Killer headlines. Either way, the deck fell silent, and I grinned at the bunch of pirates the HLA had found. I didn't trust a single fucking one.

*"What a bunch."*

"Yeah, savoury lot. Let's give them something to think about."

Mask on. Time for a little payback.

"Nkosi," I said, low, hard, looking each one in the eye. "That's right. Where are our modders?"

"Here," shouted a voice from the back, a huge, red-haired and square jawed man in a plaid shirt stepping forward, dragging a pair of unhappy looking men with him. They may have been wearing lab coats, it was hard to tell. I'll let you use your imagination.

He dragged them both forward, casting the scared scientists (I use that word loosely) to the floor. The barrel-chested HLA operative sported a huge shit-eating grin, nodding to us, pride on his face.

"These the same fuckers?" I asked.

"Yeah. Found them the same way as last time. Put out a few feelers and they bit. Money still has power." The voice was nearly musical, a far cry from the man's appearance.

"Good." The pistol barked, a bullet slamming into the big fucker's throat. Hands grasped the wound, blood spurting, and I kicked him to the floor. With barrel to head, I returned his shit-eating grin. "*This* bastard employed *these* bastards," Marc waved a tentacle at the open-mouthed scientists, "to crack whales' heads open and drill fucking probes in their brains." My finger pulled the trigger, shattering Mr Musical's skull.

I stood up, straightening my blood splattered combat jacket and patting Marc's tentacles, the metal gleaming scarlet in the ship's light. Only then did I turn to address my newly compliant crew. "Get the boats winched up the ramp. You have ten minutes."

An explosion of movement rolled over the deck. Men and women running, ropes being pulled, and the ratchets wound. Perhaps my newfound fame did have perks.

"What about these?" said Delta 1, muzzle pointing to the pair whimpering on the deck.

I so wanted to drill into their skulls, perhaps drop in a mod or two. Even a snippet of alien root tendril. But I'm not inhuman.

"Slash their wrists and throw them in the sea." A race between a cold, comfortable death, and whatever survived in the mess we'd made of our oceans. Delta 1 nodded, signalling his team.

Three off the list, now for number four.

* * *

The assault on the *Socorro* elevator platform went smoothly, after all we'd timed it based on paid info about the navy and air force capabilities. The WNF advanced frigates would take days to be within fast helicopter range, and the slower, long-range versions I so hated, wouldn't arrive until we were long gone. The level of HLA monetary resources kept on surprising us. I wanted to dig some more, find out why so many of the remaining rich seemed to be backers of a terrorist organisation. But hey, you can't leave priorities hanging around.

"Get me down. I'll do whatever the hell you want."

"Want?" I replied, nudging Science Officer Richards out a little further over the sea, the chain on the boat winch jangling in the super-hot sea breeze. "What makes you think I want anything from you?"

"Is it the MARC unit, does it need repairing? I can do that, Nkosi. Anything you want. It's not moved. Did you break the bloody thing again?" Richards coughed, dust-laden phlegm sliding from her lips where I'd cut her rebreather free. It dripped off her nose and onto her forehead, streaking a strand of hair before splashing into the seawater below. Remember the shadows on the surface? The ones we saw from the sea elevator? They were coming, we just had to wait. Be patient.

"I think Marc is fine. Are you okay Marc?" She waved a tentacle, the metal joints shuddering with a mix of fear at her nemesis, and the anger coursing inside. Perhaps there was a pinch of anticipation in there. The drift of the sea current urged the shadow our way and Richards finally clocked on.

"No, Nkosi, no. Please."

"I remember shouting that to you," I said. "That day on this very deck. No, *we* shouted, and you fucking ignored *us*." Spittle flew from my mouth. A tentacle slid around, stroking my neck but calming wasn't going to work. I had waited too long for this.

"Is that what this is about? Your fucking squid? In all that is holy, you fuck. An animal?"

You see, even in the face of death, humans remain ... ah. Fill in your own blanks.

"A cephalopod. Common Octopus, the most beautiful thing in my life. And you squashed it under your boot. A nothing, unimportant. A failed experiment to be discarded. Though you taught me a lesson, one I haven't forgotten."

For what else is humanity, but an experiment gone wrong? One that destroys with indifference. Even their own home.

"Please, Nkosi. No. Get me down."

"That's the plan." I eyed the encroaching sea shadow. A wave of blue across the surface, dark and foreboding from beneath. More modded life. Blue sea dragons riding the waves, Glaucus Atlanticus. Eaters of the man-o-wars, be they the Pacific or more famously, Portuguese. Gene modified by humans with a little help from our Drathken friends, to blanket the sea in an attempt to kill the plague of venomous siphonophores that arose as the fish and sea-life died. A vain attempt to preserve whatever food species they could. Instead, as with all meddling, they now rode the sea on the hunt in vast numbers until their food sources died out in turn. And what's oh-so special about blue sea dragons, apart from being one of the most gorgeous sea slugs on the planet? They ingest stinging cells from their victims, storing the cells in their own bodies. One sting can induce nausea, pain, vomiting, acute allergic ... yeah, you get the picture.

"Say no again."

"No, please no."

A metal tentacle reached across, tapping the ratchet mechanism, the chain spilling onto the deck and spiralling into a pile. Richards' face was a picture, her relief palpable. Until she realised the chain wasn't what held her up – no – chains are heavy. We wanted her to float.

My knife sliced the rope, and she fell. The screams lost on the dusty wind, heat searing at my skin around the rebreather, but we didn't move away until the last twitch.

"Four."

*"Do we have to finish the list?"*

"Yes. I'm sorry. I know you liked them."

*"We – we liked them."*

"We need to make people listen, Marc. Cast off our last attachment and get people's attention. Nkosi ... Nkosi is gone."

*"Has he? All of him? Because some of him lies two clicks down. Are you trying to kill what's left of him so you can face what comes next? There are some good people, Joshua."*

# Chapter 36

**A message to the world. Going out live.**

So, there you have it. You know us now, Marc and I. The whole world watching our story – Nkosi, the famous Drathken Killer. My final mask. Except Marc and I are one now and on the same path. A conscience and its bearer entwined. *We* who must be the world's conscience, because humanity has none.

Ah, perhaps there is one more thing to do, especially for our *Socorro* 'tube fans.

You people gave me a home, a place to *be*. I can see you now, Jeremiah, Nakina and Jezze. Benni, yes Benni ... Though this vid feed will cut out soon, I am pleased we could spend these last few hours with you. When I fled the favela, I feared what my life would become. How would I cope amid people who placed such value on human life? But you were like the extended family I never had. My *mae* and *pai* always provided a degree of warmth but could never show too much for fear Rocinha would use it against them. And my favela family? Gangstas one and all. And no, you do not learn to trust amid such disregard for life, doomed never to risk love or be free of thought. It was always the fight to finish on top. But here you gave me friendship, kindness. When you pulled me down, it was not to raise yourself up, but to keep Joshua Nkosi grounded two clicks under. For that, you will forever be in my heart.

But you remain indifferent to this world, and you so nearly dragged me down with you. You tear up the ocean floor, killing everything in your path, and leave a manicured lawn behind, bereft of life and hope.  A symbol of humanity's need to control, order without a care for what you take or destroy. And at what price?

Marc has begged for you to be spared, for the love you have given. He says you have *potential.* That we should save you.

The planet needs to know our name, and you are the conduit for that. Know that the world watches as we strike the first blow in this new war.  Do you hear that alarm? Marc has engaged it to give you time.

**"Emergency Evacuation Procedures Delta Bravo Two.  I say again, Emergency Evacuation, Emergency Evacuation.  To your stations."**

We hope you make it. We really do.

The Drathken hunt us. Whether it is those that wove a bomb into my spine or those I murdered. All I can assume is that our alien friends have factions and are not in agreement, denying our assumption of one homogenous consensus upon their decisions and actions. They are not the simplistic aliens of our Hollywood blockbusters, but a *people* with their own emotions and opinions. Controversial, huh?

And the WPF hound us like modded dogs on their master's leash.

We have little time left. But know this.

We are here to take the mask of indifference from your eyes.

All you are doing now is accepting the generosity of an alien race's kindness, while still manipulating and controlling the world to your own personal wants. Playing God with your animals because you are so angry at being unable to control your urges to destroy and wreak havoc, or maybe it's the pain of seeing what we all let happen to our Earth.

Marc and I don't have all the reasons.

Just the one cause.

Humanity is a stain on this world. A failed experiment.

She will heal without us. The Drathken need to leave us to our fate.

*"Thirty seconds to ignition."*

As for the rest of the world:

My parents named me Marcelo, *little warrior.* I hated it, I still do.

The WPF named me Joshua, *God is Deliverance*, after my forged credentials.

Those masks are gone. We name us Marcos, *God of War*.

Humanity, hear our roar.

Marc, before we cut to the devastation, can you explain the world's Terms and Conditions for the rest of our viewers, if you please.

*"Certainly. All views within this video are our own. All animals within this vid were harmed, and you may carry on living your lives with indifference until we find you, fucker."*

*"We accept full responsibility for our actions and reserve the right to blow your fucking head off should you in any way impede our activities. Anyone accidentally hurt or injured in the war that's coming, we don't apologise for, unless you're Drathken, in which case please just leave us to our fate. Despite evidence to the contrary, should we be captured alive, we would like it to be known that we refuse to plead 'not guilty by reason of insanity'. Look in the fucking mirror if you wish to know why."*

*"Don't forget to click like and subscribe and give us a follow on all socials."*


**The End of The Scorching: Just Press Play**

# The Scorching Series

Thank you for reading the first book in this series of three standalone novels. All three will explore aspects of a near future Earth after climate change culminates in an event known as The Scorching, ravaging the equatorial belt and heating the entire planet. As you know, an insectoid alien race, the Drathken, offers their help and the books explore the impact of humanity's wide-ranging and desperate response as the world spirals into fear-filled factions. If you enjoyed Just Press Play, a rating or a review would go a long way to support this indie author in the wild world of publishing (I kid you not - it's truly wild out there!).

Book 2 will be a mystery thriller as the future colonists wing their way from the dying Earth towards a new hope. This should be released before autumn, fingers crossed!

Book 3 will explore the Drathken, and their motivations in coming to Earth and how they cope with being so different from humanity.

# About the Author

If you have read my previous series, you will know that The Scorching is quite a departure from my action/military science fiction series Weapons of Choice. However, that series does delve into aspects of the human condition and has a reputation of being surprisingly thoughtful in its emotional depth and social conscience. It's also one heck of a ride. I am also writing a Dark Fantasy Series called, 'Warriors of Spirit and Bone.' This essentially takes my first book from Weapons of Choice and reimagines it within a world where dragons, elves and magic exist with a very dark underlayer of a people being hunted. It has been great fun to write, and I hope you delve in.

For those that don't know me, I have the usual author blurb after the link to my website below. You can also view my other books and sign up for a newsletter and a free book related to the Weapons of Choice Series:

www.nicksnape.com

# Author Bio

Nick Snape has been steeped in Science Fiction and Fantasy since his friends first dragged him from his schoolwork and stuck a book under his nose. Lost to the world of imagination he became a teacher by accident though he thoroughly enjoyed developing the joy of reading and writing in his pupils. Having retired after thirty years he thought it was high time to practise what he preached.

# Books by Nick Snape

**Weapons of Choice Series**
**(Amazon Only)**
Hostile Contact
Return Protocol
Zuri's War
Finn's War
Alien Rebirth
Invasive Species
Legion Earth
Nemesis Earth

* * *

**The Scorching**
Just Press Play

* * *

**Warriors of Spirit and Bone**
A Dragon of the Veil (to be released)

# Praise for the Author

'Stunning series. Very highly recommended.'
★★★★★ Good Reads

'Sci-fi with pace, heart and unafraid to tackle deeper questions of what it means to be human.' ★★★★★ Amazon Customer

'Wildly creative'
★★★★½ Self-Publishing Review

'I haven't enjoyed a series this much in a long time. The twists and turns keep me constantly surprised.' ★★★★★ Amazon Customer

'A truly immersive story.' ★★★★★ Amazon

# Acknowledgements

As with all authors, this book and my other series would never have existed without the dedicated friends and family who were there by my side through-out the entire process.  The least I can do is give them a mention for their patience with my obsession! My Beta readers, supporters and fiercest critics have been Pak, Claire, Paul and Mark.  Amazing friends who put that aside to make sure whatever I put out there was something they wanted to read. I have also had great support from Martin Lejeune, TK Toppin and Bryan Chaffin - authors who have given of their time during a second round of Beta Reads. Very much appreciated, and the book would not be where it is without you.

Julie, my wife, needs a special mention. Over the past years, she has kept me going, being there at every step through the dark and joyful times. I can't believe how lucky I am. Finally, the New Year and Pub Night Crews. Wouldn't be here without you.

Thank you all.